MUMMY NEEDS A BREAK

SUSAN EDMUNDS is a business journalist by day and a fiction scribbler by night. She lives in Whangarei, New Zealand, with her husband Jeremy and their two children, Liam and Olivia. Most of Susan's non-work writing relates to motherhood and the crazy experience of being left to take care of a child when you have no real idea what you're doing. When she gets the chance at some time off, she spends it with her children, exercising and trying to tackle her sleep deficit.

Mummy Needs A Break

SUSAN EDMUNDS

avon.

Published by AVON,
A division of HarperCollins*Publishers* Ltd
1 London Bridge Street
London SE1 9GF

www.harpercollins.co.uk

A Paperback Original 2019
3

A catalogue record for this book
is available from the British Library

ISBN: 978-0-00-831609-9

Typeset in Birka by Palimpsest Book Production Limited,
Falkirk, Stirlingshire

Printed and bound in Great Britain by
CPI Group (UK) Ltd, Croydon CR0 4YY

MIX
Paper from
responsible sources
FSC **FSC® C007454**

To my husband, Jeremy

CHAPTER ONE

<u>How to make blue playdough</u>

What you'll need*:

1 cup water

1 tablespoon vegetable oil

½ cup salt

1 tablespoon cream of tartar

Blue food colouring

1 cup flour

*A sharp eye to catch bits before they're ground into
the carpet

Combine water, oil, salt, cream of tartar, and food colouring in a saucepan and heat until warm. Remove from heat and add flour. Stir and knead like it's your husband's head, and he's just informed you he's working through the children's bath time, again. Warning: The kids will eat more playdough than you realise. It will turn everything in their digestive systems a deep shade of yellow. Apt really, when you're discovering what a coward the man you married has become.

It was a particularly muggy spring evening when my usually uneventful, comfortably boringly suburban life fell apart. I was eight months pregnant, sweaty, grumpy and was working late. Again.

'So, tell me a bit about what's happened.' I had tucked my phone into the crook of my neck, a pen making an indent in my middle finger as I scribbled on my notepad. Somewhere beyond the door to my makeshift home office in our spare bedroom, I could hear my two-and-a-half-year-old son, Thomas, pushing a toy truck or car repeatedly into the freshly painted wall of the kitchen. At least, I hoped it was a car. The way our day was going, it might have been his father's head.

The woman at the other end of the phone coughed. Could she hear me tapping my pen on my notebook? I eyed the clock: 6.30. My workday was meant to finish at 5 p.m., but the emails from my editor had become increasingly frantic. If we didn't want yet another front-page story about the unseasonable weather, I needed to get a quote from this woman about her burgled-for-the-fourth-time-in-a-month clothes store.

'I don't want to make myself more of a target . . .' I could hear her jangling a bunch of keys.

I deployed the most soothing tone I could muster. She sounded about the same age as my mother, but the photos I'd found of her in our files looked as if she was only a decade or so older than me. 'I'm sure you won't. You must want something done to improve safety?'

I bit my lip, allowing her silence to spread out between us. She did not take the hint to fill it.

'More security guards for the mall? Better monitoring?' I tried. 'Have you lost a lot of money?'

A wail echoed down the hallway. She didn't seem to register it. Judging by her breathing and the whir of vehicles in the background, it sounded as if she was hurrying across a car park.

'Oh, heaps. The insurance excess wipes me out each time. I'm too scared to work late here by myself.'

I swallowed. 'I'd love you to raise awareness of the problem.' I had to get the words out before she came up with another excuse to put the phone down. 'Maybe stop other business owners getting caught out.'

'I guess.' The line went silent again.

Thomas howled from the next room. I cringed. Could his father not handle one bedtime alone? 'Have you any footage? We could post it on social media, see if anyone IDs the guys?'

I nudged the door open with my foot and stuck my head through, gesturing frantically at my husband, Stephen, to reduce Thomas's noise output by a couple of thousand decibels.

He strode past, throwing Thomas over his shoulder and marching him out of the kitchen, toothbrush clenched in one hand and pyjamas in the other. He shot me a pleading look as he rounded the corner, which I pretended not to see.

4

'Just imagine how good it would feel if you found them. Plastered their names and photos around the place a bit.'

A few minutes later Stephen's voice reverberated through the walls. 'No more stories. I'm going to sit at the end of the bed while you go to sleep, okay?' Then more forceful. 'Thomas. Get back into bed. Right now. I'm not joking this time, buddy.'

I rolled my eyes. Perhaps if my husband hadn't styled himself as the *fun* parent, he might not find the process so tough. But then, bedtime wasn't a breeze for boring-strict-Mum when I did it every other night of the week, either.

The office door opened, and Thomas strutted in. Grabbing my leg, he tried to pull himself up, mountain-climber style, into my lap. Stephen appeared behind him, grabbed the neck of his dressing gown, bundled him up and carried him away. I heard a thump through the door as Stephen dropped him back on his bed. 'Water!' Thomas wailed.

'I'm sorry, you'll have to call me back.' The woman at the other end of the phone cut off the call.

I dropped the phone on to my desk and shifted in my chair. A rivulet of sweat gathered between my maternity bra and the top of the stretched skin of my stomach. All I wanted to do was lie on the couch and eat my way through the rest of the packet of chocolate biscuits I had hidden from Thomas in the top of the larder. I checked the desktop calendar lying open beside my notebook. Eight working days until my maternity leave started.

Somehow, less than half an hour later, the story was filed. I tried to push the image out of my mind of the store owner trotting to her car, wielding keys positioned between her fingers. There was still a continuous rhythm of bangs and thuds reverberating from Thomas's room as he rolled around in his bed, his knees colliding with the wall. I gathered the empty glasses and plates from around my desk and carried them through to the kitchen.

As I placed them in the soapy suds still stewing in the sink, I became aware that Stephen's phone was buzzing on the counter, the vibration moving it across the shiny surface. It was a rare sighting of his phone in the wild. Stephen's phone was normally either at his ear, in his hand or his pocket. He had even taken a brief call while I was in labour with Thomas – apparently, there was something more pressing happening that afternoon at the building firm he owned. I hadn't let him forget that one.

I kept my hands in the water, idly picking away at determined blue playdough under my nails. How long should I hang back before I ventured down the hallway and relieved Stephen? At some point, all kids have to fall asleep, right? Even with dads who were no doubt giving in to requests for one more story or an extra bedtime song.

The phone buzzed again. I turned it over. It was a message, not a call, and from a number that I didn't recognise.

'Miss you,' the message blinked. Surely a wrong number. I swiped to unlock the phone, putting in the date of our wedding anniversary as the security code. It brought up a text exchange with the unsaved contact. Odd.

'What are you up to?' Stephen had asked on Monday night. Monday night? I had been contorting myself at a prenatal yoga class, trying to maintain my zen. I'd dragged myself down for a rare class at the studio, though it would have been much easier to just stay home and do another YouTube workout on the LEGO-strewn lounge floor. Stephen had said he was working late, that night. I remembered because I'd had to send Thomas to my parents, where he'd wreaked overtired havoc.

'Just lying on the couch,' the mystery number replied.

'Lucky couch.' He signed the message off with a heart-eyed emoji. An emoji! Was that meant to be cute?

'What are you doing?'

'Sitting here, thinking about you. See you soon?'

'Of course.' Whoever the other number was, the message was ended with a heart in return.

Then the exchange had fallen dead for a couple of days. I lowered myself to the kitchen floor, the too-trendy square handle of the cabinet sticking into my back, the cold metal of the phone in my hands. *Lucky couch? Thinking about you?* I could not get my thoughts to run in order. It was like watching television when Thomas had the remote, zipping forward then doubling back. The blood had retreated from my fingertips, and my stomach had started somersaulting. The tiles were cold under my shins. What was going on?

I shut my eyes. Stephen had been away from home more than usual, blaming work. I'd assumed he was doing extra hours so that he could take some time off when the baby arrived. It had never occurred to me to question whether he might have been somewhere else.

It had been a long time since he had said anything that flirty to me. And what if there was more to it than just messages? On the one hand, the idea was preposterous. This was *my* clueless Stephen. He once tied himself in guilty knots when a woman at a party gave him her number. Later, we discovered she only wanted him to advise which type of steel she should use for her fence. But on the other, he wasn't the type to message anyone for the fun of it. I had had to show him how to set up reminders to reply to his work emails, and it had been months since he bothered to respond to any of my texts.

Thomas had finally fallen silent in his bedroom, and I

7

could hear Stephen plodding back down the hallway towards me, blinking like he'd returned from a disappointing all-night dance party. He rubbed his eyes as he emerged into the white LED light of the kitchen but stopped in the doorway when he clocked his phone in my hands. He looked at the illuminated screen, then my face and back again. 'What are you doing?'

'Who is this?' I rose to my feet.

I had to grip the cold floor with my toes to keep myself upright. 'Who are you texting?'

He spluttered, a mottled flush spreading over his face. He looked as if he'd just swallowed something rancid. 'What? No one.'

I thrust the phone at him. He snatched it from my hand and looked at the open conversation.

'What is going on?' My words were harsh in the balmy evening air.

He pushed the phone away, his hazel eyes sparkling. 'Nothing is going on. I can't believe you're going through my phone.'

I stared at him. An evening chorus of crickets had started up in the garden, highlighting the silence between us. I watched him struggle for words. My flicker of hope that there was a story to explain the messages evaporated. He had always become tongue-tied at the first hint of a lie and would avoid someone for months rather than risk a confrontation. The back of my throat was caustic with heartburn and fear danced on my nerve endings. I had only just finished getting the baby's room ready, and Stephen still had to put the cot back together. What had he done to us? To me?

He hunched his shoulders and turned away, taking cover from my gaze. 'I don't have to stand here and be interrogated by you. Am I not allowed any privacy anymore?'

He flung open the fridge, grabbed a bottle of beer and stalked over to the living room. I heard the TV switch on. Was that it? He was just going to try to ignore it? I had swallowed dozens of minor disappointments for the sake of our little family, but this one wasn't going to be one of them.

I followed him. 'You can't just walk away. Who is this?'

He stared at the television, determinedly avoiding my eyes, his shoulders drawn up to his ears.

'Talk to me.' I grabbed his callused hand and pulled him towards me. I could hear my voice becoming more and more shrill. Was he not even going to make eye contact? I stepped in front of him to block his view of the screen. 'I'm Thomas's mother. I'm about to have your second child, for God's sake. I deserve to know what is going on. I've given you fifteen years of my damn life.'

He still would not turn to face me. I could see his Adam's apple bobbing in his throat as he swallowed hard.

'Just bloody answer me!' I swiped a thick stack of magazines from the coffee table on to the floor. The clatter as they hit the beautiful grey wood (we had agonised over it when we remodelled a year earlier) seemed to rouse his attention. He grabbed his keys from the coffee table in front of him and stood up. 'I don't have to listen to this.'

Pulling a sweatshirt from the back of the couch, he strode towards the front door and marched outside. The door slammed behind him and I stared at it as I heard his boots crunch over the gravel out to his truck. He heaved the driver's door shut, the wheels spinning on the stones as he took off down the driveway.

I poured myself a glass of iced water, wishing it were wine, my hands shaking. It was only 8.30 p.m. What was I meant to do? I pondered calling a friend but what do you say:

'Hello, nice evening isn't it? I think I've just caught my husband having an affair.'

If it turned out he wasn't, it would be witheringly awkward to make small talk with the neighbours at our next barbecue. And if it transpired that he was – but we stayed together regardless – no one would look him in the eye. I could not imagine anything worse than turning up to drinks at my perfect friend Charlotte's house and having everyone look at me, the scorned wife. Poor Rachel, stuck with a cheating husband and a new baby.

I flicked through the channels on the television, but the sound washed over me like white noise. I drummed my fingers on the faded black of my overworked maternity leggings. My heart was still pumping as if I were running. I muttered a silent apology to my daughter, tucked up with her feet planted firmly in my ribs, who replied with a swift kick.

Stephen had done some stupid things in the time we had been together. There was the purchase of a boat that didn't run, which was still under a tarpaulin in the garage. He'd only started his own business because he'd stormed off a building site over some minor dispute he'd let fester for months. My reminder that we'd just signed up to our first mortgage wasn't enough to dissuade him.

But if you'd asked me even the day before if he would chuck away everything we had for a fling with someone else, I would have said categorically not. We had worked so hard.

There were men who slipped their rings into their pockets at work drinks and just needed to be offered a halfway-decent opportunity and the – often clearly misguided – belief they wouldn't be caught.

But I had always thought Stephen was in the other camp – the stoic, reliable type who dropped their wives into conversation and had cute photos of their kids as screensavers on their phones. He could be charming, charismatic – people liked him. But I knew – or *thought* I knew – he was loyal.

Who was the mystery number? There was that woman at the supermarket deli counter who always gave him a cocktail sausage for Thomas. She was quite pretty, probably, without the hairnet. There was the bartender at the dodgy bowling club he and the guys from work usually went to – but I was sure she had been flirting with me, not him, the one time we had run into her when she was off the clock.

I scrolled through the photos on my phone. It was a procession of images depicting inane domestic bliss, the sort of thing that teenage-me would have rolled her eyes at. There we were, getting married on the beach in Fiji. Posing with plates of complicated breakfasts and glasses of overpriced wine at various restaurants through the years of married life we had before Thomas. Then some floaty-dress baby bump pictures from the first time around, when I had time for wafting around on a beach with a photographer. Fitting Thomas into his car seat on the way home from the hospital. Him tottering across the lounge as he learnt to walk. Dressing up in Dad's work clothes.

Thomas had only just learnt how to line up the camera on my phone to perfectly capture all of our double chins.

It was after 4 a.m. when I heard a key rattle in the lock as Stephen returned. I was still sitting on the couch, staring blankly at the almost-silent television, tracing patterns in the textured fabric of the cushions. I held my breath as he neared the living room door. The light was on – he would know I was inside. He paused briefly but then the door to the spare room clicked shut. I sat on the couch, my fingers tracking the movement of blood through my temples.

Questions were stomping around in circles in my mind: Was she someone I knew? What was going on? What the hell was I going to do?

I knew our relationship had changed. But whose doesn't, when you have children? Years ago, I had a stash of hugely impractical, very skimpy lingerie that I brought out every night he stayed at my place. I crept out of bed sometimes before he woke to put make-up on and would go to a yoga class every night after work and twice at the weekends, coming home relaxed and stretchy. It had been a long time since I had crawled into our bed in anything other than my faded grey favourites and my yoga was now done most often in front of my laptop, with Thomas imitating alongside me, until he got bored. Although it wasn't like Stephen was auditioning for an aftershave advert each night, either – he was still sporting boxers that were dotted with holes.

Our sex life recovered a bit as Thomas got older, and then I fell pregnant with number two. Stephen was surprised if I was even still conscious once Thomas was in bed each night. Then, when the nausea of the first trimester subsided, Stephen remembered how weird he thought it was to have sex when there was a baby 'right there'. 'Especially when it starts moving around,' he complained. 'It's like being in bed with two people . . . but not in a good way.'

Lately, I'd felt like our family had divided into two camps – un-fun Mum wanting vegetables eaten and teeth brushed, and Thomas and his best mate Dad, who came home from work when the hard stuff was done, ready to play. But that was hardly unusual if my circle of friends was representative. We'd all pondered early on how our husbands seemed to regress twenty years with the arrival of a baby, while we aged ten.

Stephen and I had told each other that it was normal, and

we would get back on track eventually. We decided there was no point having a regular 'date night' – we would prefer to lie in front of the TV and see how many chocolate biscuits we could eat in half an hour, than go out somewhere public where we would have to wear pants and bribe a babysitter.

When had he changed his mind?

I should have been weeping for the loss of my family but, afraid to look into that particular abyss, I was seething for more practical reasons. I barely had time for a shower each day and beat myself up when I had to make a phone call just when Thomas needed me. I was torn between my need to work harder than every childfree twenty-something on my team and to out-parent the stay-at-home mothers I went to playgroup with on a daily basis. I pulled eighteen-hour days juggling my work–life 'balance'. It was exhausting. Yet he had managed to fit in a sexy liaison with someone else? I could kill him.

I wrenched myself up and started walking towards the spare bedroom. Stephen was still awake, staring at the lit screen of his phone as I pushed my way into the room. He quickly tapped the device to lock it, sending the room into darkness.

'I need to know right now.' I lowered myself on to the end of the bed. 'Are you seeing someone else? Is that what this is?'

He was silent. The air seemed to throb between us. I slapped his leg through the duvet. 'Stephen! You can't get out of this one.'

His voice was strangled as he pushed himself up on the pillows as if to get away from me. 'Yes.'

'Who is she? Is it someone I know?' I paused, feeling ill, as I realised the possibility. 'Have you been there tonight?'

He turned over in the bed. 'Please, can we talk about it in the morning?'

I took a deliberate breath in, then out, using every drop of my willpower to channel my deep yogi breathing I'd mastered all those years ago. 'No. We cannot talk about it in the morning.'

He pushed himself up on the pillows. I noticed his lined forehead, his short-cut hair becoming a little more sparse around the temples. 'Fine. I've been seeing Alexa. She didn't want me to say anything to you until after the baby came. But now you know.'

He flopped back and put his hands over his face. Like it was my fault that I was finding out at the wrong time. I pulled my hand back from where it lay on his leg as if I had been burned.

Alexa. The name cut through my mental fog. The too-perfect interior designer with the TV show and stupidly expensive coffee table books. She'd been working with him a lot. I should have known something was going on when he told me, completely straight-faced, that he was going to a lunch meeting with her about the colour scheme for a pet dog's bedroom at the big country house he was working on. Instead, I'd just been jealous that he got to have an expensive steak and pricey bottle of wine while I was stuck at home, trying to write a column about a proposed new tax, while I jiggled Thomas on my knee and sang along to *Fireman Sam*.

Alexa was gorgeous. Of course. If you take the average pregnant person and try to imagine the complete opposite, you have her. Tall, slim, impossibly glossy long hair with gold highlights that bounce around as she wanders about in intricately patterned harem pants. That first night we met, at an end-of-year function for Stephen's business, she had just returned from a mountain trek and thirteen-day scuba diving course and reeked of the calm confidence that it seems possible to acquire when you have more than fourteen and a half minutes a day to devote to your own interests.

Brought back to the present with a shock, I could taste my dinner bubbling up into my oesophagus at the thought of her. A scream forced its way up. I grabbed the china vase from the bedside table and hurled it at the wall. 'How could you?' I screamed. 'How the hell could you do that?' I squeaked, more softly the second time. The vase didn't even break, rebounding with a thud on the carpet.

He stared at me. 'You'll wake Thomas. Do you know how long it took me to get him to sleep?'

I stood in shock, then ran for our bedroom. A pile of his clothes lay in a heap on the end of the bed. As I curled up, I realised the whole room smelt of the aftershave I had been buying him for the last ten years.

I woke up a couple of hours later to the sound of Thomas and Stephen in the kitchen, clattering spoons into bowls as they assembled breakfast. I stretched, feeling the bones click back into place in my neck, and barrel-rolled off the bed. My baby seemed to stretch too, contorting as she found her way back to the centre of my upright body.

I edged the kitchen door open. Thomas was perched on his step stool, pouring milk into the bowl, and on to the bench, from which it was dripping on to the floor. The kettle was boiling and our dog, Waffle, nudged her empty water bowl across the tiles with her greying nose. Stephen grabbed the milk bottle from Thomas. 'I told you to be careful. Let me.'

'I do it!' Thomas glared but looked chastened. Stephen rarely snapped at him. His father tried to guide the pour. He looked up as he heard me shuffling in, my legs numb from the baby cutting off my blood supply. He quickly turned his gaze to Thomas again.

I watched the pair of them as Stephen positioned Thomas into his chair at the dining table. More cereal was spilling down the front of his T-shirt. I handed Stephen a cloth to wipe him, but he looked flummoxed, so I snatched it back and dabbed at the mess.

'I'm going to ask my mum to take Thomas out for a while, so we can talk today.' I kept my voice calm, channelling the woman who fronted the kids' TV show that kept Thomas occupied for a sanity-saving hour each Saturday morning. My husband might be trying to ruin our lives, but I was going to keep this from Thomas – as well as everyone else – for as long as I could.

Stephen swallowed, and focused on my hand blotting Thomas's T-shirt. 'I have to go to the site this morning. I can come back about eleven.'

I kissed Thomas's forehead. 'That's fine. Thank you.'

We were talking to each other as if we were business acquaintances, who didn't particularly like each other.

He had barely made a dent in his toast when he stood up and stuffed his keys and phone into a bulging pocket, whistling for Waffle to follow him into his truck.

'Say goodbye to Dad,' I prompted Thomas, who was watching a shimmer of sunlight dance across the wall. I was not going to miss an opportunity to remind Stephen of what he would be leaving behind. I would have pulled out my sonography scans and dangled them in front of him if I could.

'You shirt,' Thomas pointed at my front. I was still wearing Stephen's baggy grey T-shirt, which I'd had on the day before. There was a saucy smear across the front, where Thomas had wiped his face as I hugged him after a messy afternoon tea. He raised a puzzled eyebrow.

I arranged my face into as neutral an expression as I could manage. 'I didn't have time to get changed.' I shot him what

I hoped was a reassuring smile. He was frowning. It was time to deploy my best upbeat your-mother-is-definitely-not-falling-apart voice again. If I presented him with the wrong type of jam with his toast, it could throw him off for the whole day. Now I was turning up in day-old clothes and acting like his father was a stranger in our kitchen. 'Everything is okay, darling. You're going to Gran and Granddad's this morning. That will be fun, won't it?'

By 11.30, there was still no sign of Stephen. I paced the house, watching the driveway. Every time I tried to return to my desk, the words on the computer screen seemed to flitter in front of me. I was scanning a press release for the third time, still with no idea what it said, when my phone vibrated. A message from Stephen at last. I gritted my teeth as I opened it. 'Can't make it back this morning.'

I stabbed at the phone to call him. It rang and rang before voicemail clicked in: 'Hi, it's Stephen Murchison, I can't come to the phone . . .'

'You can't or you won't?' I growled at it and tried again. And again. At the sixth time, he answered. 'I cannot talk to you right now,' he hissed. 'I'm on site.'

Had I always been married to such a selfish coward? Did he think I could just put my own life on hold until he had time to spare for me?

'You were meant to be coming back here at eleven.' My anger reverberated through my body so hard I thought he must be able to hear it down the phone line. 'I need to know. Is that it for our marriage? For our kids? How long has this been going on for?' I spat the words at my computer screen.

'I don't know.'

There was a sound of movement, a door slammed. He must have gone to sit in his truck.

'A month maybe. Two. I've developed feelings for her.' His voice trailed off as if I was meant to just accept it. Like, oh you're in love with her? That's all right, then. Please carry on. Don't let me be an impediment to your happiness.

Instead, I let the silence hang between us. He might as well have been speaking a different language. The Stephen I knew thought 'feelings' should be approached in the same way as a particularly virulent infectious disease. The first time I'd told him I loved him, he said: 'me too'. We'd got engaged while on holiday in Hawaii because, watching loved-up Japanese couples exchanging vows on the sand, he'd said: 'I suppose you want to do that, too?'

At last, he sighed. 'I'll move out while we figure out what to do.'

'You'll move out?' I was suddenly shouting so loud it made my throat hurt. 'Damn right you'll move out. I never want to see your face again.'

I pressed the button to end the call, my hands shaking as if I had downed twenty-six coffees. A month or two? In that time, I had dragged him to midwife appointments, he had sat with me while I agonised over paint colours for the new baby's room and we had planned Thomas's third birthday party. We'd even pored over which species of dinosaur Thomas might like on his cake. All that time he had been talking to someone else, confiding in her? The crushing weight of the loss was overwhelming.

Every aspect of my life had been moulded to fit our family. Before Thomas was born, I had wanted to use an inheritance from my grandfather to set up a little yoga studio but Stephen had argued it was too risky to both be self-employed. Then, I'd passed up promotions so that I could work from home to be there for Thomas. For a while, I'd provided the only income as he channelled everything he earned into growing his business and paying the staff (he'd employed prematurely). We'd even decided the time was right to try for a second baby this year because he'd taken on a big contract that would double his workload in twelve months' time.

I gritted my teeth. If he wanted to destroy our little family, I was going to make him pay.

CHAPTER TWO

How to make a teepee

What you'll need:

Rope

Dowels

A canvas drop cloth

Screws and washers

Cut a length of rope. Drill a hole near the top of one of your poles and string the rope through it. Tie a knot. Prop your poles up in the teepee position to see where they'll need to sit to be stable. Drill a hole in your second pole where the two poles meet and feed the rope through. Do the same for the third and fourth poles. Start draping your drop cloth over the poles and secure it where they meet with a screw. If you can wrestle the cloth off your kids, who will want to pretend to be ghosts in it, screw it into each of the poles to hold it in place.

Erect the teepee in your living room or some other high-traffic area of your home where it will be sure to be in the way. You'll fall over it at least four times a day, and it will soon become a hiding place for toys you can't find space to put away. Depending on the strength of your construction, you and your kids may even be able to live in it, if you're giving up on that suburban dream that was never really yours to begin with.

I locked my phone and pushed it away from me on my desk, as if touching it again might prompt another world-destroying revelation. Thomas was still at my parents' house but there was no hope of me getting any of the work on my to-do list done. What was I meant to do next?

I tapped an email out to my boss. Being very pregnant afforded few luxuries but no-questions-asked sick leave seemed to be one of them.

I was walking aimlessly around the living room when a car pulled up outside. Through the venetian blinds, I could see a woman in sharp stiletto heels, black culottes and a spaghetti-strap pink camisole that did not quite cover her red bra, extracting herself from the driver's seat. Her long, almost puce hair caught in the door as she closed it behind her. My sister, Amy. She looked as though she was ready for a night out, not an excursion into deepest suburbia to visit me.

My shoulders slumped. Could I face a visit? I was still seesawing between a scream and hysterical laughter. I had had to bury my head in the fridge and pretend I was organising dinner when my parents came to pick up Thomas – and that was before *that* phone call. My neck was tense all the way down my spine, but I couldn't even lie flat to stretch out.

I opened the door before she could knock. She swayed slightly, her heels digging into the soft ground as she picked her way across the lawn. 'Rachel, darling.'

I gestured to her to wipe a spot of pink lipstick from her top teeth. 'Amy. You didn't tell me you were coming by.'

She kissed my cheek as she pushed past me. She was still wearing the lanyard and security pass that let her into the double-storey restaurant and bar complex where she worked. 'Are you on maternity leave yet? I figured you might be bored. Thought we could have a bit of a catch-up. Maybe get some lunch?'

'I've still got a week and a bit. Look, I've got something I need to deal with.' I shot her a look. When we were ten, she'd been able to tell when I had stashed KitKats in the wardrobe. Surely there would be no way I was hiding this one. 'Now really isn't a good time.'

She wasn't looking at me. 'What are you talking about? It's been ages since we got together.'

It hadn't, we'd had lunch last week.

Amy was picking through a pile of magazines on my coffee table. 'Mind if I take this one?' It was the latest issue of *Women's Health*, promising ten ways to bring on labour. I'd figured if my baby was still tucked up in there the day before my due date, I'd allow myself to read it.

I shrugged. 'Sure, go for it. Look, can I give you a call a bit later? We can make time for coffee. Is everything okay?'

She collapsed on to an armchair. 'I'm tired after a long, crappy night at work. Can you believe we didn't get out of there until 6 a.m.? Then I went to one of the waiters' houses for a bit . . . I really need to get a real job.'

She stretched and yawned. 'None of the losers tipped, either. Can you spot me £50?'

I sighed. 'My wallet's on the table by the door. You can take whatever's in it.'

She raised an eyebrow, seeming at last to notice something amiss. 'I was joking, mostly. I'm not that skint. What's up?'

I watched her lean back in the chair and frown at me, twisting her hair around her fingertips. She had always made fun of Stephen and me for our 'domestic bliss'. She bought me a copy of *The Stepford Wives* for Christmas one year, and an apron for my twenty-first birthday. But what would she know? Her longest relationship had lasted two years, with an artist named Frank. I couldn't even remember his last name. She had always seemed to think that the scruffier he was, the more of a genius he must be. I just thought he needed a shower.

'Stephen and I are having a few problems,' I muttered at last. The words seemed to stick in my throat.

She blinked. 'All is not well in this land of domestic harmony?'

I turned away. She scrambled to her feet and was behind me in seconds, putting her arm around my shoulders. Her skin felt vaguely sticky and she smelled fruity, as if she'd had a drink spilt on her. I wanted to offer her a baby wipe.

'I'm sorry. I shouldn't have said that,' she murmured into my hair. 'Is there anything I can do?'

I flinched as she tried to lay her head against mine and smiled thinly. 'No. Thanks, though.' I checked my watch. It was almost 1 p.m. 'I've got to go and pick up Thomas before Dad has a hernia.' I could still remember my father's face the last time I'd arrived late and walked in on Thomas. He was face down, spread-eagled on the dining room floor, screaming with every bit of breath in his little lungs, because my mother had suggested he might like to change out of his food-soaked T-shirt. It was at least a twenty-minute drive from my place in the suburbs to my parents' home by the beach. Amy grabbed my hand, twisting her fingers into mine. 'I'll come with you.'

I hesitated. This time, she seemed to read my mind. 'Don't worry, I won't make you talk about it if you don't want to. I'll keep you company. Tell you some stories about last night's sleazeballs to make you feel better. You won't believe what Heidi had to put up with.'

Thomas was doing circuits of the living room when we arrived. Overtired energy coursing through him, he was busy throwing magazines and television remotes into his favourite plastic trolley. Every time he completed a circuit, he would veer off and collide with the side of the couch. My father sat on said couch, his legs tucked up beneath him to avoid Thomas, focusing on the television, with his index fingers tracing circles on his temples.

'Hi, Mumma,' Thomas screamed and dropped his trolley when he noticed me at last. He wrapped his arms around my legs and peered up at me. 'Hello.' Then he noticed my sister: 'Auntie Army!'

It was a sweet mispronunciation that no one had bothered to correct because it was too endearing. She scooped him up and placed an exuberant, wet kiss on his cheek.

I noticed something brown smeared across the side of his face. Had my mother been trying to get him to bake again?

As I was pondering, I noticed both he and my mum were staring at me. Out of the corner of my eye, I could see a streak of mascara on the side of my nose. I hadn't thought

26

I'd cried that much in the car but perhaps I was wrong. Amy kicked off her heels and nudged Thomas towards the living room. 'Go and find your new trains to show me, buddy.'

He ambled off obediently, and we heard crashing as he upended a toy box and knocked over a makeshift teepee. 'It must be somewhere,' he shouted. It was what I said to him every time he asked me to find the latest toy that had gone missing.

'New trains?' I forced a high-pitched laugh as I turned to my mother. Thomas would soon be able to curate an exhibition of toys my parents had collected for him.

She wasn't buying my attempt to change the subject, took me by the wrists and stared at my puffy, itchy eyes. 'What's going on? You've been crying. Is something wrong at work? Has something happened to Stephen's business?'

I tried to choke out the words, but they did not make any more sense on the second retelling than they had when I gave Amy an abridged version in the car. Soon the tears were dripping off my chin. Two days ago, everything was normal. Everything was fine. I was boring Rachel, married to a nice but slightly infuriating man with one exuberant son and a daughter on the way. Not exactly living the dream but doing well enough to pass the Christmas card newsletter test. Now I was separating from a cheating husband who had taken up with a B-grade celebrity interior designer.

'What? Are you sure? I can't believe . . .' My mother placed a perfectly manicured hand over her mouth.

I cut her off. 'Yes, I know. It was a surprise to me as well.'

'But . . . you're pregnant! He can't get away with this, surely.' She pushed her small square glasses up on her nose and stared at me as if being able to see me more clearly might present a different reality.

I rolled my eyes and gestured to my midsection, where

27

my stomach was doing its best impression of a parade float. 'I'm aware of that, too. Turns out, there's no law against it. Thomas!' I shouted over her head. 'In the car, please.'

She grabbed my hand again. 'What will you do? A newborn and Thomas on your own . . . Can you imagine . . .' Her eyes were sparking with anger. 'How dare he? After everything you've done for him.'

I rested my hand on her arm in a way I hoped was reassuring. The last thing I needed was her flying off to fight my cause for me. I still hadn't recovered fully from the email she had sent to one of my university lecturers when I had failed a paper in my final year.

'I'm sure I'll be fine.' I took another deep breath, summoning up an image of my first yoga teacher, who'd spent a full session showing me how to move my diaphragm. 'Sillier people than me manage it. Thomas! What are you doing in there?'

'Darling, come and stay with us.'

My father gave up his pretence of ignoring us. 'What did you say?'

'I said Rachel must come and stay here if she and Stephen are having problems.' My mother's voice was unusually firm. 'We have the spare rooms upstairs. We can help you with the baby. I can clean out the cupboards down here, so you have room for your things. The rooms aren't big, but they should be fine for the three of you. It's quite warm in the evening on that side of the house, but I can get you a fan . . .'

I bit my lip. Would the things that drove me nuts as a teenager – my mother's anxiety about every decision I had to make, my father's need for routine – be even more grating twenty years on? Did they think I couldn't cope on my own?

I cut her off. 'I'll think about it, okay?' Thomas had

appeared at my side, stretching his little fingers around two new train carriages.

In the car on the way back to our house, I replayed my mother's words in my mind. Amy had dozed off in the passenger seat next to me, her phone clasped in her hand.

Could I manage a newborn and Thomas, alone? There were millions of women around the world functioning perfectly well as single mothers. Should I be offended that my mother deemed me unable do the same? I assumed I would need a little longer off work than the roughly four and a half hours I'd taken with Thomas. But it could be done. Perhaps I could get a flatmate. I drafted the ad in my head: Sunny room for single person to share with professional woman and two others, one prone to stomping about in the middle of the night or waking early with a rousing rendition of 'Jingle Bells'.

Perhaps a flatmate was not going to work.

'Stephen will have to pay some sort of child support, won't he?' I realised I was asking the woman with the friendly smile on the billboard opposite us as we waited for the traffic light to change.

'What, Mumma?' Thomas's little forehead crumpled into a frown. His floppy brown fringe needed a trim. I met his eyes in the rear-view mirror. 'Nothing, darling. Sorry. Don't worry, Mumma's just having a bit of a rough day today. It's going to be okay.'

He kept watching me, cracker in one hand, as the traffic light went green and I put my foot on the accelerator. The irony was, I had a tower of parenting books on the table beside my bed. Could any of them tell me how to protect a two-and-a-bit-year-old from a sudden-onset paternal midlife crisis?

What would I do if the baby woke just as Thomas was falling asleep, his little arms wrapped around my neck? And would I ever get another shower again, if I had to coax two of them through breakfast first? Thomas stretched his hand out, making a smeary print on the window. I watched him drag his finger through the crumbs left on the glass.

Back at the house, Thomas splashed in his paddling pool in the late afternoon sunshine. The leaves on the tree in the middle of our lawn had curled prematurely, dropping one by one and forming a mushy brown mulch. The lawn looked exactly as I felt. I propped myself on an outdoor dining chair and tracked back through my missed calls. One number had tried me three times already. I pressed the button to call it back.

A woman's voice answered on the first ring. 'Rachel.' She exhaled my name into the phone. 'Thanks so much for getting in touch. I just wanted to run a story idea past you. I think it's pretty neat – one of my clients is launching a new business . . .'

I yelped as Thomas threw a plastic bucket of water at my legs. I held up a finger.

'Rachel? Are you okay?' The PR woman was still talking.

'Sorry, yes. Just working from home with my son today.' Thomas frowned and backed up for another attempt.

Her laugh tinkled down the phone. 'Oh, don't worry. I know how that is.'

I would have bet anything that she didn't. I'd heard from a friend that she had employed two nannies, working in tandem, so that she could carry on with her life fairly untroubled, despite the arrival of twins. It had made me question my life choices.

Thomas took aim with his next bucket-load. I grabbed the pail from his clutches, and with a surge of anger shooting through me, threw it to the far corner of the garden. His face fell as he turned away. A twang of remorse tugged at my chest. I reached to pat his shoulder, but he ducked and darted away to the bucket.

'So it's ground-breaking, exciting stuff. Was hoping you might like to do an interview? I could set it up for any time that suits you.'

Thomas pumped his fists in the air as I watched him attempt to kick water at me from the far end of his paddling pool. I turned away from him and huddled over the phone. 'Do you think you could pop the details in an email to me?'

When the water in the pool was evenly spread across the rest of the garden, Thomas moved to his bike and propelled himself along as fast as his lean legs would permit, heading for the gate. When at last I was able to put the phone down, I stumbled after him. 'Get back here.'

He shook his head. 'Leaving.'

I dropped to his height and blocked his path. 'Sorry for throwing your bucket, darling. I was trying to concentrate on my call.'

He kicked at the ground. 'Hungry.'

I hauled myself to my feet. 'Okay, let's go inside and see what we can find, shall we?'

Of all the parenting things at which I was failing, feeding Thomas seemed the most egregious.

When he was first starting to eat solid food, I would spend every other Sunday evening cooking and freezing nutritious meals with a laundry list of clean foods like kale and quinoa. He invariably turned his nose up, and more went on the floor than in his mouth. Defeated, I'd let the most recent freezer stash run out, and now the chances of me producing more than a plate of fish fingers for his dinner were slim. The most I could hope for was that there was a handful of oven chips somewhere in the bottom of the garage chest freezer to accompany them.

I stripped off Thomas's wet things and positioned him on the couch with my iPad and one of his favourite YouTube clips, of children unwrapping Kinder Surprise eggs. Before I became a parent, I would not have believed such a thing existed, but he would always find them, even if I dutifully set up something like *Thomas the Tank Engine*. How could a child who could not read, write, or even reliably use the toilet navigate YouTube on an iPad?

I arranged the fish fingers, chips, some carefully sliced carrot and a spoonful of hummus on to one of those plastic platters designed for fussy kids who don't like their food groups to touch. I had bought a set thinking they might inspire me to serve up interesting antipasto-style meals for Thomas, with morsels of healthy treats for him to select from. Pinterest mums always provided a selection of examples to follow. But the pressure of having to come up with something for each of the spots was intense. Once I had found myself adding a few cornflakes, just so he wouldn't have an empty platter segment.

The landline phone jingled and startled me; I'd almost forgotten we still had one.

'Is this Murchison Contracting?' The man's voice was gruff. Stephen must have his work phone off. I pushed an image of him in bed with Alexa out of my mind, dabbing at an unidentified splotch on my shirt.

'Oh sorry.' I tried to hit the pitch and tone of a cheery receptionist. 'Stephen Murchison's gone out of business. Terrible thing.'

There was a pause. 'Are you sure? Stephen?'

'Quite. Allegations of poor workmanship. Awful situation. I'm just taking the calls. Should I take a message?'

The man coughed. 'Never mind. I'll try someone else.'

Thomas wailed from the lounge. My iPad had run out of battery. I ushered him in to the dinner table, helping him use my bump as a kind of step stool on to his seat. 'What you eating?' He looked at me.

I could not respond. My stomach was still doing an impression of the kitchen blender but if I threw our routine off track, I might never get him into bed. It was only the promise of a bath on my own once he was asleep that was getting me through the evening. I half-heartedly picked a limp fish finger from the oven tray and put it on a bread plate. I slid into the chair next to him and gave him what I hoped was an encouraging smile.

He frowned. 'You sad, Mumma? Daddy home?'

I had to turn my face away and pinch my thigh to stop a surge of tears. 'I'm fine, darling, don't worry. I'm not sure what Daddy's up to, but you've got me tonight, okay?'

I clenched his hand, probably a little too tightly. With three of us around the dinner table, the six-person setting had seemed appropriate. With just us two, it seemed empty. Of course, it would not be long before we would have another person with us in her high chair, throwing her own fish fingers on the ground. Somehow the thought did not make me any happier.

It turns out you can share a house with someone for more than a decade and still not really know them.

I met Stephen as I was finishing high school. It had been what one of my teachers described as a 'social year' for me, in which I spent more time getting acquainted with the coffee machine in the common room set aside for seniors than I did in the classroom. We were allowed to come and go as we liked and I duly did, erasing any classes before 10 a.m. from my timetable. Despite that, I had learnt to write an essay florid enough that no one noticed its lack of substance and I was able to squeeze out enough marks to get into a communications degree.

I would like to claim to have been following a lifelong dream, but that would be a lie. I was not good enough at maths to be a doctor, not confident enough for marketing and although I harboured daydreams about being a youth worker, who helped troubled young people find their way, I had finally accepted that it probably wouldn't all be like *Dangerous Minds*. I could never pull off a leather jacket in the same way Michelle Pfeiffer did, anyway. Kids would take one look at me and roll their eyes.

Stephen crashed his way into my world at a friend's party – the kind where for the first time one of your inner circle is finally of legal drinking age. We all felt very grown up that one of us had ventured to the off-licence and stocked up on sugary ready-mixed vodka pops.

Stephen had ended up there by accident because the friend who was meant to be taking him and his mates to the football had drunk too much and could no longer drive. He'd sidled over to me with the confidence of someone on their third beer. Helena, who had been my friend since we were in kindergarten, gave me a knowing look. We had spent ages agonising over my outfit and settled on a pair of bootleg jeans, an off-the-shoulder sparkly black top and an impossibly high pair of stiletto heels that I was not able to walk in without looking like a particularly hesitant fawn but which we decided looked incredibly sophisticated.

Stephen looked me straight in the eye. 'I snore, sometimes

pee in the shower and have been known to turn my underwear inside out to get another day's wear out of them.'

'Pardon?' I wasn't sure if he had mistaken me for someone else.

He shot me an ear-to-ear grin. 'I figure if I tell you all the bad stuff about me now, there's less chance you'll be disappointed when you get to know me.'

He settled down on to the sofa beside me and put his arm along its back. I could smell his supermarket cologne. He had shaved his head, but you could see the shadow where the hair was growing back, so I knew he was not actually bald. He was sporting the small, under-the-lip tuft of hair that was inexplicably the fashion at the time, particularly among those who needed to prove they had hair to grow.

'How do you know I'm going to want to get to know you?' I was impressed by his arrogance.

His eyes were mischievous. 'Oh, I don't. But it's not like you were talking to anyone else.' He gestured to the boys my age, who were all still milling around on the other side of the room, too nervous to try their own opening lines. Helena looked as though she might be about to rescue one of them.

That was fifteen years ago, and although I found out pretty quickly that his list of negative things was by no means comprehensive, he was correct in his prediction that I was rarely disappointed – in the early years, at least.

Through university, while my friends were ranking the various schools according to the sexual prowess of their male students, I was going home to Stephen. I would still add my cash to the fund we built up each week for jugs of second-rate beer in the campus bar, before they headed off into the night with the latest guy to get their hopes up. Whereas I knew exactly what I was getting with Stephen – and it would

35

come with an early alarm clock the next day as he got ready for work.

He even willingly attended a mock appointment with a friend who was training to be a naturopath and put us through a process in which we were asked to describe the consistency of our faeces. I had felt sick with mortification but he had chuckled at the flowchart of photographs and brought it up when he wanted to make me blush, for weeks afterwards.

There was a period when my friends and I became a bit too invested in *Sex and the City*, and I decided I needed some time as a single girl to carve my identity, preferably from the comfort of something that resembled an upmarket New York loft apartment. It took about twelve hours before I realised that my rundown flat didn't have quite the same vibe. The heel of my imitation Manolo Blahniks kept getting stuck in the cracked concrete of the front steps, for one.

Wanting to punish me, he went for drinks with his work-mates at the bar I worked at, and gave my colleague a tip that was about three times her nightly wage. I found out later he'd taken out a loan from his father to pay the rent that week.

I responded by going on a blind date offered by one of my flatmates. The standoff lasted about three weeks before I called him, manufacturing a leaking tap that needed his attention. He turned up within ten minutes, not even mentioning that he was a builder, not a plumber.

Our relationship had become so familiar I sometimes had to think twice to remember that he had not always been around. We had become so comfortable that it was not unusual for him to discuss – in detail – the symptoms of the latest tummy bug he had picked up from Thomas or to wander out after a shower to ask me whether a spot on his back was a new addition.

Now, I was working out how best to keep up my energy to read bedtime stories to our son on my own, while he spent the evening – I guessed – entwined with Alexa's freakishly long, sickeningly smooth limbs. It was as though I had landed in someone else's life.

Thomas seemed to sense my strength was waning and was a little more compliant than normal as we dragged ourselves through the evening motions. I did not argue when he merely waved the toothbrush in the direction of his teeth, and he only protested for a minute when it was time to turn out the light.

I snuggled down next to him and arranged his little body around the curve of my stomach. He buried his face in my hair, twisting some of it around his fingers. 'Daddy home tomorrow?'

I kissed his forehead hard. 'I don't think so, sweetheart. But I'll think of something fun for us to do, promise.'

He screwed up his face. I started to draw circles on his back with my finger, counting 187 of them before his breathing started to become slow and regular. I lay as still as I could, next to him, staring at the ceiling. Over the past two and a half years, I had watched him fall asleep so often I could always pinpoint the moment he finally nodded off. His body would give a little jerk and his breath deepened.

I used to count to 100 of those breaths before I started to try to extricate myself from the bed, so there was no chance I would wake him on my run to freedom. This time I allowed myself to enjoy being cuddled up next to him. The world outside his bedroom door might have changed dramatically, but I would cling on to this little cocoon of familiarity for as long as I could.

CHAPTER THREE

<u>How to make gloop</u>

What you'll need:

500g cornflour

Water

Food colouring

In a decent-sized mixing bowl, mix your cornflour and water together in a ratio of one part water to two parts cornflour. When it's reached the desired consistency, add your choice of food colouring. Perfect for adding splashes of colour to an otherwise perfect-condition white T-shirt. Never mind, though. Perhaps it's time to stop trying to keep up appearances. Worn-in is the new black, right?

The next morning, Thomas woke as the first birds started singing. He slumped out of his bed and stomped down the hallway, dragging his duvet behind him. I pretended to be asleep, complete with a faux snore for effect, as he pushed my bedroom door open. He clambered under the duvet, warm from his bed, and started driving a toy truck up the side of my face.

'Wake up, Mumma!' he shouted and giggled when I started. 'Are you stuck? Tow truck pull you out.'

'Don't you want to watch something on the iPad for a little while before we get up?' I reached for it and waved it desperately. It had taken me hours to fall asleep, battling mental glamour shots of Stephen and Alexa interspersed with little short films of my weakest parenting and marriage moments.

He shook his head and grabbed my hand, pulling me out from under the covers, towards the door. I reached for my bathrobe and tried to arrange it around my bump. The tie would not quite reach so I held it shut with one hand while he wrenched me along with the other. We stumbled out of my bedroom into the living room, where the first weak rays of sunlight were trying to push their way through the crack in the curtains. A steady rhythm of rain pelted the windows. I leant against the wall, willing my still-sleepy brain to catch up.

'What do you want for breakfast, honey?'

I could probably stretch my culinary skills to produce some toast and Marmite, and there might be a few crumbs of cereal left. I might even be able to find a banana somewhere in the back of the cupboard. I had not been to the supermarket in days.

'Crackers.' Thomas was firm.

Thomas would live on crackers if he could. But not any kind of crackers – it had to be one brand, specific to one supermarket that always seemed to stock too few of the things. Sometimes I had to check back with them two or three days in a row before they had a packet on the shelves.

'You'll have something on the crackers, though, right? Peanut butter?'

I tried to keep my voice light. Please say yes, I willed him. I needed to at least pretend his breakfast had contained more than just packaged, refined carbohydrates.

'Just crackers,' he said solemnly. 'I sit here and eat them.'

He strolled through to the dining room and pulled himself on to a chair at the table. He looked at me expectantly. I was too tired to try harder. Maybe serving nutritious breakfasts was the domain of people who were not suddenly single-parenting.

'Do you need to go to the toilet?' He was fidgeting in his seat.

'No thank you,' he said primly, a cracker in each hand.

He wriggled again.

'Are you sure?'

His eyes widened in alarm. 'Toilet!' He jumped from his seat and rushed for the door. There was a banging as he tried to get his pyjamas off and climb on to his step stool at the same time.

He re-emerged a few minutes later, his pants discarded. I shrugged it off. He'd be getting dressed before long, anyway. While he ate his parent-incriminating breakfast, I packed his lunchbox for nursery with an array of relatively healthy snacks – carrot sticks, hummus, a couple of rice crackers, some fruit. I regarded it for a minute. I had better add a serving of yoghurt and a couple of plain biscuits so I could be sure that he would at least eat something during the day.

Crackers demolished, Thomas bumbled off to my bedroom, dragging his fingers along the walls as he went.

'Where are you off to?' It was a half-hearted inquiry and I did not wait for a response. He soon started clattering and banging, pulling things down from the bedside table. I tried not to think about it – I had moved everything 'dangerous' to a shelf in my wardrobe that even I needed a step stool to reach. Somehow, I needed to get his bag packed, to find clothes for him and something clean and big enough for me to wear. Then I needed to put the dishwasher on, all before we had to leave the house at 8.30.

I figured the worst that could happen would be that he wasted some of my Chanel hand cream – bought for me as a gift and which I was using so sparingly that it was into its second year. On a scale of The Worst Things To Happen, seeing that disappear would be pretty bad – old me might even have cried – but I could sacrifice it in the interests of making it out of the door.

He appeared in the kitchen in front of me. It took me a second to realise what he had in his hand: a vibrator from my underwear drawer, the type that has a head that is attached to the main body of the contraption with a long wire. The batteries had long since gone flat.

'A skipping rope!' he shouted. 'I found a skipping rope in your drawer!'

My horror must have been apparent because he looked at me sideways and put it behind his back, scowling fiercely at my lunge to wrench it from his grasp. 'Mine! I show Kaskia!'

I could just imagine it. His teachers, one of whom was 'Kaskia', who, in fact, was a tiny German woman called Saskia, already seemed to think I was some sort of deviant because I occasionally arrived late to pick him up, usually in my faded activewear, and almost always forgot about their themed 'wacky days' – when he was meant to dress up as a superhero or paint his hair green. They would have a field day if he turned up with sex toys in his schoolbag.

I would have to distract him with something else if I was to have a hope of getting it from him. 'I'll swap you an M&M for your skipping rope,' I ventured, pushing half-empty boxes of crackers and muesli bars around in the cupboard as I tried to find them.

'Two,' he said, his eyes narrowing.

'Fine, two,' I agreed. 'If you put your raincoat on.' The deal was done.

The goodbye as I dropped him off at nursery was not the drawn-out film scene farewell that it sometimes was, where he would sit on me and hold my hair, then lean through the fence as I drove away, waving at me as if he was a castaway on an island. This time, his class was engrossed in what looked like a big bowl of blue gloop. They were in it up to their armpits, flicking handfuls at each other. All fifteen of them were filthy.

Thomas pushed through to the middle of the group and

plunged in up to his armpits. One of the teachers met my gaze as I quickly tallied up whether we had enough size three clothes to justify throwing this set out, rather than bothering to wash it. Their 'washable' paints had taken me at least a week and half a bottle of bleach to budge last time, and even then the shirts had looked like they'd been washed with some vibrant socks. 'It's a valuable learning experience. Great sensory exploration,' she shouted over their heads.

I ignored her and blew a kiss at Thomas, noticing with a jolt how the curve of his face had become that of a little boy, not the round-cheeked profile of a baby. He jostled with his best friend, Nixon. 'I'll be back to pick you up after lunch.' He did not acknowledge me. Instead, he smeared some gloop across the front of his shirt and threw some at Nixon.

The rain had stopped when I returned to my car but the sunshine was not yet sure of itself. I clambered in. Between the baby seat behind me and the steering wheel in front, there was little room left for my expanding bulk. I slammed my hand on the button to turn the car on. The fuel light glared at me. I'd usually have tried to swap cars with Stephen just at the moment when it needed to be filled. But there was a service station on the way home, so there was no excuse.

Even though I'd had this car more than three years, I always drove up to the pumps on the wrong side. The hose reached across the top – just – but left a dingy mark on the white paintwork.

'Let me help you.' A woman appeared beside me. With a deft wriggle, she moved the nozzle around so it no longer threatened to snap out and spurt across the forecourt. 'Go inside, I'll finish up here.' She gave me the sort of half-smile I assume most people saved for children and the very elderly.

Behind the counter, another woman was shuffling packs of gum into a display unit. She looked up as I approached and beamed. 'You don't have long to go.'

I felt my shoulders sag. I did not have the energy for another of *these* conversations. The only worse conversation starter was something about how enormous I was. Or a request to touch the bump always asked in the way a small child might approach a petting farm animal.

'A few weeks.' I pointedly turned my attention to the display of protein bars and chocolate. It was almost time for second breakfast, a pregnant person's most important meal of the day.

'Is this your first?'

I passed her my card and a couple of chocolate bars. 'No, I have a son. He's two.'

'Do you know what you're having?'

I had promised myself that the next time I had this question, I would reply that I was having a baby. Or perhaps hoping for a small rabbit or chicken. But at that moment, it felt a bit like I'd be telling her that Santa wasn't real. I sighed. 'I'm having a girl.'

She half-squealed. 'You must be so pleased. Daddy's little girl! Your partner must be over the moon.'

My stomach did a backflip. I backed away, trying to avoid her puzzled gaze as I fumbled my credit card back into my wallet. I could feel tears forcing their way out of the corners of my eyes. 'Sorry, I have to go.'

When I arrived home, my hands were still shaking, and the blood had left my knuckles from the vehemence with which I had gripped the steering wheel. My feet were on fire, my lower back throbbed and my throat was raspy from crying. I dropped on to the sofa, wincing as I lifted my legs on to the ottoman. I had lost all definition in my ankles, and the bones in my feet were a mere memory.

As I leant back, the wedding photo in a heavy frame on the opposite wall seemed to glint in the sunlight. I had never really liked it – my pre-wedding diet had been overzealous, and my dress ended up a little too big. Every couple of minutes, I had had to hitch it up to cover my bra. My smile was glossy white but forced. It was probably the twenty-fifth photo that had been taken in a row while we stood under a sagging tree branch. Although everyone exclaimed over how happy we looked, with Stephen guffawing at someone over the photographer's shoulder, I could see in my own face how much I'd worried about the table settings, the accom-modation, making sure my parents were not stuck in awkward conversation with Stephen's boorish newly single uncle and that Amy was not too far into the champagne before she gave her speech.

The photo was only on the wall because I felt it was what we *should* do when we finally had our – very expensive – delivery from the photographer. Suddenly, I found I could not look at it a moment longer. In two steps, I was across the room and ripping it from the hook. Without thinking, I turned on my heel and strode out to my car. I thrust the chunky frame into the boot. Looking at it lying among the detritus of shopping receipts, some empty lunchboxes and an old picnic blanket, felt apt. I was determined not to stop there.

There were holiday snaps in matching frames on our bedroom wall. A photo of Stephen and his parents, with his niece, was propped on the side table in the spare room. They could all come down too. It was not like he was around to notice.

I worked my way through the house, room by room, pulling photos from their hooks, thrusting the smaller ones

47

into rubbish bags. Only Thomas's baby photos and one of my family were left in place.

As I walked out after stripping our bedroom, I noticed the door on Stephen's side of the wardrobe had been left ajar. As usual, his clothes were spilling out, jammed on to hangers and in piles on the wardrobe floor. He would never throw anything out. I grabbed handfuls of material and stuffed them into the top of the big black plastic bags of photos.

Half an hour later, I was driving into the rubbish collection centre in the middle of town, the back of my car laden with the big black rubbish bags, huge photos in frames, T-shirts, hoodies and business shirts. The frames clinked together as I rounded each corner and crashed into the back of the back seat when I stepped on the brake.

The woman who staffed the entrance looked at me quizzically as I drove up. 'Just a carload of rubbish.' I gave her my cheeriest smile. My face was probably still streaked with make-up, and my eyes were undoubtedly bright red. She waved me on.

At the edge of the rubbish pit, I stood next to an elderly man who was dropping his own rubbish bags in, watching them flop one on top of each other. The contents of Stephen's wardrobe landed with a satisfying thump. I hurled the photos one by one, listening to the glass smash on the concrete floor below.

There went our wedding photo. Crash. The time we had lunch on the street in Barcelona. Smash. The evening we spent on the beach in Waikiki after Stephen 'asked' me to marry him. The glass in that frame blew apart into a thousand little pieces.

Thomas was swinging on the gate when I arrived to pick him up from nursery, next to a girl in a T-shirt at least two sizes too big for her. They were both filthy from the knees down, with tracks of sand in their hair.

'Mummy! My mummy!' he shouted as I hauled myself out of the car.

I pulled his bag out of the cubbyhole by the door, and a plastic bag full of wet, blue clothes came somersaulting down with it. As I had expected, almost everything in his lunchbox was untouched, except for the yoghurt and cookies, which were gone.

He allowed himself to be clipped into the car seat, wriggling as my midsection got in the way while I fastened the buckles. When he was secure, I paused, jangling my keys in my hands. I desperately did not want to go back home – and work could wait. 'Shall we go to the library?'

'Yes!'

There was something about the fish tanks, the long staircases and my insistence on quiet that appealed enormously to Thomas when we went to the library. We only had to be nearby, and he started off in the direction of the big grey and glass building. Some of the librarians knew him by name, even though I had been avoiding them and using the self-checkout system for years.

When we arrived, the front sliding doors were emblazoned with posters. Pirate treasure hunt day, dress as your favourite book character . . . When did libraries become so busy? Then I realised. It was the school holidays. Parents who had forgotten about the library all term suddenly became avid library users, wanting to drop their kids off for a couple of hours, if only to use the free Wi-Fi.

We wandered in. The noise from the kids' area filtered through, past the reference books, the magazines and the shelves of online orders waiting to be picked up.

'Can we go and look?' Thomas pointed at the children's

section and smiled in what I knew he thought was his sweetest way. In truth, it looked as if the dentist had just asked him to show him his gums.

It was some sort of 'music of the world' class, led by the same guy who did his best to wrangle a range of kids' music sessions through the week.

I had started going to one because, in the haze of terrified-new-motherhood, I had been convinced that if I did not have a full week of classes set up for my son by the time he was six months old, I would stifle his mental development. I pictured a thirty-year-old Thomas pipped at the post for the Nobel Prize, demanding to know why I had skimped on baby yoga.

At the music class, parents dutifully, self-consciously, sang the songs and did all the actions – some of the regulars were quite enthusiastic while reluctant stand-ins barely moved their lips.

The teacher was one of the librarians, and he was the one reason I persisted past the initial visit. He was about forty, with dishevelled short, dark hair that was starting to acquire a smattering of grey at the temples and rimless rectangular glasses that slipped down his nose when he launched into a song with particular gusto.

At the beginning of the class, I had not thought much of him. But the longer I watched, the more impressive he became. It's so easy to seem forced and condescending when you try to make kids laugh, but he had perfectly mastered the magical vocabulary of weird sounds and silly songs that would always get a giggle – even from the adults. He was perennially happy, but not in that fake way that lots of people deploy around kids, and his smile seemed to light up every bit of his face. I would bet the loose change in the bottom of my handbag that he'd never 'developed feelings' for someone while his wife was pregnant.

He'd won my devotion completely one morning when Thomas decided he did not want to be there. Rather than being awed by the chirpy music and enchanted by the books, he balled up his little baby fists, threw back his head and started to wail. And wail.

The teacher had stopped, and I'd thought he was going to suggest we leave.

'We're having a great time trying out these instruments,' he'd told the children, 'but the best noises are the ones that really convey an emotion.' He'd then pointed at Thomas. 'Can we all try to make the funniest noise you can think of to help this guy feel a little bit better?'

The older toddlers had responded with raspberries and popping sounds, and it wasn't long before Thomas was chortling his delicious baby giggle.

This time, the teacher was channelling Elmo for an assembled group of bored preschool-aged kids and a smattering of parents who were trying not to be spotted checking their phones. He brandished a collection of what looked like traditional Mexican musical instruments – bashing out a rhythm on one, waving another in the air. Thomas was transfixed. I tried to guide him to a seat on one of the flashing stairs.

We squeezed into a corner, next to a woman who seemed to be wrangling triplets – three little girls of about four, dressed almost identically, with blue bows in their brilliant blonde hair. She was trying to get them to pay attention but they were more interested in poking each other's eyes and whacking each other with books when she wasn't looking. Thomas was clapping to the music and nodding his head out of time. Such is the toddler way. I tried to maintain my zen and pull my best supportive smile – inwardly pleading for the noise to end.

I exhaled heavily as I leant against the glass wall, hoping my top was long enough to meet my leggings at the back. It was unlikely the rest of the library patrons wanted a detailed view of my underwear making a break for freedom over the top of my pants.

I was at peak pregnancy. My legs had ballooned with fluid, as they always did by late morning, and most of my shoes no longer fit. Even my maternity leggings were struggling to cover my bump and the singlets I had bought – that claimed to be perfect for pregnancy and breastfeeding – looked set to be able to cope with neither. I would have taken my wedding rings off, but my fingers had swelled too much. My breasts had leaked through two sets of breast pads, and I already had that distinctive old dishcloth air about me, which surrounds lactating mothers. I know people say pregnancy is beautiful, and I still held out hope that I would turn into some kind of Earth Goddess soon. But, at thirty-eight weeks, I was still waiting.

Thomas stood up and started to edge down the stairs, shaking his arms to the beat as he went.

I pocketed the phone on which I had been tapping out a text telling Stephen exactly what I thought of him. I reached down to put my arm around Thomas to try to draw him back up close to me. I could feel his body zinging with energy. Soon he had ducked out of my grasp and was edging still further forward towards the Very Attractive Man. I tried to shuffle along behind the seated parents to get closer to him, but while the audience seemed happy to let a two-year-old through, they were not so keen on having his barrel-like mother follow.

'Excuse me,' I whispered as I stepped on one woman's handbag. 'Sorry.' I ducked my head as a man grabbed his child out of my path.

But soon Thomas was a good couple of rows ahead of me, and still progressing. 'Thomas!' I hissed. 'Come back here, darling.' Some of the mothers in front of me turned and glared. I rolled my eyes apologetically. Thomas kept working his way forward. Soon, he was in the front row.

The teacher smiled at him as he stamped and clapped, getting closer and closer. Then Thomas's arms were in the air, trying to grab the instrument in the teacher's right hand. I attempted to push my way down the side of the crowd to where the man was trying to continue his show, grinning as he stretched to hold his instruments higher and higher out of Thomas's reach. But Thomas wouldn't be dissuaded.

The stares of the other parents were boring into the back of my head. I stretched over the row of children right at the front and grabbed Thomas, throwing him over my shoulder in a movement that sent a wrench of pain across my stomach. He shrieked. One of the girls who sat in a perfect cross-legged position in the front row covered her ears and scowled. 'We are going home,' I muttered.

'Don't feel you have to go.' The man taking the class had finished his song. 'Stay, if you'd like to. It's nice to see someone getting into my warbling.'

I turned, grimacing. 'He's a little disruptive.'

'He's fine, aren't you, little man? A bit of enthusiasm is what we like to see. Do you think you could give me a hand? I don't want you to take my instruments, but I'm sure I can find you some of your own.'

He shuffled over and reached for another stool, pulling it beside him. A woman handed him another set of maracas. Thomas was spellbound. 'I help.' He wriggled up. I reached

53

for my phone to snap a picture as he joined in, at the top of his lungs, with a rendition of 'Wheels on the Bus'. I must have looked puzzled because the librarian caught my eye and grinned. 'Not exotic, sorry. Finished the song sheet a bit too early.'

I became aware of a woman standing at my elbow, watching them. 'God, he's gorgeous, isn't he?'

'Thanks, I think he's pretty lovely.' I turned to look at her. Her gaze was fixed on Thomas and the teacher. Thomas's cheeks were flushed from the exertion of bashing along, wildly off-beat. The librarian was monitoring his movements and looked to be biting back a laugh.

'Oh no,' she put her hand on my arm. 'Not him, he's cute, I mean Luke. I never miss his class.'

It was almost time for dinner by the time we made it home, complete with seven new library books inside the weekender bag I suddenly found I needed to use every day. My breath caught in my throat as we rounded the corner before our house and I saw Stephen's truck parked outside. What was he doing? Only a couple of days ago he would not pick up the phone. Now he had decided to turn up?

I kept my foot steady on the accelerator. The last thing I wanted was for him to think I was rushing to see him. As we came to a stop, Thomas whooped. 'Daddy's home!' he shouted and started wiggling. I manoeuvred to the edge of the car seat and inched myself out, one hand on each side of the doorframe, in case Stephen was watching. Of all the things that become difficult when you are very pregnant, getting in and out of a car is the most noticeable.

Stephen appeared from around the side of the house, plodding towards us. He would not meet my eye but jiggled on the spot, his hands in his pockets, as I helped Thomas

54

out of the car. Thomas ran for his leg and twisted himself around his father. Stephen reached down and ruffled his hair. Waffle snuffled around our feet.

'Sweetheart, why don't you grab your bike and show us how fast you can ride around on the grass?' I nudged Thomas in the direction of his new toy.

He climbed on, hopping from one foot to the other. 'Watch me, watch me, Daddy!'

Stephen and I followed him, so we were standing side by side under the porch that ran along the front of the house. A few scraggly pansies were fading in the flowerbed opposite. We never had discovered how the irrigation system worked. Not something we were ever likely to solve now. Stephen cleared his throat and swallowed. His voice was strangled with the effort of not attracting Thomas's attention. 'Where are my clothes?'

I shrugged. 'I didn't think you were coming back.'

He grabbed my arm. 'That's ridiculous. I need my stuff. What have you done with it?'

'Chucked it. You've got money. Get her to buy you some more. Bet she's got better taste than I have, anyway.'

He grimaced. His hand was in his pocket – I knew he would be squeezing the stress ball on his key ring. I had bought it as a gift for him when he first started his business and was struggling to stay calm in difficult conversations with suppliers. We'd run through it together: 'I'll pay you (squeeze) on the twentieth (squeeze), but I need a line of credit (squeeze) until then.'

He was grinding his teeth. He looked away from me, at the overgrown lemon tree he had been promising to prune. He was off the hook there, at least. 'I want to see Thomas. Alexa says I have a right . . .'

I spluttered. 'You want to talk about rights?'

A bird took flight from the tree in surprise. 'I think I have a right not to have a husband cheat on me when I'm about to have a baby.'

Stephen stepped back as if my anger shocked him. 'I'm just asking if we can arrange for me to have Thomas, maybe a Saturday afternoon.'

Thomas was still zipping happily around the lawn. For the first time, I could understand the urge to spit with disgust.

'Is that enough for you, is it? Take his dad away but give him just enough to let him know what he's missing out on. Every Saturday afternoon to show off your awesome parenting to the world. Get some good photos for your Facebook feed.'

'No one is taking away his dad.'

'Maybe not, but it's not going to be the same, is it? You're not going to be around when he wakes up in the morning and wants someone to rest his head on when he watches cartoons. You're not going to race around with him on his bike after work. You'll have your Saturday, or whatever you decide you can fit into your new life, and the rest of the time who cares about us?'

He whirled around, and the fury in his face was shocking. His cold, angry eyes and clenched jaw could have belonged to a stranger. 'You can feel sorry for yourself,' he hissed, darting a look at Thomas. 'You keep making me the bad guy if that makes you feel better. You chuck out all my clothes if you don't want to look at them anymore. But don't pretend that this is all my fault.'

Thomas was scooting away down the far end of the lawn.

'What the hell do you mean?'

'Okay, Alexa and I started seeing each other. I'm sorry, all right? That was a crappy move.' Stephen crossed his arms. 'But you're not perfect, are you?'

I looked at him, open-mouthed, as he blustered on. Not perfect? Probably not – but who could blame me?

He was gesticulating at me in much the same way Thomas did when he was mid-tantrum. I watched him. Was this what I wanted to hold on to? Maybe he was actually doing me a favour.

'You just want someone around to help pay the bills.' Stephen was still talking. 'We never spent any time together. And it was all just going to get worse once this one comes along. I sometimes wonder if you can even remember my name.'

I had to suppress a snort of laughter. He had no idea what it was like for me. Sometimes I could barely remember my own name.

I had assumed that Stephen would pick up more of the parenting as Thomas got older but it had not happened. I had learnt how to respond to a work message on my phone, sliding around the corner of the door so Thomas wouldn't know I wasn't paying full attention to his bath-time display. But Stephen would arrive home from work and if we didn't give him ten minutes alone on the couch with his beer before Thomas requested that he play, he'd look aggrieved. While I worried about finishing meetings and interviews in time to pick Thomas up from nursery, Stephen would casually inform me the night before a trip that he was going away and wasn't sure exactly how long he'd be.

He was still speaking. 'What have you got planned for when the baby arrives?'

Did he mean the actual birth? He had rolled his eyes about every antenatal appointment I'd asked him to come to. I could not see why he would suddenly be taking an interest in my birth plan.

'I still want to be there.' He folded his arms obstinately.

'Why would you want to do that? Why would you think I'd let you do that?' The feeling that I was in an alternate reality was growing stronger with each breath I took. Everything felt so unreal.

'I'm this child's father.'

'Yeah but I'm the one who's going to be naked, in pain – what makes you even remotely think I want someone there who doesn't even want me around anymore?'

Giving birth to Thomas had been the time of my life when I had felt the most exposed. There are not many instances where you basically perform every bodily function imaginable on a table in front of a room full of people.

The idea of having this man who was becoming more like a stranger every second watch me go through that, and then go home to someone else, made my skin crawl. Thomas was scooting back towards us on his bike, his eyes wide. I gave Stephen the most withering, dismissive glare I could muster. 'We will talk about this later.'

I reached out for Thomas and lifted him off the saddle. Avoiding Stephen's eyes, I pushed past and strode around the side of the house to the front door. His footsteps crunched behind me, but as soon as we were across the threshold, I shut the door and leant against it. It was not long before I heard him whistle for Waffle. His truck door slammed and he drove away.

CHAPTER FOUR

<u>How to make a parking garage for toy cars</u>

What you'll need:

A box

Some tubes (paper towel rolls will do)

Cardboard

Sand down your box to get rid of any rough edges. Cut the tubes until they are just long enough to reach from the back of the box to the front. Glue your tubes on top of each other in rows, and stick the sheet of cardboard on to the back of them so that the cars do not fall out. Now your only challenge is getting your kids to store their cars in the garage and not on the floor where you will trip on them when you are too pregnant to get back up again, leaving you stranded like an upended cockroach on the floor. If you're suddenly single-handedly parenting, you might consider setting up a playpen in the middle of the living room and sitting inside it. The kids can then create havoc all around your peaceful island of serenity.

It was some time after 1 a.m. when I opened my eyes and saw a shadow standing next to the bed. I squinted. The shadow was short, wearing pyjamas and had hair half-flattened from sleep. 'Thomas?'

He put his hand on the side of my face. His skin was clammy. I shuffled across the bed. 'You can hop in with me, honey. Can't you sleep?'

He put his arms around my neck and squirmed in, searching for the cool spot on my pillow to lay his head. The duvet was almost over his nose when he stopped twisting. 'Did something wake you?'

He rested his head on the top of my arm. 'Noise.'

I kissed his forehead. 'It's probably just the wind in the trees. Try to go back to sleep – it's still really early.'

I closed my eyes and focused on my own long, slow breaths. It wasn't long before I felt him become heavier as he succumbed, my arm pinned awkwardly under his head and his body pressed up against mine. I watched his little chest rise and fall and his eyelids flutter with dreams, in the light of Stephen's old clock radio. At some point, as the dark gave way to the insipid grey of the first shoots of dawn, I must have fallen asleep for real because he was soon shaking me awake.

'Mummy,' he hissed. 'Daytime.'

I reluctantly opened my eyes and felt for his pyjamas. 'Do you need to go to the toilet?'

He shook his head.

'I'll give you a treat if you do . . .'

He regarded me for a minute. 'Okay.'

We tumbled out of bed and into the en-suite bathroom. It was the one room of the house that Stephen hadn't yet finished renovating – the bath and shower had been replaced but the toilet was still dingy avocado, and the new plasterboard was patiently waiting for its paint. I helped Thomas on to the toilet where he perched, looking at me expectantly. 'All finished,' he proclaimed a second later, leaping off in mid-stream.

'Good work, honey.' I hastily dabbed at the mess on the tiles as he took off out of the room, back towards the kitchen, where he would wait for me to turn on the Saturday morning cartoons while I made our breakfast.

I sat, hands cradling my coffee, as he spooned porridge into his mouth, eyes agog as a cartoon Peppa Pig schooled him in several different ways to be impertinent to your parents. Whoever wrote the series must have had issues similar to mine, I thought as I loaded the dishwasher. You couldn't trust Daddy Pig with anything.

A bicycle bell trilled in the driveway. I grimaced. There was only one person I knew who would be riding a bike around at that time of the morning with enough enthusiasm to ring a bell about it – my best friend, Laura. I know all the films tell you that the first thing you should do when you've been wronged by a man is down a couple of pink cocktails and bitch about him with your girlfriends before pashing an absurdly attractive stranger. But I was still firmly in If-I'm-not-talking-about-it,-it's-not-really-happening mode.

She knocked but didn't wait for us to open the door, sliding her own key into the lock and pushing the door open. 'Thomas, darling?'

'Auntie Laura.' He let out a whoop and barrelled across the floor to her. She stooped to kiss his cheek. A pixie-like little girl appeared from behind her long, Lycra-clad legs, fumbling with the clip on her own purple bike helmet.

'Lila wanted to come over to play.' Laura nudged her in Thomas's direction. 'Why don't you show her the blocks you were telling me about the other day?'

Laura had a bag of pastries over one arm and a steely look in her eye as she advanced towards me. I discarded my first impulse to convince her that everything was normal. She had once told me that I had distinctive 'tells' when I was trying to pretend nothing was wrong. It was when I didn't want to admit to her I hadn't been able to get Thomas to sleep more than two hours in a row for six months, while the rest of our antenatal group seemed to be operating on a perfect schedule. One of those giveaway signs was the jiggling from foot to foot that I knew I'd started as soon as she spotted me.

'I've brought you breakfast. I didn't ring, because I know you'd tell me not to come. You're not rude enough to tell me to leave now I'm here.'

She was right. I motioned for her to follow me into the living room, where the kids quickly tipped the contents of Thomas's toy box out across the floor. Both of us pretended that we could not see a pile of Thomas's energetic artworks that had fallen across the floor and a teetering stack of washing waiting to be folded in the corner of the room.

'I don't know what's happened.' She sat, back perfectly straight, on the edge of the sofa and stared at me. 'I saw Stephen at the supermarket last night, and he introduced me to Alexa McKenzie, that designer person . . .' She bit her lip. 'It was all a bit awkward.'

I cast about for something to stall the conversation while I caught up. I could feel the heat rising in my cheeks. Stephen was introducing Alexa to my friends? Already? But he had not outright admitted that Alexa was his girlfriend. I could not decide whether that made me feel better or not. Generally, he went out of his way to avoid talking to Laura at all. He and her husband, Mark, sometimes worked together and, unless she turned up with him, he usually found an excuse to do something in another part of the house whenever she came to visit me.

I had to avoid her gaze. 'Yep, for some reason, he's decided he'd rather be with a young, fit interior designer than with his heavily pregnant, hormonal wife.' I tried to smile. I wanted to be self-deprecating, but I just sounded bitter. Which, I might add, I was perfectly within my rights to be.

Laura pulled me towards her and kissed my cheek. 'I am so sorry. I didn't want to believe it.'

We sat in silence for a minute, watching the kids roll around on the carpet together. Thomas was pushing a toy car around Lila, who was trying to land a plane on it.

'What is he thinking?' Laura spluttered at last. Her words were staccato as she bit back her anger to avoid sparking the kids' attention. 'You're about to have this baby and he's off ladding about with someone who probably doesn't even do her own laundry. What a selfish, narcissistic . . .'

She was talking too quickly, as she extended her arms in

my direction. One of her deliberately mismatched earrings scratched the side of my face as she hugged me. 'It's so unfair. Being a parent is so . . . optional for them, isn't it?'

Laura and I had met at our antenatal classes three years before. Five wide-eyed, unsuspecting new mothers had assembled on plastic chairs in a hospital meeting room, where graphic descriptions of how our pelvises would have to move to allow our kids to get out into the world caused at least one of us to faint. Laura, a nurse who had spent years in the emergency department, just rolled her eyes.

Laura had been trying to fall pregnant for six months when she insisted on being sent for IVF. She was only twenty-eight at the time but managed to get Mark to do a sperm test the day after he had suffered a particularly high fever. It meant he had no swimmers to show for it, and the doctors bumped her to the front of the queue. She was pregnant with Lila after the first round.

Laura impressed me in class with her immaculate wardrobe and always-done make-up, the kind of clothes I would much rather have been rocking as I bumbled around in maternity jeans and oversized shirts. But it was not until Laura and I locked eyes, trying to quell a giggle when an instructor told us she had been qualified at the National Institute of Baby Massage, that we became friends.

'I'll cry mascara on your top.' I pulled back from her. 'I'm sorry I'm such a mess.' I twisted a strand of oily hair around my index finger. I couldn't remember the last time I'd washed it.

'I do not care about that one bit. What I care about is how hideous this situation is.' She rested her head against mine. 'If you want to kill him, I'll help you.'

I laughed weakly. 'It's bloody tempting, I tell you.'

Her skin was cool and smooth. She looked as though she

was wearing perfectly matched foundation, although I would have put money on her being bare-faced. I had never noticed before how oversized her wedding ring was on her slim pianist's fingers. She pushed a pain au chocolat at me that she'd brought with her. 'What are you going to do?'

I put my face in my hands. 'Well, I've already signed her up to a lot of email newsletters, for a start.'

Laura coughed as she inhaled a crumb of pastry. She raised her eyebrows. 'Pardon?'

Alexa's business website listed her email address in full and I'd signed her up to more than 200 mailing lists, to ensure her inbox was packed with advertising and newsletters, at least until she figured out how to unsubscribe from them all. Stephen would be no help – he still struggled to remember his email password.

There are some surprising benefits to my job. I'd written a story a couple of weeks earlier about a private investigator who told me what some of her clients did when they discovered their suspicions about their cheating husbands were correct. Some of it was genius stuff – hiding anchovies in expensive cars, selling pricey one-off designer suits at no reserve on eBay. Since Stephen walked out, I'd returned to a few of their blogs and chat groups. The inbox email idea had belonged to one of them.

'Wow.' Laura's eyes were sparkling as she leant back against the couch. 'You're right. That'll be very annoying.'

I shrugged. 'Well, it will keep them occupied.'

Lila returned and burrowed between Laura's legs. Laura reached down and stroked a stray piece of hair back from her daughter's face.

I smiled at Lila. She was only three months younger than Thomas, but she seemed so slight compared to his sturdy legs and barrel-like torso. She was wearing one of those sparkly baby pink dresses with layers of petticoat tulle that now seemed to be a daily uniform for small girls, whether they're going to a birthday party, riding a bike with their mothers, or making mud pies. She ducked back under the insufficient hiding place of Laura's athletic thighs. I suddenly desperately wanted to change the subject.

'How's everything going with you?'

Laura pushed the question away. 'Oh, fine. If the hospital could learn to fit a part-time shift into part-time hours or had enough staff to cover the workload, that would be fantastic. But otherwise, you know, we're fine.'

We sat in silence, watching Thomas tip over another box, sending a convoy of small trucks zipping across the floor. 'Good riddance to him,' Laura murmured at last. 'I mean, if you'd left him, he would have been a total disaster. But you without him . . .' Her voice trailed off.

'Yeah. I'll probably survive. I know. I just don't feel it yet.'

Lila's head snapped up. She had found some of Thomas's marker pens on the floor and had drawn on her arms and face. 'Pretty.' She smiled at us.

Laura turned back to me. 'I'm sorry. It's fine to be angry. Be furious. But can you promise me something?'

I groaned. 'What?'

'Can you please call me at least daily? I know you, and now you're going on leave with no work to think about you'll just sit around here getting pissed off, and I don't think that's going to be helpful for anyone.'

'Sorry.' I looked at my hands. 'I just didn't want to tell you until . . .'

'Yes, I know. You don't like to talk about these sorts of things until they're over and you've got everything back how you want it. But you can't get through this one alone. Now . . .'

She was businesslike. 'What would you like to do? I know you don't like a whole day with nothing planned, even when you haven't got this other stuff going on.'

What did I want to do? I had been so focused on plodding through each minute that I had not allowed myself to think much beyond the most basic necessities of getting the last bits of work done, feeding myself and Thomas, and remembering to shower from time to time. I realised she was still waiting for an answer.

I cast around for something. 'Shall we go for a little walk? See how far I can waddle along? Some fresh air might be good to clear my head a bit.'

Laura snapped her fingers. 'We can do that. Come on, children, we're going on an adventure.'

We returned to the house less than twenty-five minutes later, after Thomas and Lila shrieked at each other in disagreement about which way around the block they wanted to walk. They were horrified when we would not allow them to bring home some bits of old plastic bottles and dog poo they found while conducting a 'treasure hunt'. I pretended to be exasperated that we were giving up, but I could feel the exertion in my growing varicose veins, and my daughter seemed to have joined in with an intrauterine walk of her own. Amy's car was in the driveway as we arrived back. Laura glanced at me. 'We might leave you to it.'

When Amy and Laura had first met, Amy had lectured her – at length – about why she thought all of her customers who claimed to be on a gluten-free diet were insufferable and putting it on to be trendy. 'Trying to get attention when there's nothing else interesting about them,' I think were her words.

Laura, a coeliac with a nursing degree, had hurled a few

insults of her own. 'Uneducated' and 'narrow-minded' were the ones I remembered best. Ever since, Amy had thought it hilarious to joke about what she might have hidden in food that Laura ate at my house.

I kissed Laura on the cheek. 'Let me go and deal with her. Thanks for visiting.'

Lila gave us a shy wave from the seat Laura had fixed on to her bike for her, just behind her handlebars. 'Say bye, Thomas,' I prompted. He returned the wave.

As the bike rounded the edge of the driveway, he dropped to the ground. 'No! Lila come back. Come back!' I scooped him up and carried him inside under one arm, his legs still kicking behind me.

Music was blaring from the spare room. Amy emerged, scarves draping and spiky, scuffed stiletto heels sticking out of a half-taped box under her arm. I had not realised that she, too, had a spare key to the house.

'What are you doing?' I watched as she returned to her car and pulled out a clothes rack, which she then tried to manoeuvre through the door. 'What's going on?'

She stopped and grinned at me. 'I have a plan.'

I rocked from my heels to the balls of my feet and back again. Heat spread across my lower back. A walk really hadn't been such a good idea.

'I'm going to come and live with you.' Amy dropped a box to the ground. 'I heard what Mum said to you before you left the other day about staying there. Can you imagine? You'll be her pet project again before you know it and Dad will want to know what you're doing every time you're five minutes late. Torture!'

She patted me on the shoulder as she went to get another bag. 'You won't even know I'm here. Promise. I'll just help you when you need me.'

I followed her out to the car. I could just imagine having her as my permanent house guest. She'd assure me that she would be home to help with dinner at 5.30 p.m., roll in at 7.30 p.m. and wonder why I was upset. No doubt she still sang in the shower at the top of her voice, even in the middle of the night. Dishes would be piled in the sink and skimpy underwear added to my laundry pile. There would never be any mention of rent being paid.

'It'll be okay, honestly.'

Her face fell. 'No?'

'No. Really. Thanks for the offer, though.'

She bit the rough edge of her index fingernail. 'The thing is . . .'

I waited. There was always something.

'I kind of have to move. We've been evicted.'

Amy shared a huge, rundown warehouse apartment with three of her friends. It was barely habitable, with old sash windows that didn't close properly, floorboards like gappy teeth and holes in some of the walls that had been punched through by a previous tenant. The rent was eye-watering, but she could walk to work, and I suspected she had just been too lazy to get around to moving.

'Turns out I was paying my share to Laurel but she wasn't paying the landlord. So I have to get out, anyway. And I can't get a house anywhere else at the moment . . .'

I tried to push down a growing wave of frustration. Did I not have enough problems of my own to deal with?

'Why not? You've got a job.'

'I took out a loan to pay off my credit card last summer but my work's been so erratic I haven't been able to make the repayments – bastards sent me to the debt collectors. I won't pass a credit check for a good couple of years, they say.'

70

I stood as tall as I could and stared at her, my hands on my hips. 'How old are you, Amy?'

She looked surprised. 'I'm thirty-one.'

'Why are you still doing dumb stuff like this?'

She recoiled. Her voice was timid. 'I didn't want to ask Mum and Dad for a loan, so I thought it was the best thing to do. I was doing my best . . . I want to be self-sufficient.'

She trailed off, her eyes watering. I hadn't snapped at her in years. But I had already bailed her out of two housing-related messes. The first was when Frank had walked away, leaving her with a lease she couldn't handle. I'd paid half of it for three months. The second time Stephen and I had paid her insurance excess when someone started a fire in the bathroom at a party.

'No.' The force of my fury shocked us both. Too bad – walking all over me seemed to be the pastime of the moment and I wasn't having it.

'It's time you accepted the consequences of your actions. You can't keep rolling through life like a teenager with nothing to worry about. I've picked up after every other stupid mistake you've made, and I've got way too much on my plate right now to add you to it. Own your own mess for a change.'

She was staring at me, her mouth open.

'Other people manage to find new apartments. I'm sure you can, too.'

I turned away and directed Thomas through to the lounge, where I propped him on the bean bag. I sank on to the armchair behind him. He leant back against me, his cheek against my shin. I could hear Amy clattering as she threw her clothes back into boxes and hurled them out to the car. She stepped heavily on the accelerator, her wheels screeching as she took off from the end of our driveway.

'Daddy home soon?' Thomas looked up. I stroked his head, trying to slow my breathing. I was in danger of getting a little 'ping' from the sanctimonious smartwatch app I'd downloaded to help manage my stress. I wanted to slap the old me across the face. What did she have to be stressed about?

CHAPTER FIVE

<u>How to make a paper doll chain</u>

What you'll need:

Some paper

Scissors

If you're using A4 paper, cut it in half lengthwise. Fold the piece into eight equal-sized accordion pleats. With the fold on the left, trace an outline of half a doll on the paper. Then cut around it. When you open the paper up you should be left with four dolls, holding hands. They'll stick together, even if your family is falling apart – although some days you might wish it would fall apart a little more quickly.

Do you know what drives me nuts? The concept of 'me time'. You're meant to have a bath, or go for a massage, eat a whole block of chocolate in bed or skive off for lunch with your girlfriends and feel good about taking time out for yourself. Except I get into the bath and I can't get out, and even before I got pregnant I couldn't bear the idea of strangers massaging my body. All my friends are juggling workloads much too heavy, and with childcare far too limited, to break for lunch with me.

Between work and looking after Thomas, I manage to squeeze in a couple of minutes of 'me time' for frivolous things such as washing my hair. I can't bring myself to believe that half an hour of indulgence makes up for the fact that I do 99 per cent of the drudgery the rest of the time.

But try to explain that to anyone else, and they look aghast. 'No me time? Oh but you must have some me time. Can't pour from an empty cup . . .'

So it's another thing added to my ever-growing to-do list. No one wants to be an empty mother cup.

One thing I still do try to squeeze in between the frantic

dash for work deadlines, and the seemingly interminable bedtime battle, is yoga. Although I've long since given up my dream of being a teacher myself, I find ten minutes of stretching can turn around many of the aggravations of a day of child-wrangling. I'll never be a YouTube yoga star – while those women get the tops of their heads on the floor in a forward fold, my palms are still only halfway down my shins (I blame my short arms). But I happily follow them through the motions, and even Thomas is starting to enjoy finding his own tree pose or a comfortable seated position (although sometimes that is in front of the television).

While I still had access to the joint bank account, I decided to book in one last pre-baby session with my favourite teacher, Lani, at the studio near the paper's main office. Before I started working from home, I'd been there three out of five lunchtimes a week. The class was the kind of expense I wouldn't normally be able to justify for myself – it was about the same as one of those huge boxes of nappies that are meant to last a month – but I figured Stephen owed me. He hadn't bought me a birthday present in at least three years.

As the appointment drew nearer, I realised I was hanging out for it. Amid the chaos of managing Thomas on my own, and the frantic dash to finish my work before my maternity leave started, the prospect of an hour of peace twinkled in front of me like an oasis.

I arrived at the door to the studio only half a minute later than I had booked. Lani greeted me in the foyer. 'You look wonderful.' She kissed my cheek.

'You're sweet but clearly lying,' I whispered, as I put my bag down, and switched my phone to silent.

Lani gestured me to a mat in the closest room. 'Let's start with some gentle loosening exercises.'

I eased down on to a mat and leant back, propped against a bolster cushion. I was well past the cut-off for most pregnancy yoga classes. 'I don't think I can even cross my legs these days.'

She smiled. 'That's fine. Let's just go with what you can do – it's just about getting you super relaxed and in tune with your body. Nothing strenuous today.'

She guided me through a slow flow. It was one I was familiar with but only in a not-pregnant state. Every time I lunged even gently my leg would collide with the bottom of my stomach. When I lowered to a squat, I couldn't get back up again and had to lean forward on to all fours, before I would roll over on to my back like an upturned crab.

Lani directed me into a hip-opening, severely modified swan pose. 'Just if you can . . .'

I grimaced. 'It doesn't hurt . . .'

She smiled. 'You're always so graceful. When are you coming back to yoga properly? We miss you down here.'

I shrugged. 'Probably never. I don't know how I'm going to have time to eat with two kids and work.'

She nodded. 'It's definitely a juggle.'

Lani reached for my leg and rested her palm against my shin. 'Try and lean forward a bit more; pull your right leg in towards you. Don't push too far – you know how pregnancy hormones can make everything a bit too stretchy. Just go as far as you're comfortable with. Even a gentle movement will help.'

I took a deep breath in and out and sank a centimetre further into the stretch. I wiggled it around a bit, feeling tightness release in my upper thighs. As the seconds ticked by on the clock on the wall, I paused. 'I think I'm stuck.'

One of my legs was bent in front of me, and one pushed back behind me. I was on a lean, accommodating my bump.

77

Lani grinned. I tried to straighten my front leg, but it wouldn't move. I shifted, trying to release the pressure at the back.

'No really. I don't know how I'm going to get out of this.'

A surge of panic rose in my chest. Her smile faded. I could feel sweat beginning to pop up on my top lip. It had started out mildly uncomfortable, but the pose was becoming painful. The room was uncomfortably hot. What was I thinking, trying to run through a routine at this point in my pregnancy? I should have known something would go wrong. Lani reached out a long slim hand again and tried to pull me towards her. I rolled a little to the left but couldn't get traction to take the weight off my legs.

'I think you're going to have to help me up,' I muttered. She positioned herself behind me, her hands under my upper arms.

'I don't think you're strong enough to lift me. I'm a decent twenty kilos heavier than I normally would be.' I must have been twice her size.

She chewed her lip, shooting desperate glances around the room for an object to help me. I was sure there used to be some straps that people used to get into awkward positions. Could they not set up some system of pulleys for me?

'I'm so sorry, Rachel. I shouldn't have encouraged you into this position. I'll see if I can get someone to help.'

She looked around the door and called to one of the other teachers to come in. I didn't recognise her – tall, with her long black hair scraped back in a severe bun. She shot Lani a stern look. 'I thought you had done a prenatal refresher.'

They each slid an arm under my armpits and hauled me to my feet. The other teacher frowned at me. 'Just do some lunges to finish up, okay? Maybe some warrior ones. You can't put yourself through that sort of thing in your condition.'

When she left the room, Lani and I locked eyes. I could see she was trying not to giggle, waiting to see how upset I was. 'Sorry,' I muttered. 'I shouldn't have pushed myself.'

'No, it was all me. I'm sorry that was a bit embarrassing.'

I allowed myself to laugh. 'What? No, being lifted up like a stranded whale was totally on my to-do list this morning.'

Lani grinned. 'Let's just cruise through a little bit more then I'll let you be on your way.'

The air outside the studio carried the scent of blossoms that were still popping up on trees on the other side of the road. It had finally started to feel like summer couldn't be far off. An image flashed into my mind of summer the year before – Thomas collecting old fish skeletons at the beach with his dad, demanding to know which were dinosaur fossils. When was the next time Stephen would spend a day like that with him again?

I checked my watch – despite the disaster, Lani and I had kept to time but no doubt once I returned to the car, there would be a long list of emails and voicemails waiting for me.

I slid behind the steering wheel and pulled my phone from my bag. My prediction was correct – I'd missed nine calls. I pushed the button to bring them up and stared at the screen. They were all from the same number, and one I recognised – Thomas's nursery.

Any reduction I'd managed in my heart rate at yoga was soon gone. My pulse thudded in my ears as I stabbed at the number to call back. The phone rang and rang until at last Saskia answered.

'Rachel, thank goodness you called. It's Thomas . . .'

'What's happened?'

'He had a fall. He and a couple of the other boys were playing on the fort, and we think Thomas must have stepped backwards. He hit his head, he seemed to lose consciousness for a second, and he's been vomiting.'

'Poor baby,' I groaned. How could I have thought my yoga class was more important than being able to answer the phone? 'I'm coming right now.'

'Actually, he's gone to get checked out.' Saskia sounded tentative. 'We couldn't get hold of you or Stephen, and we didn't have any other emergency numbers, so Kelly's taken him up to the medical centre. You don't want to mess around with head injuries, and he seemed a bit dazed.'

I bit my lip. That was at least another ten minutes in the other direction. How was he coping without me? 'Okay, you did the right thing. I'll talk to you later.'

The machine in the car park next to the doctor's rooms was so slow it might as well have been writing tickets by hand. By the time the barrier arm finally creaked up, I was almost ready to ditch my car and run in.

A bored receptionist looked up as I finally burst through the doors. 'My son is here.' I stumbled towards her. 'I need to see my son.'

She tapped on her keyboard. 'What's his name?'

'Thomas Murchison.'

She tapped again, then stopped, seemed to look to her basket of pens and fished around for a piece of chewing gum.

I stared at her. 'Can you tell me where he is?'

'Just a minute please.' Like I was being the unreasonable one, wanting to know where they had put my child.

'He's in the room first on your left down the hall.'

I pushed past a man having his blood pressure taken and a young woman pacing the waiting room floor with a wailing baby. 'Thomas?'

I thrust the door open.

'Mummy!'

He was curled on Kelly's lap on a thin bed at one side of the room, looking at a tattered book. His eyes were puffy. He stretched out his arms to me but I clambered on to the bed and pulled him on to my lap before he could move.

'My poor darling,' I breathed into his hair. I looked across his head at Kelly. 'Thank you for looking after him.'

She stroked his arm. 'Of course. Poor little guy. They've had a good look at him, and it seems like he's going to be fine. They just wanted him to stick around for observation for a little bit longer before going home. It looks like a mild concussion, but the nurse has been checking on him every twenty minutes or so. The doctor gave him a number to remember . . .'

'Eight!' Thomas chimed in.

'And he's had no trouble with that. They just asked that we try to keep him as calm as possible and not to let him watch any screens for forty-eight hours.'

'I'm so sorry I wasn't able to answer the phone.'

Kelly patted my hand. 'It's not easy – you can't be everywhere at once. And look, he's going to be fine. You had a great time coming in my car with me, didn't you, T?'

I grimaced. If anyone was taking Thomas to the doctor, it should have been me, or at least his father. But it seemed as though Stephen had completely checked out.

Kelly stood up. 'I'll leave you to it. I'd better get back to work.' She gave Thomas a peck on the top of the head. 'See you soon, okay?'

I leant back against the pillows, balancing Thomas on my chest. 'Let's try to call Dad, shall we?'

I pushed the icon to initiate a video call. It had become our unspoken way of showing him that it was Thomas wanting to talk. It rang interminably before he finally picked up. I turned my phone away from Thomas so we wouldn't break our screen ban within the first hour.

'Hey, buddy, how's it going?' He wasn't looking.

'Dad!' I patted Thomas to try to keep him calm. 'I'm in hospital.' The way he pronounced it sounded like hobs-stable.

Stephen seemed to flinch. 'Really? I saw I missed a call from nursery.'

I took over. 'You didn't think to call back?'

Stephen shrugged. 'I assumed they'd get hold of you. We were out.'

'We?'

He swallowed. 'Alexa and I were just having lunch. She thought it would be unfair for me to jump in, to make it seem like you didn't have it under control. You know?'

Unfair? It would be unfair, would it? I wanted to slap her perfectly made-up face. Unfair for her to give up her presumably expensive lunch out somewhere, more like it.

'I'm sure I would have coped,' I bit the words out.

He seemed to put the phone down on the centre console of the car. 'What happened?'

'He's had a bad fall. Probably concussed. We're at the doctor's. I'm hoping we can go home soon.'

Stephen said something I couldn't make out.

'Okay, well, it's been great talking to you . . .'

'Hey, Rach.' The signal weakened and I lost the video connection as I went to hang up but his voice cut me off. 'I might pop round soon and check in on him if that's okay?'

I paused. 'Really?'

'Be good to see him. I'll drop in on my way home.'

There was a knock on the door and a doctor peered in. 'How's everyone going in here?'

She smiled broadly at me as she checked Thomas's chart.

'He's doing really well. I'm happy for you to go – just try to wake him every two hours once he goes to bed tonight, and don't hesitate to get help if there's any sign that he's hard to rouse. Don't let him get too worked up about anything. We don't want to mess around with head injuries. You'll be okay to handle all that? You've got someone at home with you?'

I frowned, feeling my pulse pick up. 'No, it's just me now.'

I avoided her eyes, looking down at Thomas. 'But I'm sure I'll be fine, thanks. Waking up regularly is something Thomas has never had a problem with.'

She gave me a look. I was still wearing my yoga tights, a camisole top and a hoodie that must have once belonged to Stephen. My hair had shifted from curly to outright frizzy in the growing humidity and I knew had developed a new row of spots where my glasses sat on my face because I'd been too tired at night to bother with my skincare routine. 'Okay, well don't be afraid to call if you're worried.'

As we were collecting our bags, the receptionist appeared behind us. She put a pamphlet in my hand. It was for a parenting course. 'I'm giving them to all parents of this age,' she offered weakly. 'You know, give you some extra strategies.'

I pushed it to the bottom of my bag. My experience with parenting 'strategies' was that they worked brilliantly when you had had a good night's sleep, were full of energy and had unlimited time. Then you could stop a meltdown mid-flight by pretending to be a plane coming in to land or a dinosaur eating a tree. But since I hadn't actually had a proper sleep in about three years and was continually oper-ating at the sort of energy level that made other people ask whether I was sick, my reserves for perfect parenting were depleted. Clearly, that was obvious.

'Hey, Thomas.' I took him by the shoulders as he tried to hop off the bed. 'You're going to need to be super relaxed tonight, okay, sweetheart? Lots of big deep breaths.'

He looked at me, puzzled. I might as well have told him that he had to master French on his way home.

My parents were pulling up as we arrived back at our house. I'd only sent Mum a text as we left the doctor's but she was zinging with worry as she leapt out of her car and opened the back door of mine before I'd even completely stopped.

'How are you, Thomas my darling?'

She unclipped him from his car seat and, propped against her shoulder, carried him towards the house.

Rocking him as if he were a newborn again, she turned to me as I thrust my key into the lock. 'What happened?'

'Fell over!' Thomas pushed back from her and grinned. 'Kelly took me to doctor.'

Mum raised her eyebrows. 'Who's Kelly?'

'Nursery teacher.' I gestured for her to go in. I could see my computer screen flickering accusingly in the next room. 'I missed their call at first so I met them there.'

I avoided her eyes, swiping at the light switch to illuminate the room.

She stared at me. 'What were you doing? Why didn't they try me?'

'I guess I haven't listed you as an emergency contact.'

'You'd better do that.' She lowered Thomas on to the sofa as if he was made of glass. He promptly wiggled off. 'If you're going to try to do this on your own you're obviously going to need our help. Have you thought any more about coming to live with us?'

I rolled my eyes. Why had everyone decided it was time for a parenting intervention? 'Mum, I think I can cope. But thanks. And can you imagine Dad with two little kids full-time? I wouldn't be the only one heading for a divorce.'

She frowned. 'Don't be silly. We always have room for you. I don't know how you think you're going to manage when you can't even pick up your son in a medical emergency.'

'That's not fair. It was a one-off. I had my phone off for half an hour . . .'

She sighed, following Thomas as he started circling the lounge. 'Just think what it will be like when the baby comes.'

The arrival of Stephen's truck on the gravel outside interrupted us. I'd hoped there might have been time to move my parents on before he arrived but we heard his door slam then his boots crunch to the front door. He seemed to pause, perhaps wondering whether to knock, before pushing it open. I scuttled over and positioned myself in the entranceway, so he had no option but to see me as he entered. I knew I didn't look very imposing – being about as wide as I was high and still dressed in my morning workout gear – but I was determined to maintain my composure.

He didn't make eye contact with any of us as he entered the room, swooping down behind Thomas and wrapping him in a bear hug. Thomas squealed with happy surprise. I coughed. 'Keep him calm, remember?'

He ignored me. 'You okay, little guy?'

Thomas twisted around and buried his face in his shoulder. 'Fell over.'

'I heard, I heard.' Stephen was clinging tightly to Thomas's lean back. 'I'm sorry I couldn't get to see you earlier.'

He perched, half-kneeling on the floor and they held each other as if neither wanted to let go. I shifted my weight from one foot to the other and gestured to the table. 'Are you planning to stay for dinner? It's not much . . .'

He stood, brushing off his jeans. 'No, I'll get something later.'

Surprise, surprise.

'I just wanted to see that Thomas is okay. How are you going, my man?'

Thomas shrugged. 'Okay.'

I smiled. 'He's doing really well. The biggest problem will be trying to keep him from bouncing off the walls, I think.'

Stephen rolled his eyes. 'That will be tricky. How is Mummy going to do that?'

Thomas grinned. 'Treats.'

Stephen laughed. 'You know, you're probably right.'

I watched him carry Thomas back to the couch and curl into the corner. Stephen drew circles on Thomas's hand with his finger, trying to make him smile. For a minute it felt just like old times.

I could feel my mum watching me. Her words were still on repeat in my brain. How was I going to manage?

After ten minutes had ticked past, Stephen shifted to extricate himself from Thomas.

'I actually wanted to talk to your mum for a minute, buddy. Is that cool? You could go and play with Gran for a second?'

My mum and dad were sitting in armchairs at the other end of the room, pretending to read magazines, still refusing to acknowledge Stephen.

I raised an eyebrow. 'Okay?'

My mother stood, gestured for Thomas to come with her and shunted him in the direction of his bedroom.

'We need to sort out the house.' He spoke when all three had finally left the room. His gaze was over my shoulder and out the window.

'Do we? Already? After the day we've had?'

'I'm sorry the timing isn't great. But he's fine, right? I can't afford to rent anywhere else and pay the mortgage here.'

The mortgage payments were still coming out of our joint account. I'd noticed he'd stopped transferring any money from his business account, but I just assumed he'd pitch in a bit when the time of the month rolled around for the next payment. Perhaps I'd been wrong.

'Okay . . .'

'I'm not sure how you're going to be able to keep up paying even your half when you're off work with the baby, either.'

Clearly – no leeway then to help out the mother of your child through her maternity leave?

'And we thought looking after the house on your own might be a bit much, too. This place needs a lot of mainten-ance. The bathroom's not even finished.'

'We?'

'Alexa thought . . . we thought . . . that if we moved in here, it would take some pressure off you. You can stop paying your bit of the loan while we work out what's happening. Then we'll get a proper legal deal done a bit later on.'

'Wow.'

He seemed to think I was pleasantly surprised and smiled tentatively. 'Yeah, she won't expect any compensation for the mortgage payments she makes while we are working through the settlement – it's not much more than her rent.'

I wasn't surprised. She probably lived in an incredibly expensive, incredibly tidy apartment in the middle of town.

I stared around the room. There was the couch that had had the Thomas treatment, with a couple of suspect stains across its centre. The pile of decorating magazines I'd bought in a nesting fit. It was my home. Why was everyone suggesting I just give it up?

But then again, maybe everything that really made it my home was already gone. That would always be the kitchen where I found out about Stephen and Alexa, the bedroom he came back to after being with her. And no one seemed to think I could cope with Thomas and the new arrival on my own, anyway.

I exhaled. 'Okay.'

I turned away from him and plodded towards the kitchen to make a cup of tea.

'Okay?' He followed me.

'Yeah I give up. I'm too tired to fight you all. You can pay my moving costs, though. I can't move this stuff on my own.'

'Right.'

'And what do you want me to leave?'

He brushed away the question. 'Take whatever you need. Alexa . . .'

'Yeah, I imagine she's got her own stuff. You can go now.'

He seemed about to argue but thought the better of it. 'I'll go and say goodbye to Thomas.'

There was something about being pregnant that made me veer between *why does everyone want to treat me like an invalid* and *why doesn't anyone care I'm pregnant?* The over-attentive people who demanded I put my feet up always seemed to arrive just when I had restored my energy levels. But I would only meet those who pretended the fact I was carrying a baby was nothing more than a minor inconvenience when I was reaching the end of a twelve-hour day. After a day of standing, the only thing aching more than my feet were my newly sprouted haemorrhoids.

My mother was rooted in the former camp and treated

both my pregnancies like nine-month illnesses. Usually I fought it vehemently. But as I watched Stephen close the door behind him, I figured, for one night at least, I would let her fuss over me.

I lay on the couch and pulled the throw blanket up to my chin while she convinced Thomas to eat a plate of sausages and mashed potato – where she'd found the sausages I was still not sure.

'That was well done, Thomas, thank you.' She patted his shoulder as she cleared the table.

He nodded thoughtfully. 'All part of the service.'

We locked eyes. 'Where did Thomas get that one from?'

I shrugged. 'Who knows. TV?'

'I'll just get him into bed. Would you like us to stay, tonight? Since someone will have to check on him every couple of hours?'

Thomas had jumped down from his seat at the table and was watching us.

'I'll be fine. It's not like I'm sleeping any great stretch as it is.'

She pursed her lips. 'You need to get some sleep before the baby comes . . .'

I stared at her. 'Can you tell that to my passenger? She has ballroom dancing practice every forty-five minutes.'

Thomas climbed on to my thighs, perching on what was left of my lap. He rested his head against mine. My dad was wandering about the room, tidying magazines into racks and putting toys back in toy boxes.

I sighed heavily. 'Hey, sweetheart, how would you feel about staying with Granny and Granddad for a bit?'

He looked up. 'You?'

'And me, until we get ourselves sorted a bit more, the three of us.' I kissed him. 'Seems like I could do with the help.'

My mum looked up from where she seemed to have found a discarded nappy behind the TV. How long had that been there? 'That's a wonderful idea.' That was decision made: we were moving in with my parents. Whether it was the right decision remained to be seen . . .

CHAPTER SIX

How to make a rag doll

What you'll need:

Pencil

Paper

Scissors

Some fabric – an old pillowcase is ideal

Pins

Needle and thread or sewing machine

Stuffing

Markers

Draw an outline on the piece of paper of how you want your doll to look. A fairly simple figure is the easiest. Cut this pattern out and pin it to the fabric, folded in half. Cut around the pattern. Pin the two pieces together and sew around the outside. Turn inside out and fill with stuffing. Use your markers to draw a face. You can also use scraps of fabric to make clothes for your doll if you are a talented sewer, or particularly patient. Use your rag doll in attempts to deflect your first child's attention when you're focusing on a newborn. If you're lucky, it might work for about twenty-three seconds. Unfortunately it probably won't work as a decoy to distract your husband's grasping new girlfriend, who seems focused on getting hold of all the things you cherish.

By half-past nine on Saturday morning, I was biting my lip as a couple of large, singlet-clad men manoeuvred my antique dressing table, sideways, through the slightly too small front door. 'We could try to take it out the garage?' The chances of it fitting through the doorframe seemed marginally better if they opted for the biggest door possible.

'It'll be fine.' The bigger one smiled broadly as they turned it, end-over-end, to get it out. He had a missing tooth, which I hoped had not been taken out in a collision with someone's bedroom furniture.

I had marked everything that I wanted to take with an orange Post-it note. But I was still performing a constantly revolving circuit of the house, checking each room every time they took something to the truck.

I had taken Stephen at his word that he was no longer concerned about material things in his newly liberated life. I left him the horrendous pink floral lounge suite that his aunt had given us when she could not get the local charity shop to pick it up. It had spent most of its life in the garage, for when his mates came over to play their out-of-tune guitars and drink bourbon and Cokes, but I had elevated its status to the living room. If he did not like it in there, he could buy another. Alexa probably had her own collection of trendy Scandinavian furniture that was just *waiting* to move in, anyway.

I was taking the bed, which we had spent far too much money on but justified with the assumption that we would be able to use it for at least a decade. The saleswoman had promised two decades. It was the most expensive piece of furniture we owned.

I had also managed to make a case for taking all my favourite bed linen and towels, our small collection of art picked up from various holidays before we had children, the fridge, TV, washing machine and dryer.

But it would be a while before I saw them again. The truck was taking my things to a storage firm on the other side of the city, rather than my parents' house. My mother had quickly cleared out her spare rooms, and we would probably only be able to fit the contents of a couple of suitcases and Thomas's toy boxes in them. I wondered if I was going to have to book in some afternoons visiting my own furniture, just to feel like an adult with my own stuff again. Culling back to just the clothes that would fit in her spare bedroom's wardrobe had been difficult enough. I had been wearing the same four items of clothing on high rotate for the past three months, but I liked to have the reassurance that there would be other options there when I was able to wear them again.

When the last pieces had been loaded into the truck, I stood at the doorway and watched as it made its way down the driveway and out into the street. Thomas was already at his grandparents' house, so I had time to do one last circuit of our home. Without my things in it, it already felt foreign.

I sat on the floor in what had been Thomas's room. It still smelt like him, the air tinged with the scent of his sleeping breath. My baby turned over lazily in my stomach, her elbows stretching the sides of her increasingly snug lodgings.

There was one last thing to do. If Stephen thought he could just move us out and set up his new life here without a hiccup, he was in for a shock. As long as Alexa thought it was a good idea for them to live in my home, she could have the *full* experience.

I pulled a couple of cans of tuna out of my bag. I'd already slipped the curtains off the rails earlier in the day and unstitched the hems. I carefully added smears of the slimy fish, stitching the material back together and squishing the oily mess through the folds of material. I arranged the curtains back on the tracks as I went, making sure the fishy bits were in the gathers. Choosing such a dark pattern had been a wise move. By the time Stephen moved in, they would be completely dry from the warmth of the sun. It could take him and Alexa a while to work out where the smell was coming from. I silently thanked the women on the online revenge groups. What a goldmine of ideas they had been.

I worked through the living room, bedrooms and spare room. Someone else had suggested leaving a particularly pongy nappy under the furniture, but I couldn't cope with the thought of one of them finding it and blaming Thomas.

I carefully washed out the tuna cans and put them into the bottom of my handbag, throwing my keys in on top. When a large chunk of money appeared in my bank account, I might consider giving up access to the house, but certainly not before.

Thomas was waiting outside when I pulled up in the car outside my parents' house, waving so hard it looked as if he might take off. His head injury had left him with nothing more than a good-sized bump. The most torturous aspect of the experience had been trying to keep him calm and away from the TV for two days.

He seemed to regard our move as just another stint with his indulgent grandparents, where his chances of ice cream were significantly higher than on any given day at home. Here, they would let him set up a sleeping bag in front of the television on the living room floor.

My mother was behind him, her wary hand resting on his shoulder. When I clambered out of the car and waddled over to them, they both pulled me in for a hug. I held my breath. Did I smell a bit like an old fishing boat?

A banging from the back garden distracted me. 'What's that?'

My mother rolled her eyes. 'Your sister. Putting up some sort of shade contraption. She's moving into your father's study for a bit, and she thinks that'll make a nice sort of patio for her when she wants to sit outside and do whatever it is she does.'

'She's here?'

'Yes.' My mother grasped my forearm. She still smelt of the perfume she had been wearing – one bottle after another – since she and my father bought it on their honeymoon forty years earlier. 'We're all back here together. Isn't that lovely? She had some trouble at her place, had to move out. Something about someone taking rent they shouldn't. Your father's already suggested she take it up with a lawyer.'

Dad appeared from within the house. I felt the rasp of his grey stubble against my cheek as he kissed me. He leant around me to look for Amy. 'Is she okay over there?'

My mother put a hand on his arm. 'I'm sure it's fine. It's

just a temporary gazebo. She'll get the stakes in the ground and it'll be sorted.'

'Are we going to be left with big holes in the lawn?'

She patted him. 'It'll be fine.'

I peered around the corner. A man was helping her, facing away from us. 'Who's that?'

'His name's Luke. He owns next door, just moved back in. Somehow Amy talked him into helping. He seems lovely . . .' She dropped an eyebrow and moved her head in what I think was meant to be a meaningful way – she looked like a character in a clichéd rom-com.

'Mum!' It came out shriller than I had expected. 'I literally just moved out of the house.'

She smiled. 'I know, I know. But you know . . . one day . . . you or Amy . . .'

I turned away from her.

Thomas trotted behind me to the car, as I pulled our suitcases out of the boot. For something carrying some of our most important belongings, they seemed very light. My father reached out for a bag. 'Let me. In your state . . .'

I brushed him away. 'Not an invalid, remember?'

Once in the house, I could hear my parents talking in their bedroom as I ferried some of our belongings up to the spare rooms. The biggest of the bags I left at the bottom. There was no room for both bump and bag up the narrow staircase. They were speaking in hushed tones but since my dad stopped wearing his hearing aid, he hasn't been anyone's pick for a co-conspirator. My mum was deploying her best soothing tone, but I could hear every third sentence he said.

'You will need to make sure you get enough rest. Thomas runs you ragged.' 'Are we going to have enough hot water for us all?' Clearly, he thought I still took teenager-length showers. 'How long is it all likely to last?'

'I wish I knew,' I muttered under my breath.

The house had barely changed in the seventeen years since I had moved out. They had given the lounge a coat of paint to hide a garish orange wallpaper from the 1970s that I had endured. The shredded lounge suite had been replaced when the offending cat died, and one of the bathrooms had been given a new vanity after one of my friends spilt black hair dye all over the wooden doors during a sleepover. My sister's paintings still adorned the hallway, lounge and most of the bedroom walls – big abstract creations that she had spent hours slaving over through her teens and twenties. Precisely the kind of thing that would turn someone like Alexa's stomach when it came to fitting them into any interior design scheme.

I pushed open the door to the room that had been mine for the first couple of decades of my life. The furniture had changed, but the walls were still painted off-taupe, which I had considered the height of sophistication when I was thirteen. The dark blue curtains were still accumulating a smattering of mould where they touched windows that seemed permanently covered in condensation, no matter how often you left them open. At least they weren't the curtains hanging up in Alexa and Stephen's new love nest.

The carpet was the same dark brown that it had been when my parents moved into the house and I could still see an aged sticky grey mark where some glow-in-the-dark putty Amy and I had played with had sunk into the fibres.

It was both overwhelmingly familiar and suffocatingly strange. I would have to set up the bassinet for the baby under the window I used to climb out of, on to the garage roof and down the fence, when I was sneaking out to meet friends when I was fifteen. Thomas would be next door, in what had been Amy's room. I wouldn't need a baby monitor to keep an eye on him – Amy and I had proved many times that it was possible to communicate perfectly through the paper-thin wall between the two rooms.

I smiled at the memory – when had we stopped talking like that? It must have started about the time her ex, Frank, started telling her that people like me didn't understand 'creatives' like them. Magic Frank – she hadn't been willing to hear a word against him.

Thomas could have his little art table in the corner of one room, and most of his toys would stack against the wall of the larger room. As long as he had train set pieces to tip out, he would be happy. But I was not sure we could contain our mess to just these rooms. I could already imagine my father's face as he followed Thomas around, picking up the toys and putting them back into the right box, only to have them immediately tipped out again.

I could hear Thomas in the guest bathroom across the hallway, rifling through the cupboard under the basin. He was endlessly fascinated by his ability to squeeze moisturiser out of bottles and smear it on his legs. At home, I had moved all but one bottle well out of his reach, but my mother still had not learned the fine art of good-stuff-protection, and there was an array of top-of-the-line Yves Saint Laurent cosmetics just waiting to attract his attention.

I strode across the landing to pick him up. 'Why don't we go outside and play for a bit?'

The concrete of the driveway was warm under my feet as I stood, watching Thomas on his scooter, balancing precariously on one foot as he tried to stretch his body sufficiently to reach the handlebars and the ground at the same time. He pushed tentatively and looked up at me, beaming, as he started to move. 'Are you watching?' he demanded. 'Watch me!'

I had managed about seven minutes of obediently watching his scuffling scooting, resisting the urge to check my emails, when we heard a dog bark through the fence. Then there was some intent snuffling under the gate and a little snout became visible beneath the wood.

Thomas leant his scooter against the fence and dropped to his hands and knees, peering back under the fence at the animal. He recoiled with a delighted shriek when a dainty, wet tongue licked his face. 'Oh sorry.' The man still helping Amy dropped his hammer with a bounce on the hard lawn. 'That's my dog, Limbo.' He ducked down to look under the fence. 'It's okay, Limbo. Calm down.'

The dog seemed, from what we could see of him, to be a designer fluff ball, with the kind of fur that had to be brushed regularly just so that the animal could retain some vision. The man dusted his pants off and advanced towards us, extending his hand to shake mine. His close-cut salt-and-pepper hair and intensely blue eyes were familiar. Was he from a television show? Or a film? Then it hit me.

'Oh, it's you!' I blushed. 'The man from the library. Hi . . . Are you the neighbour?'

He laughed. 'I am indeed, and you're with the little one who was so intent on being part of my performance the other day.'

He watched as Thomas scooted across, in front him. 'I don't think I've seen you around here before. I would have recognised you.'

I could feel my face turning an unattractive shade of pink. 'I'm really sorry about that. I was hoping you wouldn't remember.'

He laughed a warm vibrato chuckle that made me want to lean in to him. 'You wouldn't believe how often one of the little ones tries to take part. Honestly, I love it.'

He turned and gestured towards Amy, who was now reclining on a lounger in the sun on the patio. She lifted a hand a fraction, her face expressionless.

'I've just been trying to help your sister with her mad plan for an outdoor entertaining area on the windiest part of the lawn.'

'She wouldn't be deterred?'

He pushed his glasses up his nose. 'Nope. Your dad is looking a bit worried. I bet she regrets asking a librarian to help now. Your parents really need to find some more practical neighbours.'

Thomas scooted back towards us, squinting into the sun. 'I'm fastest.' Thomas frowned at me.

'Yes, you are.'

He turned to Luke. 'Faster than you.'

Luke nodded obediently. 'I'm sure. Maybe we could have a race sometime.'

Thomas looked at him for a minute. 'I am Thomas Murchison.'

'Well, it's nice to meet you, Thomas Murchison,' he said. 'I'm Luke Tee, I live next door.'

Thomas nodded as if he had decided this information was acceptable. He was still circling back every couple of minutes to try to reach under the fence to pat Limbo.

Luke smiled at me. 'I'd better be going. Limbo's losing the plot with me over here and I'm no further use to Amy. It was nice to meet you two properly. Are you visiting for the day?'

'We're here for a little while.'

He gave Thomas a sort of half-salute. 'That's excellent

news. We might see you at the library again sometime soon, young man.'

Thomas headed back out again on his scooter, wobbling slightly as he resumed his pace. I found I was still staring in the direction of Luke's house several minutes later when the front door had closed with a click behind him.

My mother appeared at my side. 'Told you he's nice.'

'Mum!'

About six months earlier, I had sat hurling abuse at the TV one night because the programme had shown mothers of young kids living what had seemed like a fantasy life: taking an afternoon nap after a rough night sitting up with the kids, drinking a coffee in the sunshine and getting their nails done. 'No one has time for that,' I had shouted at Stephen. 'That's ridiculous. I'm lucky if I get to drink my coffee while it's still vaguely warm. My nail polish is the quick-dry stuff I put on while I was sitting on the toilet two weeks ago.'

But six months later, now that we had split up, I had to face the realisation that I was in for more than just a few hours without Thomas – and the prospect was not as welcome as I might have thought a couple of months before.

Stephen and I had agreed, with the briefest of communication, that he could have his wish to take Thomas for a day at the weekend. He would come to pick him up some time between 8 a.m. and 9 a.m. on Sunday and drop him back in time for dinner, bath and bed that same afternoon. The idea was that would give them time to do lots of 'dad things' – a trip to the cricket, or a ride on the train. Before I remembered it was no longer my problem, I'd wondered whether Stephen would know what to do. Usually, if he was having a day with Thomas in the past, it had been because I had organised an event for them.

Handing Thomas over had seemed almost okay when I was firing off an email among the arrival of ten others in my inbox during the week as I raced from nursery to a midwife check-up to organising my life into boxes for the move. But as the time for Stephen to arrive clawed ever closer, and Thomas's day away from me became a reality, I felt my body start to buzz with anxious energy. By Sunday morning, I was pacing across the kitchen, winding my necklace through my fingers, as Thomas tentatively spooned cereal somewhere in the direction of his face.

'You be good for Daddy today, okay honey?' I dropped in front of him to get his attention, squatting with my hands on his shoulders, thrusting a toothbrush in the direction of his teeth as soon as he had finished his breakfast. I tried to smooth the bit of his hair that always stood determinedly vertical. He looked at me quizzically but nodded.

The rumble of Stephen's truck pulling up outside interrupted us. Thomas gripped my hand. 'Come, Mummy. Dad's here!'

I scooped him up to carry him towards the door on what was left of my hip. 'You'll have a great time.'

I tried to keep my voice upbeat as I strode outside and into the driveway so Stephen would not have to enter the house and confront my parents. I was not sure whether I was protecting him from them, or them from the disappointment he had created for them. Either way, I was positive I did not want them to meet again for as long as I could avoid it. He was clambering out of the driver's seat as we walked down the front steps. 'You didn't have to come out.'

'It's fine.' I threw a backpack at him. 'I've put together a little bag of stuff for Thomas, just little treats for when you need a bribe and a change of clothes in case you get wet or anything. Just call me if anything happens . . .'

I was speaking too quickly and avoiding his eyes. I looked up and froze. Sitting in the passenger seat of the car was a woman. She had her head bowed, and was fixated on her phone. Her perfectly smooth, glossy hair had fallen over the side of her face, but I knew who she was.

'You brought *her*?'

The tremble in my hands had turned into a full-body shake. 'You're taking Thomas out with her? What are you thinking?'

Stephen rubbed his face with his hands. 'They have to meet at some time. She said she'd like to have a chance to get to know him – Alexa thinks it'll make it easier on him if they're friends.'

'But now? You've literally just moved us out. Now you're going to play happy families together, with her?'

Thomas was squirming in my arms and frowning at us. I buried my face in his hair.

'Can you run and get your coat from the box in the lounge, sweetheart?' I nudged him back towards the house. It was a brilliantly sunny day but Thomas didn't question me.

Stephen cleared his throat once he was out of earshot. 'Do you expect me to hide her from him? She is part of my life now.'

That was precisely what I expected him to do, at least until I was convinced this was not a temporary bout of madness, or I had accepted a marriage proposal from a handsome billionaire. I pushed him aside and approached the truck. She looked up as I placed my palms flat on the window, tapping my fingers against the glass to get her attention. 'Open the door.' I kept my voice level.

She obliged but said nothing. Our eyes locked.

'You've got balls, I'll give you that.' The words dripped from my mouth. 'Breaking up a family and turning up to rub my face in it.'

She put her hand to the thin choker around her slim, olive-skinned neck.

'I only hope that one day when you've got kids of your own someone else rips the ground out from under you, just so you know what it's like.' I stared at her.

Her gaze was unflinching. 'He told me you never believed he made his own decisions.' She gestured to my stomach. 'A pigeon pair, right? It'll be great when we can spend time with both of them. We need some kids around the house. It's too empty with just the two of us.'

'You're not taking my baby.'

'Oh no, not taking.' She smiled thinly. 'I've told Stephen 50/50 is fair. Especially when they're so little. We can't have him missing out.'

I looked to Stephen. Was he hearing this? This woman, a stranger, was suggesting my baby should live with her for half of her life. And not me. Not me! He seemed deliberately not to be listening.

My hands were shaking with rage. 'The lawyers have a lot to discuss, obviously.'

Thomas bounded out of the door behind me. 'Got it.' He handed a T-shirt to his father. He skipped over to the back door of the truck and tried to reach for the handle, which was well above his head.

I turned to Stephen. 'Don't you dare upset him. He's the sweetest boy in the world and he does not deserve any of this.' I needed to get back into the house quickly. My peripheral vision had disappeared and it was like I was staring down a tunnel.

'I would never do anything to hurt him.' Stephen brushed me away.

'How nice for him. Pity you didn't feel the same way about me.'

I turned on my heel and scurried back inside. I watched out the window as the truck pulled away.

I sat on the couch, watching the gold hands of the slate clock my parents had bought on a family holiday inch around the face. Alexa's words went around and around in my head. Amy had fallen asleep next to me, her phone in her hand. What time had she come in from work? Thomas had already been stirring and the sun was definitely up. I turned the television on, and the volume up. She grunted and rolled over. Her seemingly untroubled sleep sparked rage in me. She had nothing real to worry about in her life and yet she'd still managed to make a mess of it. I switched to a music channel.

Finally, she turned over and opened one eye. 'What is wrong with you?'

I shrugged. 'Did I wake you?'

She sat up. 'Don't be such a bitch. Just because your life's gone to crap. I'm going upstairs.'

'Feeling a bit tired?' I was sarcastic. She should try three years of interrupted nights and nine months trying to sleep with someone thrashing around in her abdomen. 'Better get some rest, you've got another shift at your big job tonight.'

I regretted it as soon as the words were out of my mouth. It was a sore point. When we were little and dreaming about the future, she'd wanted to be an artist – elevating to becoming an art teacher as she got older – not a bartender. She would never admit it but I knew from the way she ducked questions from our relatives at Christmas and told random surveys she was in customer relations that it was a sore point. It was probably why she was mean to Laura. She didn't look back as she left the room. I didn't even have Barbies these days to offer as a peace gesture.

I picked up my phone again. Still no messages, just a couple of Facebook notifications – someone was going to an event near me that looked a bit like a run of some sort, and someone else was having a birthday.

I found my mind tracking back to Luke. Discovering he was my parents' neighbour was the only bright spot in a dire week. It wasn't just that he was good-looking. There was something about him that pulled me in. Where Stephen had always made me feel vaguely incompetent when Thomas was on a roll – quick with the criticism of my parenting methods though he offered no alternative – Luke made it seem as though the whims of my two-year-old were the most delightful thing in the world.

I pulled myself up. What was I doing? I was extremely, debilitatingly pregnant. The time to fixate on a new man was not when your tummy button brushed your knees when you sat cross-legged. And my personality wasn't going to win him over – Stephen had done a pretty good job of dampening my sense of humour when he made me the boring, responsible one in recent years. And despite how much effort my mother put into hoping, there was no way a man like that was single.

But Stephen clearly hadn't let that stop him and, anyway, it was a harmless crush if it was anything. Some women spent the early weeks of new motherhood swaddling or baby-wearing; perhaps I could keep myself entertained chastely lusting after the neighbour.

I clicked on the browser and put in Luke's name. I owed it to my journalist training to dig a little deeper. There was an obscure singer from the 1970s who shared his name, and a fashion designer. But there were only a couple of entries that looked like they could be for Luke-next-door – one was a LinkedIn profile that showed he had gone to university in

Australia and worked in a law firm library before his current job. Bingo.

There was a news story where he had been interviewed about a school holiday project that had been held at the library. I switched over to Facebook. There he was – the only Luke Tee anywhere nearby. I started to scroll through the pictures.

Over the past couple of years, most of his photos were only of scenery. He had done a lot of travel – the intrepid kind requiring backpacks, which always made my anxiety spike. There were a couple of selfies, but he was alone in them. I kept going further back. It looked like he had made a cursory effort at locking down his privacy settings but there were still a lot of photos visible. As I scrolled, images of a woman began to appear. She was tagged in them as Angela Tee. That had to be the wife. Unless it was a sister?

There they were having dinner at a restaurant with an elaborate floral arrangement. There she was on top of a cliff, laughing at the camera. Shopping. Drinking cocktails. And there it was – a wedding snap. So if he wasn't married, he recently had been. Perhaps he too had been ditched by someone with a newfound surge of confidence? Somehow he didn't seem the type. I scrolled through the rest of my Facebook newsfeed. My cousin had liked a post from Stephen. Traitor. I knew I should have unfriended her when she sent an 'I'm a breast man' shirt for Thomas when he was born.

My finger hovered over the link to Stephen's profile. He had not changed his cover photo. It was still Thomas's cheesy grin, taken while he was in a bubble bath with bubbles that threatened to spill over his head. I clicked.

He was not a regular poster but there had been a flurry of photos taken since we split. One at a music festival, taken the previous weekend, probably around the time I had been dealing with one large-scale toddler meltdown because we had not been able to go on the miniature trains downtown. A music festival! Who did he think he was, Bruno Mars? It warmed my heart to see that he was easily the oldest in the group photo by a decade.

Alexa was leaning against him in what looked like late afternoon sunshine, wearing big, rose-gold-framed reflective sunglasses, with her perfectly styled, now caramel blonde hair, pulling a half-fish face and a peace sign at the camera. I could tell she had practised her photo pose. She was positioned slightly side-on in every shot I could find, with her hand balanced on her hip.

Not that she needed to make her waist look any smaller; it was about the size of my wrist. Was this really a woman who wanted a house full of kids – my kids?

What had I posted lately? I checked back through my profile. A recipe for fudge made using jellybeans, an angry opinion piece about the gender pay gap and a photo of Thomas prancing around in the garden, just after he had tipped his dinner on his head.

Four hours until Thomas came back – and counting.

I opened my email program to send a message to Kyle Matthews. He and I had started at the newspaper together when we were new graduates out of university on the intern programme. I'd been put on the police round, which I'd hated, and he'd been added to the sports reporting team, despite not knowing a basketball from a football. We had regular Friday debrief drinks where we plotted ways to get out.

Ten years later, by then a senior entertainment reporter, he had taken redundancy and set out to work as a freelancer. His latest project was a new gossip website designed to carry the most salacious of news. It showed promise but was yet to get its first big break.

'Have you heard,' I typed quickly. 'Apparently that celeb (ish) designer woman Alexa McKenzie is a total diva – demands only brown rice and cucumber served on set, for the whole crew when she's filming? I heard people quitting in protest. Might be worth a story xx.'

CHAPTER SEVEN

<u>How to get your baby to sleep</u>

What you'll need:

Lavender essential oil

White noise machine

Socks

*Merino onesie to raise baby's temperature
by exactly half a degree*

Sleeping bag

Moses basket

A magic wand

Put a drop of oil on each of your baby's feet. Set the white noise machine going at approximately 70 decibels. Slowly massage both feet and legs. While massaging, pat your baby's bottom 92 times and rub her back anti-clockwise 49 times. Dress her in her socks and onesie and put on her sleeping bag. Lay her in her Moses basket, and without stopping your rhythm, hold your tongue at a 90-degree angle as you extract your hands. Complete this manoeuvre perfectly and you'll get a full night's sleep. Fail and you'll never sleep again.

The house was still quiet when I woke the next morning. It took me half a minute to realise where I was. Every day when I first opened my eyes, I expected to be in my bed at home, Stephen snorting and farting beside me. The morning sun sent dappled shadows across the floor in the same way I remembered from when I was a teenager. Back then, I'd have been going to bed at this time. There was no noise to indicate that Thomas had stirred yet.

I wiggled my toes. How long would it be before I could sleep on my stomach again? There was only one sleeping position I could bear, with a pillow wedged under my stomach and another between my knees. Still, every morning I woke up with a different part of my body tingling with pins and needles. My hips throbbed.

'Make your entrance any time you like, littlest one.' I put my hands on either side of my stomach. A foot, or maybe an elbow – I could never tell, even though the midwife had patiently tried to show me each visit – pushed back at me.

There was a clatter at the front door. 'S'all right, I can do it.' Amy. I checked the time. Just before 7 a.m. Was she just arriving home from work? I rolled out of bed, to look out the window. She was concealed by the eaves over the front door but I could make out a shape behind her. It looked a bit like Luke. I quickly checked my reflection in the full-length mirror on the wardrobe door. There was no getting around it, I was heavily pregnant and wearing a pair of old pyjamas. But if she kept rattling around trying to get her key in the lock, she was going to wake everyone up.

It took twenty seconds to get down the stairs and to the front door, in which time Amy seemed to have become so frustrated she had hurled her keys into the front rosebushes. When I opened the door, she was leaning on the frame, her head in her hands.

'What is going on?'

Luke put his hand on Amy's shoulder and nudged her towards me. 'Here's your sister – she'll help you.'

Amy pushed him away. 'Don't need help.'

I looked at him. He made a gesture of helplessness. 'I found her sitting on the kerb this morning when I went out for a run.'

'She's been drinking.'

He snorted. 'You could say that. The best I've got out of her so far is there was some sort of function after work. Seemed to involve tequila. Someone dropped her off and she decided getting into the house was just a bit too much effort. You okay to handle her from here? I can help you get her into bed, if you like.'

'It's fine. I lived with her for a bit while we were students. Come on, Amy.'

I put my arm around her and pulled her towards the house. He was still watching us. I shot him what I hoped was a reassuring smile. 'We'll be okay. I'll talk to her when she wakes up.'

I gave him an awkward wave. He was wearing rather more than he had been in the dream I'd been wrenched from twenty minutes earlier. Could she not have waited until I had at least cleaned my teeth?

I pushed her towards the couch. 'Lie down. I'm not carrying you to your room. You can sleep it off here.'

She grunted and swatted at me but lay down. 'I'm fine. Piss off.'

My parents still kept a store of neatly folded blankets in a chest at the end of the sofa, which they pulled over their knees as they watched their television dramas on a Sunday night. I retrieved one and draped it across Amy. She emitted a guttural snort, her mouth slightly open.

Thomas had appeared on the staircase. 'Morning, darling.' I scooped him up. He peered over my shoulder at Amy. 'Auntie's a bit tired, sweetheart. Let's get you some breakfast and off to nursery, shall we?'

I was scrolling classified ads on my phone when Amy stirred four hours later. She cracked open one eye. 'What are you doing?'

I shrugged. 'Just shopping.'

She struggled to sit up, wincing and massaging her temples. 'For what? Don't you have all the baby things in the world by now?'

'Not for me. For Stephen.'

She screwed up her face against the light streaming through the living room windows. 'Am I still drunk?'

'Probably. Now, what do you reckon, five cubic metres of topsoil? Or a couple of big boulders? These guys say they'll deliver, leave them right in the middle of the driveway at home for me. Or here, what about this huge old truck body? Nothing working, free to a good home. Alexa would love that as a piece of outdoor art. Probably would be a bit of a pain when they're trying to move her stuff in, too, or throwing a housewarming party.'

Amy threw a cushion at me. 'You wouldn't dare.'

I put my phone down. 'Try me. How are you feeling?'

She hauled herself off the couch. 'I've been better, been worse. I'll be all right after an aspirin and a hash brown. Spare me the lecture.'

She teetered towards the kitchen.

'Amy.' I reached out for her as she walked past. 'Do you remember his name?'

She snorted. 'Who?'

I made an expansive gesture. 'You know, the guy you brought home.' It wasn't exactly a lie. Luke had been at the doorstep with her.

She went pale. 'What?'

I focused on keeping my face neutral. 'You don't remember?'

I could see her running an inventory of her memories. Finally, she turned away in disgust. 'You're just winding me up.'

I smirked. 'Sorry. Just trying to entertain myself.'

'Sort it out. You're just grumpy because your baby isn't here yet.'

She pointed at the calendar as she stalked away. It was my due date. No matter how many times people told me that only 22.4 per cent of babies – or something – are born on even their due week, that due date seemed to bore into my brain. I had counted down the days and now it was here – and nothing.

It did not help that my mother had taken to watching me intently, always looking for signs that 'something might be happening'. She would regard me before she left to do the supermarket shopping or to go for her morning walk around the block. When I at last managed to convince her that I was not on the very verge of delivering, she would insist that I kept my phone by me and send her a message at the first sign of a twinge.

I just rolled my eyes. I had given up trying to convince her that she would get more than ten minutes' notice to get home from the shops in time to help me.

Amy returned to the couch and offered me an open packet of chips. I took a handful and we sat, facing the wall, the only sound the overly loud crunching of saturated fat and sodium.

'This sucks!' she exclaimed at last.

'What do you mean?'

'We're both over thirty. We're back in our parents' house. You're planning some sort of mad revenge on your crappy husband and taking it out on me. It's Monday morning and I'm already hungover but I have to go to my awful job.'

'It's not that bad is it?' I tried to reach for her hand. A wave of guilt turned my stomach. 'I'm sorry I was horrible when you wanted to move into my place. I'd just had it that day, you know? Like it didn't have to be you. If the laptop froze, I'd have chucked it out the window. I just get to the point where there is so much in my brain that I have to worry about that there's literally no room for anything more.'

She squeezed my hand so briefly I wasn't sure if I'd imagined it. 'It's okay. I know you're going through some stuff. It's just, you don't know what it's like, you know? To think things have got as tough as they're going to get and then to discover there's still a bit further to fall. At least for you this is a temporary blip.'

'You think?' I gestured to my stained T-shirt and straining maternity jeans.

She smiled ruefully. 'In ten years you won't even remember

all this. Your kids will be amazing little people and you'll have some important job somewhere. What if I never get going? Not so cool being fifty and living with your parents, is it?'

Before Thomas was born, I asked a friend what it felt like to give birth. Hollywood would indicate it's a burst of water on the floor – usually at the supermarket – a few minutes of shrieking and swearing, then a blissful smile. Some mums groups on the internet had seemed to want to convince me that the pain was so bad I would feel like I was going to die, or that that would be preferable. Others claimed it was nothing a bit of floating about in hot water wouldn't fix – and if I was to take drugs for the pain I might as well have them injected directly into my newborn's bloodstream. Weakling.

My friend, Alison, had looked at me sideways. 'Ever had bad period pain? It's like that, only worse.'

She was the most accurate. Except about a thousand times too kind.

It was not until two days later that I felt the first pain-that-might-have-been-something. Thomas had gone to bed and I was sitting in the lounge with my parents. It was meant to all come back to you, wasn't it? Like some sort of horrendous cycling episode. But I wasn't sure. I had been having a lot of indigestion.

I looked at my parents, each nursing a cup of coffee, their feet propped on a coffee table scattered with magazines and Thomas's picture books. Once I said something, there would be no going back. I would wait to see what happened. My worst fear was being one of those people I had heard about being turned away from the delivery ward because they were only a couple of centimetres dilated. Right then, I could not imagine anything more embarrassing than showing up at the hospital thinking I was in fully fledged delivery mode only to have a doctor tell me that it was going to get much worse.

A couple of minutes later, the niggle was back, tapping on roughly where I thought my cervix might be, and stronger.

'I'm going to have a bath.' I hauled myself out of the armchair and started to shuffle towards the bathroom.

My mum sat up. 'Are you feeling okay?'

'There might be something happening, I'm not sure. I'll just sit for a bit and see what happens.'

As the water filled the spa bath, I had to stop and bend over, holding on to the side, to ride out a wrenching cramp. It felt a bit as if I had sat on the expensive vacuum cleaner Stephen and I had been talked into buying by a pushy salesman, who demonstrated with a cup of sand that he tipped on to the ground.

I counted down in my head. Sixty seconds, right? A contraction should last a minute. It subsided after about forty-five seconds. Maybe not labour, then. I hauled my shaking body over the side of the bathtub and into the water and watched as my stomach tightened to a peak as another cramp soared up from my lower abdomen. I pulled my knees up as close to my chest as they could go. (Not very.) Perhaps lying in the water was not going to work. I turned on one of the jets and tried to position my lower back in front of it, but it was itchy and irritating. I gave up and pulled myself up. Another contraction pulsed through me. I curled over into the foetal position and counted again. This time, I got to sixty.

'Mum,' I shouted.

There was silence. I tried to pull the bathrobe around myself, breathing fiercely through my clenched teeth and concentrating on the feeling of the lino on my feet. A book had told me that the body could focus on only one pain at a time so if I made my feet or my hands uncomfortable I should be able to feel less discomfort in my cervix. I would like to meet a person who can work out how to make their feet uncomfortable enough to put up a distraction from labour pains.

'Mum!'

I could hear footsteps outside the bathroom door. 'Is everything all right in there?'

'I need you to call the midwife and see if you can get her to come out here and check me,' I said, leaning against the bathroom door. 'I'm not sure what's going on but I think the baby might be coming.'

I could hear her scurrying away. I doubled over as another pain built inside me. My toes were curled on the floor and my hands had balled into fists, which I thumped against my thighs to count down the minute.

Minutes later she was back. 'She says she's going to come here to check you first. Are you sure you don't want to go straight to the hospital?'

'No, I'm sure I'm not ready for that yet.' I stopped as another cramp washed in. I stamped and hummed under my breath until it subsided.

I was hunched on the bed, completely naked, rolling the duvet between my hands and furiously counting under my breath when the midwife, Tina, arrived.

'We'll just check you and see how far along you are,' she said, guiding me on to my back and then sticking what felt like her entire hand inside me.

'Well.' She was businesslike. 'You're fully dilated. It looks like we're having this baby here.'

'What?' I sat up on the bed. I was not ready for that. I had just changed the sheets. Wasn't it only hippies and new-agers who had their babies at home? And probably ate the placenta afterwards. I had wanted the hospital, where they would look after me and give me a cooked breakfast and make cups of tea for at least a good couple of days afterwards.

'You do not have time to make it to the hospital,' she said. 'I'll just get my tools together. Are you feeling the urge to push?'

The pressure had been building with every contraction for the past twenty minutes. I had thought I was in for an explosive bout of diarrhoea but it turned out it was just my baby trying to make her way into the world. I nodded word-lessly as another one racked through me, making me feel as if I had to rush to the toilet and fall apart into a hundred pieces at the same time.

Tina placed a foetal heart monitor on my stomach and watched as it calculated its reading. She muttered something under her breath and made a note in the pad next to her. Positioning my knee so it was against the red satin of her shirt, she looked firmly into my eyes. 'Your baby's not very happy in there so you're going to have to push this kid out,' she said. 'I'm going to need you to focus.'

'What? What's wrong?'

She shook her head. 'Everything is fine, but we need to get her out. Next contraction, you push.'

Somehow my mother had appeared at my other side. They each took a leg and, as the next wave hit me, I pushed as though I was trying to expel my brain through my pelvis. The energy required to propel the baby from my body made my eyes burn.

'Okay, one more push and your baby will be here.' Tina

looked at me in what I think was meant to be a reassuring way. 'It's a bit stretchy right?'

Stretchy was not the word. I could feel where my baby's head was sitting just inside my body. My skin zinged with heat. Another pain hit and I pushed as if I wanted to turn my body inside out. There was a rush and a slither and then – at last – a cry.

'Is she okay? Can I hold her?'

I sat up. Tina was doing something slightly out of my sight. 'Please? Can I hold her?'

'Just a second.'

She turned to me and presented the small, kicking, purple, wrinkled body. I noticed her hands first – seemingly too large for her body and pale against the mottled skin of her torso.

'She had her cord around her neck. Twice.' She saw my face. 'But she's fine. She's a beautiful, healthy little girl.'

I held my baby to the shivering skin of my chest and watched as she snuffled. She was covered in sticky vernix and had her eyes firmly scrunched shut. Her head glistened with a mixture of blood and mucus. I guided her to my breast, where she snorted as she bumbled around, trying to latch on. I held my nipple to her mouth and looked at my mother. 'I never want to do that again.'

When Tina had gone and my mother had returned to her bedroom, I lay back against the pillows. Baby Amelia's entrance had not been what I expected, but then, none of my new existence was what I would have predicted even a month ago.

The only sound in the room was her snuffly breathing. It was still warm and the bedside lamp was on its lowest setting, sending a soft glow across her face. She lay in her

Moses basket; the oversized beanie my mother had retrieved from my box of baby gear jauntily askew on her head. Her wrinkled face was serene with sleep, her lips slightly pursed. She was so beautiful it made my fingertips tingle.

Her chest was rising and falling quickly, like an out-of-practice runner's. Every so often her breath would pause and she would give a little cough before it started up again.

Every tendon in my body was sparking with energy. I needed to sleep – I remembered the dreaded second night after Thomas's birth when he refused to shut his eyes for almost fourteen hours straight – but as soon as I put my head on the pillow I leapt back up to check whether I could still see the movements of her breath, or whether the blankets were still covering her adequately, whether the store of nappies and wipes was sufficient or even – at one point – whether I had remembered to turn the oven off when I had finished cooking dinner earlier in the evening.

It is like expecting someone to run a marathon and then immediately tuck themselves up in bed. I felt so under-prepared for the care of this little person. How could I ever be enough for two of them? I was barely sufficient for one. She was so trusting and I felt sure it would only be a matter of time before I let her down in some way. How could I not have seen this coming? What good was I as a mother if I couldn't manage to hold my relationship together long enough to bring her into a world where her father was still around?

I bit my lip. I would have to somehow find a way to be both mum and dad and show her that flaky fathers were an entirely optional extra.

Thomas was still asleep – the boy who can hear an Easter egg being opened from a mile off had missed the commotion of his sister's arrival.

When he was born, we had been shifted to a hospital ward's bed within a couple of hours, me clutching him to my breast nervously, unsure of how to hold him securely, how to convince him that my breast, which suddenly felt very inadequate for the job of nourishing such a small person, was worth sampling. Someone had mentioned holding my nipple as if it was a burger I was offering him to bite. I still hadn't figured out what they meant, even the second time around.

Then, I counted the clicks of the clock's second hand until Stephen was allowed back in and I could relinquish some of the parental responsibility for a while. When he sent me a text first thing the next morning to tell me that he would be late in because he had to wait for an electrician to turn up to fix the oven, I cried. The nurse weighing Thomas had patted my shoulder. 'You'll get used to it.' I still wasn't sure if she meant the whole business of motherhood or just my husband running late. Either way, she was right.

This time, there was no end in sight. Even my Facebook newsfeed, which had got me through many a lonely Saturday night so far, had fallen silent. I still had not told Stephen that Amelia had been born. Somehow, it was the saddest bit about the whole split, delivering such news via a text message. I had drafted it several times in my head. 'Congratulations, your daughter's been born,' seemed too chirpy. 'Baby here,' seemed too perfunctory.

I tried for the truth. 'Baby came faster than expected,' I tapped on to the screen. 'Accidental home birth but all well. I'll call you tomorrow to arrange a time to visit.' I pressed send and tried not to imagine him getting the message. His phone would be lying on the bedside table next to him, where it always was. On the other side, I assumed, would be her. She would be asleep, her perfect hair spread across the pillow and not a trace of mascara smudged under her eyes. She'd probably had permanent make-up done. Those tattooed eyeliners and brows I was too scared to go near.

What would she do when they got the news? How weird it must be to congratulate someone you are sleeping with on the birth of their baby – with someone else. I did not have to wait long to get a reaction. My phone buzzed in my hand almost instantly.

'Are you serious?' he replied.

I groaned. I had no reply.

He sent another message: 'I'll come around in the morning. You can't keep me out of the baby's life.'

'I have no intention of doing so,' I fired back.

Another message followed: 'And what the hell did you do to the curtains?'

I left it.

I found I was crying big, ugly tears. My whole body shook. I tried to push them down but they kept forcing their way out, bubbling up and wailing out of me. My nose was streaming and my stomach heaved. There was a knock at the door and my mother pushed it open. I buried my face in the pillow, my arms around my deflated stomach. She reached out for me and leant her face against the top of my head.

'Shhh,' she soothed under her breath in the same tone I used to calm Thomas mid-tantrum. 'Shhh.'

I couldn't. The sobs just kept coming. 'I don't understand how he could give it all up,' I choked out. My pillowcase was soaked.

'He's an idiot.' My mother's voice was harsh. I looked up. It was the first time I could remember having heard her so furious. 'You'll get through this, darling. You're better than them both.'

I fell asleep leaning against her, still trying to balance on the pad the midwife had left on my bed to soak up the post-birth blood flood.

A couple of hours later, I startled awake when I dreamily opened my eyes and spotted Amelia in her basket next to me, twitching and snorting in her sleep. She was here. I was suddenly a mother of two.

More messages had pinged up on my phone overnight. I'd told Laura the baby had been born and she must have relayed the message to the rest of our coffee group, who each had sent me a little message of congratulations. There were three promises of meals for the freezer and two offering babysitting or playdates for Thomas.

I stared at my phone. They were so kind – it had been at least a year since I had seen some of these women and now they were offering to adjust their lives to help me. Usually my instinctive response would be to say no. I took pride in managing my own life, not needing the hassle of relying on others. But was that what normal people did? I tentatively tried a reply to all. 'I'm with parents so sorted for meals, but would be lovely to catch up.' Not too needy, I decided.

Thomas was stirring in his room. He had begun to start the day with a sort of anguished cry, as if he cannot quite believe that he is awake and must endure another day of playing for hours and getting whatever he decided he wanted. I waited until I could hear him slithering out of bed, and his feet hitting the floor with a thump.

Calling out to him, I kept one eye on Amelia. She would wake any minute for another attempt at a feed. She was still testing the world; working out how her jaw worked was the first hurdle. Then she would need to think about fingers, toes, hands. If I thought about it too much the challenge ahead of her seemed insurmountable.

Thomas peeked around the door, one curl of hair flopping down on to his forehead and one of his eyelids slightly drooping. I gestured for him to clamber up into bed beside me. 'I've got a surprise for you.'

He sat up. 'What?' He was probably hoping for a new *Paw Patrol* truck.

'Be very quiet and gentle.' I reached for Amelia and lifted her from her basket. 'It's your sister.'

'What? Me see.' He climbed over me, so that he was leaning with one hand on my stomach and the other touching her head. I had to bite back a yelp. The after-pains rippling through me were like the start of labour all over again.

'Be gentle honey. Isn't she sweet?'

He stroked her smattering of fine hair. 'Sweet little baby.'

'You're going to be such a good big brother.'

I could feel tears pricking at my eyeballs again. After two and a half years of registering only Thomas as my baby – and, if I'm honest, the only child I had much interest in at all except when I could compare Thomas favourably to another – I was now looking at two little people who each felt like a part of myself laid out in front of me. We lay side by side, Thomas leaning on my shoulder, watching Amelia breathe.

'Doesn't she have tiny lips?' I drew the outline of her mouth with my finger.

He giggled. 'Can she play?'

'You'll have to wait until she's a bit older, sorry, darling.'

A vehicle roared into the driveway, its engine humming in a way that seemed obnoxious in the early calm of the morning. The only person I knew who sat in his truck for what felt like hours before turning it off was Stephen. He was usually on his phone.

'Is that Daddy?' Thomas looked up at me, his eyes hopeful.

I was already halfway to the window, maternity pad lodged like a phone book in my underwear and Amelia in the crook of my arm. I pulled the curtain back and watched as Stephen climbed out of his truck and stalked towards the house.

He wouldn't ring the bell, surely? It wasn't even 7 a.m. It rang.

'Can you go and let Daddy in, honey?' I asked Thomas.

I was too late. I heard my father open the door. 'Oh, it's you. She's upstairs. Does she know you're coming?'

Stephen had already pushed past him and was on his way up.

'Rachel!' my father bellowed up the stairs. 'You've got a visitor. Are you ready? Do you want me to tell him to come back later?'

I was walking like a cowboy from an old western and my stomach shook like jelly. I still expected to feel a kick or a somersault in there any minute and every so often I got a little shock when I remembered that she was now out in the world wearing a little merino onesie that I had bought on sale six months earlier, when the world was quite a different place.

Stephen crashed through the bedroom door. Thomas leapt up and threw himself at him, like he was running defence against a football player aiming for a goal. Stephen scooped him up on to his shoulder.

'I came to see my two babies.'

Thomas giggled. 'I'm baby number one.'

I gestured towards our daughter, still fast asleep in my arms. 'Amelia.' He shot a glance at me. Amelia had been my pick for a name throughout the pregnancy but Stephen had never got around to agreeing to it. Too bad – I hadn't agreed to an evil stepmother, either.

He reached out. 'Can I hold Amelia?'

I blanched but he was already lifting her out of my arms. He gazed down at her adoringly. 'She's got a lot of hair.' He looked at me. 'She looks so much like Thomas did . . . Do you remember?'

I could not meet his eyes. That was the same little boy he'd walked away from. 'I'll go and make a cup of tea.'

CHAPTER EIGHT

<u>Make your own fairy garden</u>

What you'll need:

A planter pot

Soil

Flower seedlings

Rocks

Doll's house furniture

Glitter

Fill the pot with soil and plant your seedlings – look for plants that won't grow too big, if you can. Position some rocks in the middle and your doll's house furniture around them to create a space for your fairies to hang out. Chuck some glitter over the top to give it a touch of magic, and to provide something to vacuum out of the carpet for the next three weeks. Be prepared to do this entire exercise yourself.

Either the kids will get bored before the seedlings are planted, or they'll plant their stuff in such a haphazard way that the perfectionist in you will have you rip it all out and start again when they are not looking. Don't worry – if you no longer have your career to worry about, you will need something to occupy your mind.

After two months had ticked past, I resigned myself to the idea that I'd had no clue what I was talking about when I complained that looking after one child was hard work. Amelia was what the healthcare professionals called 'high needs'. She would sleep only if she had been awake for exactly the right amount of time – not a minute longer. Once she was six weeks old, she would feed only when there was no distraction, even a peep from a sparrow would put her off.

'I'm a perfectionist,' I told her one morning when she screamed while I was trying to get her to latch on. 'But this is ridiculous.'

It didn't help that my mother seemed to think the best way she could apply for the World's Best Grandmother award was to give me helpful tips and endless little nuggets of advice that probably were accurate thirty years ago.

'Oh she's got a bit of a sniffle? Just pop a slice of onion in the bottom of this sock I've just knitted for her.' I'm not joking.

My favourite was her endless insistence that it was hunger that stopped Amelia settling easily for naps and bedtime. As if anyone would know more than I about her routine of seven-and-a-half-minute feeds every twelve minutes, day and night.

And no matter how often I explained to Thomas that I really needed him to be quiet when I was getting her to sleep, it was like he had a sixth sense of exactly when her eyelids were starting to flutter shut. He would use just that moment to pounce upon us.

I was hiding in my bedroom, feeding her to sleep for her morning nap on the first day I was due back at work, when I heard him pacing the hallway outside. The footsteps thumped past. Then a police car was scooted along, with Thomas providing the siren sound effects. Then he was walking again, dragging his feet.

Amelia's eyelids were drooping. I tensed my fingers on the sides of my rocking chair, willing Thomas not to shatter the few magic seconds I had to hustle her off to sleep. I was due to log in for work in exactly nine minutes. The door cracked open. 'Mumma!' Amelia started, screwed up her face and bellowed.

'Thomas!' I stood, pulling her towards me.

He stuck out his bottom lip. 'Play with me.'

'Honey.' I jiggled Amelia on my shoulder. 'I can't right now. Your sister needs to sleep. I'm going to have to work soon. Granny is here somewhere, isn't she?'

He locked his knees and crossed his arms.

I forced down the urge to scream. 'How about I help you find something on the TV?'

I took his hand and guided him down the stairs to the living room, Amelia complaining loudly as she nestled against my shoulder. Amy was slumped against the cushions on the sofa, a magazine over her face. I cleared my throat.

'Do you think . . .' I spat the words at her '. . . that you could bring yourself to mind your nephew for a minute while I try to get Amelia to sleep?'

She sat up. 'What have I done?'

'Nothing.' I turned to take Amelia back upstairs. 'You've done nothing.'

I grimaced. My resolve to be nice to my sister hadn't lasted long but, seriously, my family was either over-helping and interfering or completely oblivious.

'Do you think maybe you should relax a bit? Go a bit easier on yourself? Might help.' Amy shrugged and returned to her magazine.

'Relax?' I was incredulous. 'You try dealing with two little people and an obliterated marriage and tell me how relaxing you find it.'

When I returned to the living room half an hour later, Thomas was lying on his stomach across the ottoman, eating Wotsits and staring, saucer-eyed, at the television. Amy was in the same position with her magazine. I opened my mouth to complain but decided against it. Who was I to argue about his choice of snack when there'd been days of late where I'd basically existed on additive E100?

My hair was still unwashed. I was wearing the T-shirt I'd slept in and I could feel a leak of milk spreading from my feeding bra. But I had my first post-maternity leave Monday morning phone conference with the editorial team and if I tried to redirect Thomas's attention, there was every chance I would miss it. I cursed myself for feeling too guilty to increase the number of Thomas's nursery days.

I plugged my headset in and settled on to a dining chair. Out the window, I could see across the valley to the school Amy and I used to trudge to daily. Now it looked more like an expensive law firm, with two shiny new buildings. During

135

our time there, we were lucky if our prefab classrooms didn't leak.

The phone connected. 'Rachel!' My editor boomed down the line. 'How lovely to have you back. You've been missed.'

I smiled. She was one of the best parts of my job – the kind of person who buried criticism so deep in a 'compliment sandwich' that you sometimes had to read an email twice to work out that she was telling you off. Her requests for work were constant but she had a way of asking that made you think just doing your job was doing her an enormous favour.

'How are you feeling?'

I paused. How much should I tell her? That I spent my evenings reading news stories about women who set their cheating exes' houses on fire? One only got a fine – I thought that seemed eminently worth it. Or maybe that I had not slept more than fifty minutes in a row in two months? 'Oh you know, bit tired but fine.'

Little blips signalled the others joining the call.

'Right, we've got a few things to get through this morning,' Aileen's voice rang out across the muffled sounds of clattering typing at desks in newsrooms around the country. Thomas clambered into my lap and put his arms around my shoulders. I switched the earpiece to the other side of my head and leant my cheek against his warm hair.

'We're going to reassign a couple of rounds,' Aileen said. 'I've been thinking about how we can use our strengths a bit better and I'd like Rachel to take the lead on health, supported by Trent. You'll be able to learn a lot from her.'

I pushed the button to unmute my phone. 'Okay.' The health round involved a lot of interviewing scientists and trying to turn pages of academic waffle into something that a normal person could understand. Could I do it?

136

Thomas let out a guttural, manly burp just as I went to press the mute button again. There was a pause before Aileen started talking again. 'I'd also like you all to think about what we could do to support you towards your professional development goals over the rest of this year.'

One of the juniors asked a question about training courses. Aileen laughed humourlessly. 'Sorry, I should have said – this can't be anything that is going to cost anyone any money.'

I pressed the button again to unmute my microphone. Thomas blew a raspberry. I quickly muted it again.

'Are you all right there, Rachel?'

I waved at my sister as though I was directing a plane to a gate. She picked up the remote and the *Thomas the Tank Engine* theme song rang out at top volume. 'Sorry, yes. I'm fine.'

Aileen paused again. 'I'd also like us to make a time to have you come into the office this week, to reconnect, if we could? Couple of things I'd like to discuss.'

'Oh – yes. Of course. You name the time.'

'ASAP, I think. Let's get you back into the swing of things.'

I fell out of the lift into the foyer of the *Sun-Herald* offices almost on time the next morning. The receptionist looked up from an iPad and gazed at me expectantly. I did not recognise her. But it had been at least three months since I'd been in the office and the management seemed to have a policy of not letting anyone get too comfortable in a reception role. If you didn't fit the description of whatever their latest vision for the future of media was, you were shunted off to some other part of the building.

'I'm here to see Aileen Cameron,' I told her as I inched down on to what must have been the most uncomfortable chair in the world. It was straight out of the pages of an interior design magazine but was all hard edges. And white. Very white.

She tapped on her screen. 'I'll let her know. And you are?'

'Rachel Murchison. I work here, actually. Well not here, but, you know . . .' I tried to give her a smile and made a vague gesture that could be interpreted as working somewhere outside the building. My mind drifted to my mother at home with Amelia. I drummed my fingers on my handbag. I could see the outline of people darting back and forth through the opaque glass behind the icy receptionist.

The doors slid open and a tall man in a slim-cut suit strode through. He adjusted his fedora hat. My old friend Kyle Matthews.

'Kyle!'

He looked around. 'Rachel! How lovely to see you.'

The smell of expensive cologne enveloped me as he kissed me on each cheek. 'What are you doing here? And what's with the hat?'

He smirked. 'Trying out a new look. What do you think?'

I cocked my head. 'To be honest, I'm not sold.'

He swatted me on the arm. 'What do you know about fashion?'

I pretended to be affronted.

'I'm here for a meeting with the commercial team this time, if you can believe it,' he whispered, watching the receptionist, who was examining her fingertips. 'I'm trying to get some cut-through with the site, you know. If I can get some sort of partnership going on – maybe get the odd bit of content rolling out in the paper and online here, it will make a big difference.'

I nodded. 'How's it all going?'

He shrugged. 'Just got to get some people willing to talk.

Thanks for your tip, by the way. I've heard she's a nightmare, that Alexa woman.'

I snorted and dropped my voice to a whisper. 'Tell me about it. She took off with my husband.'

His mouth dropped open. 'No!'

The door behind the receptionist burst open, interrupting us.

Aileen strode out, wearing a vintage-style full black skirt, red silk blouse and cropped jacket. She would have been the picture of polished if the hair on the right side of her head was not sticking up at an odd angle, as if she'd been raking her fingers through it. She had a folder clamped under one arm. 'Rachel, it's so lovely to see you.'

I stood up and tried to brush out a crease in my skirt, giving Kyle a half-wave. He made a signal with his hand that I assumed indicated he was planning to call me. 'And you. You look busy.'

I followed her through into the newsroom. The organisation had recently turned to hot desking, so I had no idea where any of the people I would know would be sitting. It was meant to build efficiencies but it just seemed to manufacture confusion. The sea of faces swam in front of me, so I studied my toes – in high heels for the first time in almost a year. Aileen led me into a glass-walled room on the far side. We had a view of a disused alleyway.

'Thanks for making the time to come in.' Aileen smiled. 'I know you must be so flat out with Thomas, and the new one . . .' She made an awkward rocking gesture that I assumed was meant to indicate a baby.

'I muddle through. I have my parents to help me, anyway.'

I put my iPad on the table between us. I had better make it look like I had given this meeting a bit more thought than the twenty-minute car trip in. I could already feel my breasts starting to leak. I tried to check my watch under the lip of the table. I needed to be back in time for Amelia's next feed.

'I'm really excited about you taking on the health round. There's lots of potential to try to educate readers and give them something useful. I know you said last year you wanted the opportunity for some more responsibility. This seemed a good option.'

Had I? I couldn't recall. 'I hope I can do it justice.'

Aileen raised a finger. 'You'll be fantastic. But I just need to talk to you about something else first, make sure we're on the same page before you plough ahead.'

I raised my eyebrows. Her tone had shifted.

'I'm not sure whether this will be welcome to you or not.' She was looking at her chipped red fingernails. 'The company has decided that we no longer think we are getting the synergies we need with staff working remotely as a permanent arrangement. Everyone is going to be asked to come back into the office at least four days a week to work from here. Boost teamwork, morale and so on. The latest staff engagement survey was abysmal.'

I swallowed. 'Right. When?'

'Ideally immediately but I know this is a shock so I'm not expecting you to make the change this week.' She clasped her hands on the desk in front of her in a sort of pleading gesture. 'I'm sorry to do this to you right now. I hope you'll find it's actually a pretty cool place to work. We make sure we always have Friday night drinks – it's compulsory. You can have a night off from the kids. We'd love to see more of your face.'

She shuffled the paper in her folder while she waited for me to reply. She'd suggested the night off in the way that only someone who had never tried to juggle such a thing without a willing co-parent could manage.

'I can't do that,' I managed to croak at last. The room was spinning in front of me.

'Are you sure? I know it's a big change, but we can't really make any exceptions with this sort of thing. The big bosses, you know, they're worried that there are too many distractions for people at home all the time, people not staying on task . . .'

I had to fight not to roll my eyes at her. It had been years since I had come close to missing a deadline but I guessed, after my display at the editorial meeting, I couldn't argue I was working in the most focused environment. I opted for the only card I had left to play.

'It's unprofessional of me to tell you . . .' This was mortifying but I could not see any way through apart from the truth. 'Stephen and I have split up.'

Her hand went to her mouth. 'Oh, Rachel. I'm very sorry to hear that.'

I avoided her eyes. 'There is no way that I could handle juggling a full-time job in an office with dealing with the kids at the moment, with everything going on. I just couldn't keep things ticking over at home if I was not there all day. I have to work from home – at least for the next couple of months. Amelia's only just two months old. Is there any way I could have some leeway on this one?'

I didn't say it but – Friday night drinks? It would be a long time before I could consider anything of the sort. The only Friday night drink I was involved with was warming up milk for Thomas after feeding Amelia to sleep.

Aileen shuffled her papers again, avoiding my eyes. 'I'm sorry, Rachel. This is coming from a lot further up the chain.'

I was sure it was. 'I could probably manage part-time?'

She cringed. 'Sorry. If I make your role part-time, the higher-ups won't let me hire another part-timer so we'll just be down half a person. Even though you're wonderful, even you can't do the work of a full-time role in half the hours. Nor should you, really.'

'So, you'll want me to hand in my notice, then?'

She rested her chin on her hands and stared at me. 'I'm very sorry, truly. I hate to lose you.'

She pursed her lips. 'Let me see if I can get you any freelance work. A column, perhaps. Budgets are tight but you never know. Maybe you could provide your insights on balancing work and kids? That's a very hot topic at the moment.'

I ducked my head to avoid her eyes. 'Yeah, that'd be great.' As if I had any work to balance.

I let her lead me back through the crowded floor to the main doors. A junior reporter raised her hand in greeting as I passed. I couldn't even remember her name.

My car was parked in a visitor's spot in the car park below the building. Normally, reporters were not considered important enough to have a space, so my little hatchback was tucked in among big, shiny sales managers' vehicles. The one I had inched in next to, holding my breath as if that would make my car slimmer, belonged to the general manager, Tim Bleaster. It was a dark green Lexus that looked as though it was washed every night.

I opened the door to my car and threw my handbag on the seat. The shimmer of the green paint glinted in my wing mirror. Anger boiled up in my throat. How dare he have a flash car and a pretty wife and two stupidly cute kids – whom I was almost positive had been born sleeping through the night – when his decisions were costing me a job?

I grabbed my handbag and rifled through it for the lunchbox I had pulled out of Thomas's school bag but forgotten to deal with before I left home. In it was an old yoghurt pot that had been open for at least a couple of days. I stood over Tim's car and watched the globs of now-grey yoghurt splat on to the paintwork. The smell wasn't as overpowering as I had hoped but the effect was a bit like super-charged seagull droppings. The anger that was becoming more and more a regular setting in my life hammered away behind my eyes.

At times over the next few weeks, I wished so intensely that I had taken the offer of a job in the office – however I had to work it. It was so difficult to leave the house with the two kids in tow that I rarely bothered to try. Who can force themselves to make an effort to go out for the fun of it when you have to pack a full nappy bag with at least three changes of clothes, wipes, a change of clothes for yourself, toddler snacks . . . You might as well be packing for an expedition across the desert. Instead we would stay in and watch *Pingu* and Thomas would pick up an entire useless vocabulary to honk at me with.

I would sometimes pace the floor with Amelia, wondering if there was a precise time that Stephen had fallen out of love with me. Was it the time when, heavily pregnant and hormonal, I cried when he bought strawberry ripple ice cream instead of boysenberry? Maybe it was the day I tried to talk to him about our supermarket shopping list while we were having sex. He had not been particularly keen to agree with me that we needed rubbish bags.

When I was planning our wedding it had seemed that every statistic I heard was about how many marriages failed. Even as I was buying a big meringue-y white dress, all I heard was that I was only likely to stay married 14.3 years and I was statistically most probably going to die alone with four cats. You are more likely to be hit by a meteorite than to remarry over forty, remember. But when you realise abruptly that you are going to become one of those divorce statistics, it all feels very lonely.

Had we just got married too young? Just because it was what everyone else was doing? For some reason, which now seemed ridiculous, my university friends and I had set ourselves a timeline. Engaged by twenty-three, married by twenty-five, first baby by twenty-eight. At twenty-one, we had decided that would be our measure of success. I was the only one who really stuck to it and now whether there was any success to claim seemed entirely debatable.

I missed being married. I missed knowing I had a place in a little family. I even missed the old Stephen, who had laughed and holidayed with me pre-kids. But the more time we spent apart, the more I knew I didn't really miss the man he'd become. The one who expected me to manage everything so his life could carry on as if Thomas wasn't there whenever he needed it to. The one who would sneak Thomas ice cream just before bedtime and then accuse me of being grumpy when I got frustrated that he couldn't calm down to sleep. The one who wanted us to be able to go to Christmas parties at his friends' houses that ran late into the evening and was then surprised when Thomas got overtired and burst into tears when someone popped a balloon.

Still, he'd picked the worst time to make me realise it.

My mother quickly got sick of me mooching around the house. I only ventured out when, spotting Luke in his garden or heading out for a run, I managed to corral Thomas to play in the garden.

She positioned herself on to the couch next to me as I sat, one child on each arm, staring out the window, one Wednesday morning. 'Anything planned today?' Her voice was bright.

She still had dirt in the creases of her hands, from where she had been helping Thomas make a fairy garden that looked to have already been taken over by Transformers.

I shook my head. 'Don't think so. Laura is busy. Seeing her tomorrow.'

Despite my best intentions, I still had not worked up the courage to see any of my friends apart from Laura. The humiliation was searing. It felt as though everyone in the city knew my family had been built on a lie – and I was the last one to find out. But then Laura had taken on extra hospital shifts and it had left me bereft.

Mum put her hand on my knee. 'I think you need to get out and do something. Take Thomas to the library – Luke's music class is on, isn't it? That might be fun.'

She seemed to like him almost as much as I did. One afternoon I had arrived home from a rare trip to the shops to find him and my parents outside on the balcony – a glistening bottle of iced tea on the table in front of them. Luke had been lying on the ground with Thomas, showing him a spider that was making its way up the side of the table.

He'd clambered out as I emerged from the house, dusting off the front of his pants. 'Sorry, I've borrowed your boy.'

I snorted. 'Borrow away. It looks like he's been having a great time.'

Thomas popped up next to him. 'Mum! The spider's making a special house under the table.'

'Unless I get to it first!' My mother had almost sounded as though she was giggling. My father scowled.

Luke had grinned. He had very sparkly eyes. And smile lines. I'd self-consciously brushed my hair away from my face and wished I had put some concealer on the bags under my eyes.

'Unless your mother gets to it first,' he'd repeated.

The exchange with Luke had played back and forwards in my head for days afterwards.

But going to one of his music classes? It seemed a little desperate. My mother was looking at me expectantly.

'What do you think?' I prodded Thomas. Mum seemed to be willing a response with telepathy.

He grinned. 'Yeah! Luke! My favourite.'

I had to drive around the car park three times before a space became available anywhere near the library. Just as I was almost at the point of giving up, an elderly couple I had not even realised were sitting in their car started up and backed out, almost reversing straight into the side of my vehicle.

I coaxed Thomas out, carrying Amelia in her baby seat. 'You can walk,' I told him. 'Strong legs, remember?'

He looked doubtful but jumped in a puddle while I tried to arrange Amelia's contraption against my hip. Whoever thought they were a convenient travel option was misguided. You ended up with one very strong arm and a leg absolutely battered with bruises. It was almost easier to leave it in the car and move the baby.

I could see through the car window that the milk Thomas had spilt on the floor was starting to curdle in the sun. I had tried to dab at it with a couple of baby wipes but it just seemed to move the mess around.

We squeezed into the back of the class as Luke was launching into the second verse of 'You Are My Sunshine'. The front row was looking at him with a mix of adoration and awe as he swung his props deftly.

'Hi!' Thomas was climbing on a chair, waving frantically. 'How's Limbo? Spider's still there!'

I waved self-consciously.

'My mummy put make-up on!' Thomas shouted, just as the song reached its end. Luke nodded in a way that I assumed was designed to show Thomas he had heard but not to encourage him to continue. A woman sitting next to us shot me a sympathetic look.

He pulled himself up to his full one metre tall. 'She's wearing undies too!'

How was I going to survive this? I found a seat and dragged Thomas on to my lap.

Luke appeared at my elbow as I was repacking my bag to leave. 'Thanks for coming.'

I could not meet his eye. 'At least we didn't try to grab your instruments this time, right? And everyone knows I've got underwear on. Good to have that cleared up.'

Did that sound like an innuendo? Why was I so flustered? Now I knew why I didn't leave the house.

He laughed. 'It's been boring without you.' He reached down to stroke Amelia's cheek. 'She's so little.'

I felt the familiar warm pride of new motherhood sweep over me. 'Twelve weeks now.'

I had only done what thousands of women do literally every minute of every day but all you had to do was tell me she was lovely and you might as well have informed me I had single-handedly negotiated world peace. Luke touched one of her tiny fingernails. 'So cute.'

'Thanks. You – um, you're really good at managing all the kids. How did you learn to do that?'

He shrugged. 'It's not that hard when you get to say goodbye to them all after twenty-five minutes. Even the diabolical ones are manageable for a little while.'

'Like my one?' I grabbed Thomas's shoulder to stop him rushing up the staircase.

He laughed. 'I keep telling you, there are some so much worse than Thomas. He's just . . . charismatic. Aren't you, buddy? How are your seeds coming along?'

'Good!' Thomas gazed up at him. A few weeks ago, Luke had put Thomas's tomato seeds into pots along the fence line next to his house. Every time Thomas went into the garden, Luke shouted instructions to Thomas over the fence. The seeds were getting a lot of water as a result.

I tucked the blanket around Amelia and checked that our haul of belongings was still in my nappy bag. Luke placed his hand on my arm to stop me turning for the door.

'Would you like to get a coffee?'

'Me?' I winced as soon as I had said it. It was a stupid thing to say but the request was so unexpected. A coffee? Just me and him and the kids? Did he somehow know about my online stalking? Was he going to gently tell me to get over my crush? I tried to sneak a glance at my outfit. If I had known he was going to pay me more than a second's attention I would have spent a lot more time getting ready.

But he laughed. 'Yes, you. And Thomas and . . .'

'Amelia,' I finished for him in case he had forgotten, but we said the name in unison. 'Yes, that would be lovely.'

He directed us to the café in the front of the library, where a smattering of students sat with laptops and elderly couples sipped cups of tea while scanning months-old magazines. It would have been a great place for a coffee when I was still a normal, childless person. But if you're planning to take a third wheel on a coffee date, I do not recommend a toddler.

Not that it was a date. It was a couple of neighbours getting together, sharing a hot beverage. While the offspring of one of them systematically destroyed the library café.

I ordered Thomas a glass of milk, which was my first

mistake. Had I not learned from the car incident? As soon as it was placed on the table, Thomas poured it in his lap. Then he dipped his finger in what was left in the glass and started to draw stripes on the glass tabletop. Asked to stop, he leapt down from his chair and started darting under other tables, informing the clientele that he was going through tunnels like Superman. Of course.

He stopped short in front of a large man whose paunch spilled out over his thighs. 'That man's got a baby in his tummy!' he shouted back at me.

I hid my face in my hands. 'You must be regretting this.' Amelia, mercifully, was asleep, her rosebud lips hanging open, emitting an occasional soft snore.

'He's certainly a character.' Luke was laughing. 'But if you can't get away with it now . . .' He gestured for Thomas to come back to the table and pulled a book in the shape of a dinosaur out of his bag. Thomas was briefly captivated.

'I really don't know where he gets it from.'

Luke's stare was playful as he looked up from turning the pages for Thomas. 'Really?'

My cheeks flushed. Again. Why did Thomas not look so spellbound when I tried to get his attention? 'It must be his father. I'm very well behaved.' I grinned.

Luke looked up and fiddled with his napkin. 'Is his father staying with your parents, too? I haven't seen him there. That must be a full house.'

I shook my head so quickly my earrings rattled. 'No, his father and I have split up. Has my mother not told you? I thought that she would have been dying to share that information.'

'Not at all. I'm sorry to hear that.' His gaze was soft. 'That must be hard with everything else you've got on.'

I put my latte down a bit too hard. 'Don't be sorry.'

His smile was cheeky. 'Okay, I won't. I wasn't really, anyway. Good riddance to him.'

I ducked so he couldn't see my face. Amy would have thrown up her hands in despair. Had I completely forgotten how to deal with a mildly – and this was very mildly – flirtatious conversation? Thomas scooted under the table. I could hear him rustling through my bag. 'Mummy, what's this?'

His head popped up over the edge of the table. He had a box of hair ties in his hand. 'Um, they're for my hair.' I turned back to Luke, who reached for the ties and started to try to twist them around small tufts of his own hair. His head looked like the scalp of a Cabbage Patch doll I'd had as a child.

'This?' Thomas reappeared with a tube of bright pink lipstick.

'That's lipstick, honey.'

'What for?'

Luke took it from him deftly. 'It's for putting on your lips.' He drew a dot on Thomas's lower lip. He looked puzzled.

'Why?'

I spread my hands. It was not an opportune time for a lesson about the burdens of the patriarchy. 'I guess . . . it makes you look prettier.'

He disappeared back under the table. I could hear more of the contents of my bag spilling out on to the carpeted floor. 'Oh! A monster truck!'

Luke laughed. 'You came prepared, clearly.'

There was a single hot pink gerbera in a small white vase in the middle of the table. I remembered Stephen's mother once telling me how much she hated them because they were a 'made-up' flower, and owed their existence to human intervention. It had been just as I was about to suggest them for our wedding. I had always liked them, and their sort of perennially smiley faces. Luke caught me looking at it. 'Pretty colour. I saw them bringing in a bucket or two of them this morning. You never really think of it but there's a whole industry dedicated to keeping offices and cafés around this town stocked with flowers.'

'I think they're my favourite.'

The wedding picture I had seen was boring its way into my brain. How could I get it into conversation? Was his wife about to return home from a glamorous work trip? Did she just like to stay indoors a lot? While my mother was not shy about telling me that she thought Luke was highly eligible, she'd been too polite to ask him directly for the truth.

Perhaps Mrs Tee was just scared of my family. I wouldn't blame her – since Amy and I had moved back in, we all seemed to have reverted to the roles of twenty years earlier – me and Amy bickering, Mum prodding us to try harder or do better or generally be nicer people – and Dad just keeping out of our way in his favourite spot on the sofa.

'What about you?' I spluttered finally.

He looked puzzled. 'What about me what?'

You would think after thirty years of practice I would be able to make conversation but my incompetence still surprised even me from time to time. 'Are you married?'

'Oh.' He stirred his coffee. 'I think your mother was hinting about that when I had a drink with them the other day. No. My wife, she – she passed away a couple of years ago.'

Oh God. Why did I ever open my mouth? I had not even considered that as a possibility. 'I am so sorry.' I put my face in my hands. 'Trust me to say the wrong thing.'

He reached over to pat my arm. 'Don't be.' He gave me a wry smile. 'And I mean it. It's okay. It was tough for a while, but it really is okay now. I just don't talk about it much because people never know how to react.'

I swallowed hard. That did not make me feel any better.

He put his hand over mine. 'Really, Rachel. Don't feel bad. You weren't to know. But I'm glad that I've told you.' He grinned. 'And you can tell your mother for me.'

CHAPTER NINE

<u>How to make a family tree</u>

What you'll need:

Paper

Pens

Some knowledge about your family or an active imagination

Get your kids to draw a big tree with lots of branches. Write their names at the base of the trunk. Then work your way up the branches, filling in the names of their parents, grandparents, cousins, great-grandparents and so on. If you're still on speaking terms with your in-laws, get your kids to ring them and fill in the details about their side of the family. You might take great pleasure in drawing a large X through marriages that are dissolving.

I woke four or five times that night as Amelia's sniffly nose turned into a full-blown cold. Then Thomas leapt out of bed thanks to a bad dream at 5 a.m., only about half an hour after I heard Amy arrive home from her shift at the bar.

By 7 a.m., I was confident that the happy buzz I'd been riding since my hour with Luke had completely worn off. The rumble of the water boiling for my coffee seemed to take a lot longer than normal. I watched the two children as they lay on the floor, playing a game that seemed to involve Thomas trying to squash his sister's limbs until she squawked. The day stretched out interminably ahead of me.

My parents appeared downstairs as it got closer to 7.30. Amelia was fixed on my breast as I struggled for the second time to down a hot drink before it went cold. Thomas was lying under the table, playing with a car that was just the perfect size for someone to skid on later.

'Are you okay, Rachel?' my mother asked. 'You look dreadful.'

I avoided her eyes. 'Nothing like a compliment to start the morning off right.'

A lump had appeared in my throat that got bigger with every swallow as I tried to fight it. No doubt Stephen was waking up luxuriously, stopping for a cup of takeaway coffee on his way into work, having a chat to someone about sports or the weather or basically anything that wasn't Pokémon.

I felt tears start to track down my cheeks. It was the first time I had cried since the night Amelia was born.

My father looked horrified and retreated towards the lounge. 'I'll just go and see if the newspaper's in the box.'

My mum reached out and pulled Amelia and me towards her. It was an awkward one-armed hug as I tried to balance my baby against my chest and lean against my own mother at the same time.

'It's just baby blues.' I managed to choke out the words between heaving breaths. My nose was running and Thomas looked at me in wonder. 'And a bit of career concern. And maybe some lack of sleep.' I blew my nose. 'And possibly a bit of cabin fever.'

'Sweetheart, you need a proper break. A good night's sleep.' My mum's voice was surprisingly firm. 'Even when they're not sick you're up and down all night, checking on them or worrying about something. Your dad and I will take the kids out this weekend, you invite a friend around and have some fun.'

'But Amelia . . .'

'You can bottle up some milk for me like you did that time with Thomas. She'll be fine. We'll all be fine. Even the most devoted mothers deserve the odd bit of time to themselves, you know.'

She looked at me. I searched for another excuse. The idea of both the kids being away still made my skin crawl. But then the prospect of maybe spending a couple of hours in the company of a friend without a small person swinging on my leg was so appealing that it made my stomach ache. I straightened up. 'Where will you go? Where could you take them?'

'We'll just go and stay with your uncle Peter. He'd love to see the children.'

I suppressed a snort. Peter was much more at home with cats than he was with humans of any sort and small ones seemed to bring out a new level of discomfort. He also lived in a very small, two-bedroom apartment filled with technical gadgets that he hated other people touching.

'Can I think about it? I don't even know what I'd do.'

Late that Saturday morning, Amy and I were in the garden, watching as Thomas chased a cricket ball to the far end of the garden. 'At least he's a bowler who does his own fielding.' She squirted water from her drink bottle into her mouth.

He scuttled back towards us. 'Ready?'

I assumed position in front of the wickets. The ball connected with my hip. 'Try again, darling.' I threw it back to him.

Thomas was still half-dressed, in a hoodie and his underpants. Initially, he had refused to put anything but his bike helmet on and then consumed a good chunk of toothpaste while I had tried to stack the dishwasher. But it was proving a long summer and the warmth in the sun kept the goosebumps from his little legs.

There was a scrabbling behind the fence and a little wet nose stuck out from underneath it. 'Hi, Limbo.' I reached down and scratched it.

Luke appeared behind him, raising a hand in greeting. Thomas leapt up. 'Play?' He threw the ball at Luke, who ducked to avoid it connecting with his left eye. Limbo barked deliriously. I had to fight down a grin. It had been a long time since the mere arrival of a man had made butterflies dance in my stomach.

'That looks like fun.' Luke winked at me. 'Do you want another pair of hands?'

I gestured to where Amelia was lying on her back in the grass, her feet kicking up at the blue sky above us. 'I think Amelia could do with someone to shield her from some of the more enthusiastic batting.'

He nodded. 'I'll run defence.'

He reappeared a minute later, pulling a long-sleeved T-shirt over his head as he strode up my parents' driveway, Limbo trotting along beside him. He shot me a half-smile as he bent to pick up the ball and throw it back to Thomas. 'Morning.'

I felt my cheeks redden. 'Hi.'

'I'm coming,' Thomas shouted as he ran towards us, one arm in the air to attempt to bowl. Luke ducked in front of Amelia as the ball connected with my bat and shot off towards the house. Thomas sat down.

'I guess I'm going to get it, am I?' I jogged towards it, pulling my singlet self-consciously over my exercise leggings. Pre-kids-me would have regarded the idea of participating in any game involving a bat and ball as marginally less appealing than cleaning the bathroom after a big party. But it was – if you ignored the unattractive sweat on my top lip and the number of times I had to pretend I wasn't actually trying to catch the ball anyway – surprisingly fun. Stephen would have enjoyed it, I realised, as I threw the ball back to Amy. Perhaps Thomas would have had more chances to perfect his ball skills if he'd stuck around. He certainly wasn't learning any from me.

Amy wolf-whistled when she saw me adjusting my pants for a second time. 'I thought breastfeeding was meant to reduce the size of your bum.'

'Hey!' I glared at her. 'You could put everything you own in those bags under your eyes.'

She sniffed and turned to Luke, tossing her hair over her shoulder: 'Did she tell you her husband left her when she was like forty-five weeks pregnant?'

He studied the ball, which I'd thrown back to him. 'Nope. Wasn't aware of that.' He threw it back to Thomas, who was preparing to run at us again. Luke shrugged. 'I think she looks great.'

We watched Thomas hurl the ball behind his head.

'This is really good for his spatial awareness, you know.' Luke smiled at him. 'Even if it feels like not a lot of actual ball-to-bat action is happening.'

He put his hand on the small of my back. I looked at him out of the corner of my eye. Was he making fun of me? He was looking directly at me, with those eyes – they were almost navy.

'Oh, thanks. That's really kind of you to say.'

He shrugged. 'No problem. You're a good mother, Rachel.'

I was summoned away from the game by the jingle of my phone ringing.

Still buzzing a little from Luke's attention, I pushed the button to answer it immediately. Then I realised who it was – Stephen.

'Hey, Rach. How's it going?'

I bounced Amelia on my hip. 'Just calling for a chat, were you?'

'No.' He sounded cautious. 'Hey, I heard you had a change on the job front.'

Bloody Amy. One of Stephen's staff was dating a girl she worked with. She must have let it slip.

'Yep. A temporary blip.' I tried to keep my tone light. This was a guy who had gone two months without a single client and didn't think anything of it. 'You know what it's like.'

'Yeah . . .' He clicked his tongue. 'We thought maybe we should thrash out that custody arrangement, get the legal bit done.'

'Now? Why? Because I've got all this spare time? And all that disposable income for legal fees?'

He cleared his throat. No doubt the trusty stress ball was getting a serious workout.

'Well, you know, the longer we leave it, the harder it is to change, right? Better to get it sorted. If we have the kids more often it gives you time to find another job.'

I could have thrown the phone at the wall. He should just say it. He didn't want a settlement that was going to be too expensive. If the kids stayed mostly in my care while I was not working, he would have to pay me significantly more child support than he would if I were earning, or the care of the kids was split more evenly.

That would mean less money for glamorous trips with Alexa. No doubt she wasn't ready to let that happen.

'You can take it up with my lawyer,' I hissed at him, trying not to attract Amelia or Thomas's attention.

I hung up. No job, no husband, now it seemed like they wanted to make sure there was no money, too. Maybe my mother was right, and I needed a little bit of space to vent and then sleep. If I was going to war against my husband and that woman, I would need all the ammunition I could find.

'Mum?' I called up the stairs. 'Am I too late to take you up on that offer?'

* * *

'Are you kidding?' Laura had answered her phone on the first ring. 'Of course I'll come and hang out with you. Maybe I could leave Lila with Mark, and we could go into town. Surely Amy could shout us a few drinks?'

'Oh, I don't know about that.' I patted Amelia's back as she started to complain. 'I don't think I could handle anything too raucous. But maybe you could come around for a film or something, then I could sleep. For a long time.'

She laughed. 'I could definitely do that. I'll be there as soon as I get Lila to bed.'

My mum was watching me from the doorway. 'All set?'

I nodded.

She pulled out a notebook and pen from her handbag on the edge of the sofa. 'I'm going to need a list of what you'd normally do, and when. And how much to feed Amelia. Should she have a bottle before bath, or after? Is she still in one of those swaddle things or just a sleeping bag? You know I think it'd be a bit easier on you if you didn't have all these sleep accessories to worry about. We just used sheets and a blanket, and you were fine.'

My confidence wavered. 'If it's too much trouble, you don't need to go . . .'

She put her hand on my arm. 'No, don't worry. I just know that your father will find this all much easier if there's a set timetable we can follow. Now, talk me through it.'

Laura pulled her car into the driveway just as I was waving my parents and the children off. Thomas gazed tearfully through the window, pressing his hand against the glass. Amelia obliviously batted at toys in her car seat.

Laura emerged from the driver's door of her seven-seater car, an elaborate plate of snacks in one hand and a bottle of wine in the other.

'Ready to roll?' She had a full face of make-up on and had blow-dried her hair. I was still in the leggings I had thrown on that morning.

'Ready to roll over there and pick the kids up again.'

'Don't be silly. Give it ten minutes and you'll be fine. I'll even let you text your mum in half an hour to make sure they're okay.'

I took the plate from her. As we were turning for the house, Luke jogged past the end of the driveway, Limbo straining on his lead in front of him. He raised a hand in silent greeting, using the other to wipe a trickle of perspiration that was threatening to drip from his eyebrow.

I flushed. 'Hi.'

Laura was watching me, waiting for an introduction. 'Sorry. Luke, this is my friend Laura. Luke's my parents' neighbour.'

He wiped his hand on his running shorts and reached for hers. 'Nice to meet you.' He gestured to our arms. 'Big night tonight?'

My tongue felt too big for my mouth as I racked my brain for something intelligent to say. It was so much easier when the children were around.

'Just a quiet night in.' Laura leapt to my rescue and gave him her most dazzling smile. I knew what she was thinking: Here was a good-looking, seemingly ordinary man, fantastic with kids and right there – I could not find anyone more convenient. How could I not even rustle up the words to make conversation?

At last, I managed to form a sentence. 'Are you up to much this weekend?'

He gestured towards the garden. 'Nope, I'm just trying to get on top of this mess.'

Daisies and dandelions had sprouted across the lawn, and

162

a few weeds were sending their tendrils into the sky among what looked like a once-well-tended flowerbed.

'I'm hopeless at gardening.' I hoped it sounded humble rather than uninterested. I scuffed at the ground with my shoe. 'We might head over to the beach if you'd like to come? Just me and Amelia – Thomas is probably with his dad tomorrow.'

As soon as the words were out there, hanging in the air between us, I regretted them. What sort of offer was that? What man would voluntarily attend a beach outing with a small child he was not responsible for? Going to the beach always sounds like a fine idea, but anyone with children knows that, in reality, it involves a lot of sand chafing and cold wet kids shivering and complaining all the way home.

Luke looked away quickly. 'That sounds nice. But I'd better crack on here. Lots to do, you know? If I'm not careful, my compost bin will get a life of its own and walk away.'

I brushed his explanation away, but my stomach sank. Naturally, dealing with a compost bin was a better option than spending time with me. 'Yeah, of course.'

'Okay, well, have a nice evening.' He gave us a polite wave and headed back towards the house.

As soon as we were inside the house, Laura rounded on me. 'What was that?'

'That's Luke, he's the guy from the library . . .'

'I know who he is. I've been to those classes with you, remember? But why were you being so awkward and weird?'

I decided it was better to be honest with her. 'We've been hanging out a bit. We had a coffee the other day after the music class, and it was . . . nice. I was hoping that we might do it again, I guess. But he's clearly not interested.'

I put a couple of glasses in front of her, and she sloshed wine into them. 'I'm okay with that. I've got other things to worry about.'

'I wouldn't be so sure that he's not interested.' Laura's eyes glinted. 'He was still looking at you like he thinks you're pretty special.'

I shrugged. 'Oh well. Funny way of showing it.'

She reached for my hand. 'And what's the other stuff?'

I fixed my gaze out the window. 'I think I told you I lost my job.'

'You'll find something else, sweets. I know you loved it, but there's so much you can do. Aren't you like a fully qualified yoga teacher or something?'

'Oh, that.' It felt like a lifetime ago. 'I gave up that dream – not as bendy as I used to be.'

'You'd get it back.'

I shrugged. 'Maybe. I might be able to get some contract communications work or something like that. Probably pays a lot better than yoga.'

Laura's lip gloss was sparkling in the sunlight that blazed through the living room window every late summer evening. I self-consciously smoothed my hair down.

'To be honest, I'm more worried about the kids. Stephen's on my case to sign a custody agreement. But I really question his motives. And Amelia's so little. I can't bear the idea of her being away from me.'

Laura turned her wine glass stem between her fingers. 'Have you got a good lawyer? Surely they can point out the obvious – little kids deserve to be with their mums. It's not like you're stopping him seeing them.'

I had thought about it – but no. Whatever he had done to me, I wasn't going to get in the way of Stephen being around for his children.

'I doubt they'd stick with it, anyway, would they? Alexa doesn't look like the kind of woman who wants small kids around disrupting her beauty sleep. And Stephen has always been more like your oldest child than your husband as far as I can see.'

A little while later, Laura poured the last of the second wine bottle into my glass. She had made a valiant effort at polishing it off – after a year of pregnancy, then tending to a newborn, it only took a few glasses before my world started to wobble. We had consumed her plate of crackers, quince jelly and cheese but had not had a proper dinner. I was beginning to regret it.

She grimaced. 'That woman, Alexa. Could he have picked anyone worse?'

I studied her face. Had they met again? Mark and Stephen were working together on a couple of projects. I assumed that meant Laura would have seen Alexa again at some stage – Stephen seemed to be doing a round of introductions with all his friends. Did they share cosy double dates? Go out for dinner and try to avoid talking about me?

'She's so swishy and skinny and shiny, and everything she does in her entire life seems to be tailor-made for her vapid blog or awful Instagram account.'

'I bet she'll do it again.' Laura studied some sediment that had fallen to the bottom of her glass. 'He'll get boring and she'll chuck him aside and move on to someone else.'

I swished the sauvignon blanc around the bowl of my glass. I could imagine her face if he tried to bring out his stash of Kenny Rogers albums at one of her parties. Or show her his dance moves. 'He's blocked me on Facebook.'

She snorted. 'That's ridiculous.'

'I know. I accidentally liked one of his photos, so he knew

I had been stalking him. But it's pointless because I know his password and he hasn't even been smart enough to change it.'

I had set up his Facebook account years ago when his brother moved overseas and wanted to share photos of his kids. I wanted Stephen to have his own account, so I was not inundated with messages from the in-laws trying to get me to organise everything from birthday parties to weekends away. It had not worked. I still had the kids' birthdays imprinted on my brain whereas he would only occasionally remember mine.

'Are you serious? Do you ever log in?' Laura's eyes were sparkling.

I smiled. 'Sometimes. I replied to a couple of client messages telling them that he couldn't do a job because he had violent diarrhoea. I deleted them so he couldn't see. But since then it's just seemed a bit like punishment. He's always in photos prancing about in the sunshine, and I'm here, up to my elbows in baby wipes, fretting about whether someone's going to try to take away the baby I'm wiping.'

She pretended to study the wine bottle. 'There's so much you could do with it.'

I watched her. She was flicking furtive glances at my laptop. 'What are you suggesting?'

Laura's eyes were glinting. 'What harm could there be? I'm here to make you feel better if it's awful, and I bet there's something there that will be hilarious.'

I reached for my computer, still perched on the edge of the sofa where I had been trying to juggle a freelance story pitch email to a magazine editor while breastfeeding earlier in the afternoon. My parents' living room, previously so pristine, was covered in the detritus of my life, whether it was bits and pieces from my attempts at work or the accoutrements of the smallest members of society. A dummy lay next to my father's *Economist* magazine.

The website sprang into life, and I entered Stephen's email and password as easily as if it were my own. His newsfeed appeared before me. Much of it was identical to mine – the bulk of each of our friend lists were still mutual. He had seven unread messages in his inbox. 'Some more projects to derail?'

Laura scooted around beside me. The top one was from Alexa.

'Go on, this will be good,' Laura hissed over my shoulder. I selected the message.

We stopped short. It was as if we could not quite understand what we were seeing. She had sent Stephen a string of entirely nude photos of herself.

'Wow,' Laura breathed. 'I feel like she should be sending these to her doctor, not her boyfriend.'

I snorted and could feel wine burning the back of my nose. 'This is hideous.'

'What would possess you to send something like that?' Laura looked stricken. 'I can't imagine why someone would do this. You could never know whose hands it might fall into.'

We stared at them in silence. It had been a long time since I had a wax as thorough as Alexa's.

Laura coughed. 'What are you going to do with this?'

I leant back in my chair. 'What could we do with them?'

Laura tapped her finger on her lips. 'Send them to her clients?'

'She'd probably get more work out of it.'

'Her parents?'

I made a face. 'Yuck. Maybe we should just leave it.'

Laura stood up and started pacing the room. 'But don't

167

you think we need to teach her a lesson? What if she decides to ruin someone else's life? Think of everything she's done to you.'

'My life isn't ruined . . .' I protested.

She brushed my complaint away. She was on a roll, striding around the room, gesticulating wildly.

'Because of her, you've ended up back at your parents' house looking after two little kids on your own. You lost your job. You haven't been out on your own properly in months. And she hasn't even attempted to apologise for her part in any of that. She's just trying to take over your family. She needs to know that there are consequences if she is going to be such an outright bitch.'

I studied my battered, nail-bitten hands. Laura had already taken over my laptop and was methodically working through the photos. 'An anonymous threat maybe? A blackmail note? I see she's got a butterfly tattoo on her hip – you could start to talk about butterflies a lot when you see Stephen. Really mess with his head.'

I watched her. I needed something that was one step removed. My brain was piecing the plan together. Kyle. He was looking for a big story and had sent a couple of emails asking if I'd talk about Alexa's role in my break-up, but surely this would be even better for his clicks.

I reached for my laptop. 'Pass it to me.'

In a couple of seconds, the email was gone. Kyle would wake up to his first X-rated scoop. I looked at Laura. 'Whoops.'

CHAPTER TEN

<u>How to make a stamped shirt</u>

What you'll need:

Some veggies: potatoes or peppers are good

Some paint or clothes dye

A shirt

Chop your potatoes or peppers into halves. If you're using potatoes, you'll need to carve your own patterns into them, but peppers can be used as is. Dip the vegetable pieces into the paint or dye and then press them on to your shirt. Once you're happy with the pattern, hang the shirt out to dry. Don't stand in the rain in this shirt, ever, unless you want multi-coloured, splotchy socks. Some things, it turns out, are hard to undo.

I woke the next morning with the bed sheet stuck to my skin. One of the many joys of breastmilk. One breast was much bigger than the other, but both were rock-hard. I had thought Amelia had dropped most of her night feeds, but that clearly was not the case.

A rush of remorse flooded through me as I turned over to check the time. What would Kyle do with those photos? He would know not to reveal his source, but anyone who thought about it for more than half a minute would suspect it was me.

I sent Laura a message. 'Was that a really bad idea? Even she probably doesn't deserve that.'

Her reply was instant: 'No idea what you're talking about.'

I could hear Amelia wailing as my parents' car pulled into the garage. I was downstairs, opening the car door before my father had even turned off the ignition. His forehead was beaded with sweat. Scooping her up from her car seat, I held my baby against my cheek. Her cries slowed, and she cooed as she nestled into my hair.

'She's been fine.' My mum was at my side. 'Hardly cried at all until we got in the car to head home.'

She pulled out her notebook. 'She had one bottle last night, half in the middle of the night – then I got your father to pop to the shops, and we gave her some baby cereal, actually, because she seemed hungry.'

'You what?'

She frowned. 'Was I not meant to do that? She was a little unsettled, and I thought perhaps the milk wasn't enough.'

I sighed. Amelia was probably close enough to four months old. 'Did she sleep?'

My father snorted.

'She had a couple of decent stretches, but I imagine she'll be ready for a good long nap this morning.' My mum tickled her under her arm, trying to elicit a smile. 'Stephen picked Thomas up quite early, so we've been on the go for a while now.'

I looked at my mother. 'I dealt with him.' She ducked her head. 'It was fine.'

'Was she . . .?'

'There was no one with him. He said he'd bring Thomas back before five so that we can get an early night tonight. I think he said they were going to go fishing.'

Fishing? Fishing with Thomas usually involved catching sprats in a net, examining them and then throwing them back off the wharf. He and Stephen would spend most of the morning sitting on wood that was coated in fish scales, blood and seawater. I could just imagine Alexa's reaction when they returned to the house.

Amelia had cuddled into the crook of my neck and was gently mouthing my skin. 'Okay, I'll take this one upstairs.'

Mum smiled and turned to get a bag out of the car. I put a hand on her arm. 'Mum?'

172

'Yes, darling?'

'Was Thomas really okay?'

She kissed my cheek. 'He's doing fine, honey. You just focus on getting through this, and he'll bumble along with you. Kids are surprisingly resilient, although I know you find that hard to believe.'

I paced the room for what felt like an hour trying to get Amelia off to sleep. Her breathing had just become more rhythmic, and her hold on my shoulder softer when a car engine roared outside. I held her against me, waiting for it to pass. A door slammed. She started and cried. I positioned her back on my breast, biting back a string of swear words. 'Go to sleep!'

Another door slammed. I stood and craned to see out the window. Thomas was standing beside Stephen's truck, parked in the street. I watched as his father lifted him on to his hip and marched him to the front door. He didn't knock but instead threw the door open. I could hear voices as my parents and Amy realised what was happening.

When I reached the bottom of the stairs, Amy was blocking Stephen's path. 'Let me talk to her,' he spat.

'Come with me, pet.' My mother ushered Thomas towards the kitchen. 'Your day with Dad's finished a bit early this week, has it?'

'What's going on?' Amelia was still whimpering against my chest.

Stephen's eyes flashed. He held up his phone. 'Did you do this?'

On the screen was Kyle's website. Front and centre were the photos Laura and I had discovered the night before. They were even more explicit in daylight.

'What do you mean?' I winced and took a step backwards.

173

'Don't play dumb. I know you had something to do with this.'

Amy and my father were openly staring at us. 'What is that?' Amy mouthed at me.

I jiggled Amelia. 'I don't know what you're talking about.'

His eyes narrowed. 'I know you log into my accounts. I didn't think you'd be sick enough to do something like this. You sent them to your mate. I've always known he was a shifty bugger. Couldn't get a girl even if he wanted one.'

The photo had been given a full-page treatment, with links back to her TV work. From what I could tell, it had been shared more than 100 times already. The black boxes that might shield what was left of Alexa's modesty were tiny and completely absent once you clicked through to the main article.

I exhaled through my teeth. 'You're picking on the wrong person.'

He grabbed my shoulder. 'I know you did this.'

I turned away. 'It'll be gone by tomorrow. You know how long these things last online.'

'You think? How long before someone else picks this up?' Stephen's eyes were sparking. 'Your friend is out to make a name for himself. He'll make the most of this.'

I shrugged. What did he want me to do?

He let go of me as if he could not bear to touch me another minute and turned towards the door. 'I thought you were better than this.'

I stared as he strode out, letting the door slam behind him. Amy raised her middle finger at it once he was gone. 'What a dick.'

I tried to laugh. 'Is Thomas okay?'

My phone buzzed. It was a message from Stephen. 'All future communication only through lawyers and Jan.' Jan was his PA, a sixty-five-year-old woman who acted like his second mother. She had never taken to me even though I had been the one to hire her in the first place.

'Fine,' I replied. 'What am I going to tell Thomas? That you're just going to dump him here whenever you're pissed off at me?'

Another message pinged through. 'Tell him what you want. It's not my fault his mother's a nutcase. I don't want anything to do with you. We're going to the cops.'

I felt cold. The police? Surely they wouldn't be bothered about our silly domestic dispute.

Yet another: 'And the media. Alexa wants to front-foot this thing.'

When did he start talking like that?

Thomas wailed. From the kitchen, I could hear my mother trying to calm him. In three strides I was with him and scooped him up into my arms. He tried to rain blows on my head, his hands curled into hard little fists. 'Don't . . . want . . . to!'

'I just asked him to wipe his face . . .' my mother attempted.

I pinned his arms down by his sides, suddenly furious. 'Thomas. Listen to me. You will do what your grandmother says.'

I held him, as he writhed around, while she darted the cloth in the direction of his face, apologising under her breath. When she'd finished, I let him down on to the floor. He scampered to Amy and buried his face in her lap. She stroked the back of his head and whispered something in his ear, frowning at me and shaking her head slightly as I moved towards her to try to reach out for him. 'Give him a break, Rach.'

My stomach lurched. 'I'm going to my room.'

*   *   *

I was helping Amelia into her Jolly Jumper when there was a knock on the door. I leant back so that I could see down the side of the house to the driveway. There was no sign of Stephen's car, so at least I could be sure we were not in for round two.

I looked down at my outfit. I had changed into pyjama bottoms and a T-shirt that belonged to my father after Amelia had flung her lunch at me.

I opened the door. Luke was on the doorstep. He looked surprised. Or shocked.

'Oh hi.' I folded my arms across my braless chest.

'Sorry to interrupt you. I can come back if it's not a good time.'

I shook my head. 'It's fine. I look like this a lot of the time.'

He seemed to swallow a laugh. 'I just came to see . . . I was wondering whether you still planned to go to the beach any time soon?'

I shrugged. 'I'm not sure. Thomas is here after all, and he's being a bit difficult. We might just stay around here and yell at each other.'

He gave me an uncertain look. 'Oh. Right. Well I just wanted to check that you didn't think I didn't want to come when I saw you last night.'

I raised an eyebrow. That was exactly what I had thought.

'That sounds odd, sorry. What I meant was – would you like to get together today? I saw Thomas in the garden earlier – maybe we could take him for ice cream.'

'Oh.' It took me a minute to register what he had said. 'He would love that. I would love that. That would be great.'

I looked down at my outfit. 'Were you thinking soon? Can you just give me a few minutes to get changed?'

'Of course. Meet you outside at half past, maybe? We could just walk down to the shops with them.'

Somehow I was smiling for the first time since Stephen's visit. 'That sounds great.'

'Great.'

'See you soon.'

He was backing down the stairs, probably trying to avoid looking at my chest again. I hoped against hope that there was no sign of a milk leak spreading across it.

I was desperately trying to wash my hair and shave my legs at the same time in the shower, all while listening for sounds from the room next door when I realised that since I had added children to my life it had made me appreciate the most basic things.

There must be some sort of smoke signal, visible only to children, which is triggered by my entry into any bathroom. It compelled Thomas to immediately abandon whatever he was doing and find me. I could not lock the door because he would bang on it and shout very loudly: 'Mummy, are you in there? Mummy, I need you. Mummy, come here!'

He would also demand to know in detail what I was doing. This was okay when we visited Stephen's parents in the country. Not so good in close suburban quarters and definitely not acceptable in public toilets. Sure enough, he peered around the door.

'I'll be out in a second,' I pre-empted his question. He sauntered in and wandered over to press his nose against the glass shower wall. At least our argument seemed to be forgotten for the time being.

'Where's Amelia?'

'She's on her play mat, sweetheart.'

'I get her?'

'No . . .' I was cut off by the door slamming. The one time I did not want him to leave and he was already on his way. I quickly rinsed as much of the conditioner out of my hair as I could and ran after him, pulling a towel around my dripping body. He was leaning over Amelia, who was lying under her play gym, next to my bed. She let out a squeak as he pushed his face up against hers. I rummaged through a drawer trying to find a clean T-shirt and jeans, one eye on Thomas. 'You be careful with your sister, please.'

'Yeah, Thomas.' Amy stuck her head around the corner of the door as she walked past. 'Sisters are awesome.'

I rolled my eyes. 'Some of them.'

When I had managed to throw on enough clothing to be seen in public, I checked my reflection quickly in the mirror. My hair could do with a brush. It had dried as I had chased after Thomas and floundered around trying to get into my jeans. While one side was mostly under control, the other had twisted into curls that almost seemed to levitate above my head. I tried to push it down behind my ear.

Before Thomas was born, I had strict ideas that I wouldn't let myself go. I'd be like those women on *Real Housewives of Whatever* – somehow finding time to style my hair every morning and find a fresh, white linen shirt whenever smeary fingers got near me. I'd accessorise with tasteful gold jewellery and talk about having a capsule wardrobe. Clearly I was also planning to get a major new look as well as a couple of extra hours in the day – I had always been more a comfy polyester girl than a linen wearer.

Once Thomas had been in the world for more than a couple of weeks, I realised that just being adequately dressed was an accomplishment. No visible excrement on my clothes or body? Had I remembered to put on some pants? I was ready to leave the house. It had been so long since I had gone on a date that I had no idea what was appropriate. But was it possible for this to be a date with two small humans, too? And why was I even thinking about it when I still had so much to sort with Stephen?

I had settled on a pair of skinny jeans and a loose-fit blue spotted T-shirt. I wasn't going to win any fashion awards but the high cut of the jeans held all my wobbly bits vaguely in place and the T-shirt had no noticeable stains. My make-up was still in a big box that I'd had vague ideas of tackling when I one day got a minute to myself. Obviously, that day had not yet arrived. I ripped the sticky tape off the top. Something had spilt and everything in the box was coated in a foamy blue liquid.

I thrust my hand as far through the sticky contents as I could, to my mascara and eyeliner lying at the bottom. There was once a time when I would have refused to even leave the house without these two products applied. I had been mortified and turned around to head home once in my first job when I was halfway to work and realised I only had the white under-layer of my mascara on and had left off the all-important black layer that was meant to go over the top. But since we moved in with my parents, I had barely worn any make-up at all. I hastily pushed the wand in the direction of my eyes. I still looked tired, but at least you could now see that I had eyelashes.

Luke was waiting outside, as promised. Limbo scuttled in circles around his feet, so every few seconds he had to stop and unwind the lead from his legs. He smiled when he saw us emerging from the house. Amelia was tightly fitted into a wrap on my chest, so my concerns about which shirt to wear turned out to be entirely academic. Thomas determinedly rode his bike down the front steps. He had demanded to put on a shirt that he and my mother had painted earlier in the day. The paint was flaking off already.

Luke reached out to try to help him but was firmly pushed away. 'Not my best mate today, then.'

I used my hip to steer Thomas's balance bike back to the garden as he careered out towards the road. 'Don't take it personally. He's a bit disappointed that things didn't work out as he'd hoped with his dad.'

I felt a pang of guilt. Whose fault was that?

We watched as he shot off ahead of us. Luke frowned. 'Does he know where he's going?'

I shrugged. 'He'll stop soon enough.'

We watched as he started to get speed wobbles.

'Stop!' I shouted as he got to the intersection.

Thomas turned and scowled at me.

'I wanted to explain last night,' Luke attempted. Limbo buried his head in a shrub.

'Honestly, don't worry.' I tried to give him half a smile but could not take my eyes off Thomas. 'I wasn't offended.'

'I really do need to get on with the gardening,' Luke tried again. 'I'm putting the house on the market and all those things that I haven't been able to keep up with over the past couple of years are coming back to bite me.'

I knew what that was like. If Stephen and I ended up having to sell our house, there would be years' worth of work to get it ready. I pulled my mind back from thoughts of Thomas, Alexa and Stephen living there. I tried to keep my voice uninterested. 'What has made you want to move?'

'I just think it's time. We used to rent it out – my wife and I. Then when the tenants moved out a few months ago I thought I would move in and do it up before I sold it.'

'You don't want to be a landlord anymore?' I raised a hand to indicate to Thomas that he needed to slow down.

'I just think there might be more fun things to spend money on.'

Thomas skidded to a halt outside the shop on the next corner. It was one of his favourite places, selling ice creams, sweets, milkshakes and sandwiches alongside an array of overpriced knick-knacks. 'Go in?' he shouted to us.

We nodded, and he propped his bike against the rubbish bin outside and scaled the step to the door. Luke looped Limbo's lead around the bin.

Thomas was at the glass of the ice cream display, palms splayed and nose pressed against it, when we arrived. The assistant was smiling indulgently.

'He's cute,' she said as we walked in the door.

Thomas was agonising over his decision. 'Green one,' he told her. 'Oh, no. Pink.'

Her smile started to fade as he wandered along, dragging a sticky finger across the glass. 'No, orange.' The way he said it made it sound like 'roh-rage'.

She looked to me for help.

'Make a decision, Thomas. The orange one?'

He nodded.

'Orange?' She pulled out her scoop. 'Red or brown sprinkles?'

I saw him getting ready to start another internal debate.

'He'll have brown ones.'

'And a cup or cone?'

'Cone,' I snapped.

Luke was still grinning. The woman dusted Thomas's ice cream liberally with sprinkles and passed it to Luke. 'I'll just give it to your dad, okay? I can't quite reach you.'

Thomas looked perplexed. 'That's not my . . .'

'Thanks very much.' I cut her off. 'Let's go and find somewhere to sit.'

*　　*　　*

181

We settled around a table outside. Thomas's ice cream had already started to drip over his hand. He was licking one side, not noticing that the other was sliding off the cone. I reached over and scooped some off with my finger.

'You're not my dad,' he told Luke.

Luke shook his head slowly. 'No, I'm not.'

'She called you my dad.'

'She was just confused, honey. How's your ice cream?' I tried to change the subject, but he was determined.

'Dad's not here.'

'Sweetheart, she just didn't understand.'

Luke patted Thomas on the leg. 'I'll let her know we're just good mates next time, hey?'

I tidied Thomas's ice cream again. 'Tell me about your work. How long have you been with the library?'

Luke looked thoughtful. 'Just a few years. I used to work in a law firm.'

I tried not to let my face reveal that I already knew this. And where he went to school. And that he'd fallen off a snowboard eighteen months earlier and broken his leg. 'What made you give it up?'

He studied his hands. 'When Ange was sick it made sense for me to find a job that didn't have the long hours. I used to have to be there from seven in the morning sometimes until eight or nine at night if we were working on something big. That doesn't really suit when you have someone who needs you at home.'

I put my hand on his arm. 'I'm sorry, it must have been really hard.'

'It was. But it was also amazing. I'm glad I could do it. Be there for her, I mean.'

'I can't imagine.'

'When she died, I wasn't sure how I was going to carry

on. Everything in my life was her by then, you know?' He looked at me. 'But it was also almost a relief. It was so hard on her at the end.'

'Was it cancer?'

'Breast cancer. She was only thirty-two. I felt guilty for a long time that I was able to carry on with my life while she wasn't. She would have been such a great mother, and she was about to start working as a doctor when she was diagnosed. You would have liked her.'

I gave a weak smile. She must have been extraordinary. 'I guess she would have wanted you to have a good life.' I mentally scolded myself for how trite that sounded. And would he think I meant with me? How self-centred.

But he grinned. 'That's what I decided, too.'

After Thomas had finished his ice cream and zipped around in circles outside the shop a couple of times, we headed back to the house, mostly in silence. Anything I thought of to say seemed silly and inconsequential. Thomas filled in the gaps by testing my nerves – coming far too close to moving cars on his bike, and Amelia started to complain when we were halfway back.

We stopped outside Luke's house. He gave Thomas a wave. 'Thanks for having an ice cream with me, buddy.'

Thomas returned the gesture. 'You welcome.'

Luke leant over and gave me an awkward kiss on the cheek. 'I've had fun. See you soon?'

'That would be lovely.' My hand had travelled to the spot on my face that he had kissed.

He fixed me with a look, then smiled. 'I'll be in touch.'

My phone rang the next morning as I conducted a surreptitious Google search to see how far Alexa's photo had spread. It had clearly been Kyle's biggest success to date, shared hundreds of times from all his social media accounts. As with most things in my life at that minute, it seemed as though once it was out in the world, it was out of my control. The thought that I might have given Stephen and Alexa another piece of ammunition to fight me with made me feel ill.

My mother had dropped Thomas off at nursery, and Amelia was asleep in her bassinet in the spot of sun on the far side of the living room.

The voice on the other end of the phone was gruff and a bit nasal, as if the man was battling the flu. 'Is that Rachel Murchison?'

I tried to swallow my mouthful of water from my drink bottle. 'Yes.'

'This is Sergeant Tony Macalister.' He cleared his throat. 'I'd like you to come down to the station if you could. We've got a couple of questions for you.'

The ground wobbled beneath me. I grabbed the edge of the table. Already? 'Can you tell me what this is in relation to?'

He coughed. 'Yes, Alexa McKenzie.'

The sinking feeling that had been brewing in the base of my stomach swept over me. I wondered briefly if there was somewhere I could hide. Or run. The only other time I had been in trouble with the police was when I was fifteen and drove through a stop sign on the way to an English exam. My father had written a letter arguing that I shouldn't get a fine. If only he could try that trick for me now. 'When do you need me?'

'As soon as possible please.'

As I collected my things and thrust them into my bag, I racked my brain for a solution. Would I carry on the pretence of having nothing to do with it? Or was it better to just come clean?

* * *

As I drove to the station, one eye on the road, I scrolled through my phone to find the number for Thomas's nursery. Saskia answered.

'I'm going to be a bit late picking Thomas up today.'

She cleared her throat. I could hear kids laughing in the background. 'Okay, can't be helped. I'd like to have a chat with you when you get here if that's okay.'

Her too? 'What's up?'

'Nothing to worry about, Thomas is just being a little unusual, and I wanted to find out whether there's anything going on I should know about.'

I sat up straighter. I could offer her a shopping list of things. 'What's he doing?'

'Nothing major, just not being himself. He and Nixon keep getting into physical altercations over the smallest things. Then today he's taken all of his clothes off and refused to put them on again.'

I sighed. 'I'll be there as soon as I can.'

The waiting room at the police station was empty when I arrived. A couple of magazines from three years earlier lay on a coffee table next to a row of plastic chairs. I knew at least one of the couples on the covers had already split. I thumbed through one but my eyes glazed over. Amelia, mercifully, had nodded off again in her car seat.

After ten interminable minutes had passed, a tall, stocky man strode over to me. His shirt was pulled too tight over his chest, and I could see flashes of skin through the holes between the buttons. 'Mrs Murchison? Please come with me.'

I followed mutely into an interview room, Amelia's seat banging awkwardly against my shins. There was not enough space to sit at the table and place her at my feet. I propped her on my lap.

'I'm going to need to take a statement from you in regard to some photos of Miss McKenzie that have been distributed online,' he said. 'We have reason to believe that you may have had something to do with it. As you may be aware, this sort of harassment is a serious crime that carries a potential prison sentence these days.'

I was more than aware – I had written a feature that led to a campaign calling for stricter rules on revenge porn. I'd been outraged on behalf of women hurt by vengeful ex-boyfriends. I had never imagined that those same rules might be applied against almost-middle-aged women like me making stupid decisions after a few too many glasses of wine. Did it really count when it was sent to a gossip site? Surely that's just slightly dodgy journalism.

He looked at me, emotionless. 'Do you know what I'm talking about?'

I bit my lip. 'Yes, I do.'

He raised his eyebrows but reached for a pen and wrote the date on the top of the notepad on the table in front of him, with an elaborate flourish.

'You tell me in your own words what happened. I'll write it down, and then you'll get a chance to look over it before you sign it,' he said.

He underlined the date and cleared his throat. 'Okay, Mrs Murchison. I'm here talking to you about intimate photos of Miss McKenzie, which have been posted, without her permission, for public consumption on a "gossip website" online. You have the right to remain silent, you do not have to make a statement, but anything you say will be recorded and may be used in court. Do you understand?'

I nodded dumbly.

'Please begin. Do you know how these photographs became public?'

Sergeant Macalister's expression never wavered as he dutifully took notes and fired questions to me.

'Did you know the photos would end up online?' 'Why did you download them?' 'Who is Laura?'

I stumbled over my words. 'It was all my fault. I needed to do something to get back at them. I thought it might help Kyle's website. I should add Laura had nothing to do with it.'

'Please just stick to the facts.'

I spread my hands helplessly. 'That's all I can tell you. It was a silly mistake, and I regret it. I didn't realise the photos would spread so fast or that there would be so much interest in them. I wasn't even sure Kyle would want to run a story. But you must understand a bit, right? Why I was so angry?'

Macalister looked at me out of the corner of his eye. 'I believe there's sometimes a payment from some websites for so-called "good ones". That wouldn't have tempted you, at all?'

'No, I promise. It was an impulsive thing, on the spur of the moment. I didn't plan it.'

He shuffled his paper. 'Well, it's a severe invasion of privacy. They were sent between the couple in confidence.'

I opened my mouth and shut it again. What would he know? Perhaps he wanted someone to send him nude photos?

Finally, my humiliation complete, I signed my trembling signature on the bottom of the printed statement. I fumbled for the words to ask the question that had been bubbling around in my mind since I first answered his phone call. 'Is this going to affect my custody arrangements, for my kids?'

He did not meet my eyes. 'I could not say. That's a matter

for the lawyers to work out between them. Thank you for your co-operation with this. We will be in touch.'

As I turned to open the door, he cleared his throat. I froze. 'Mrs Murchison, I'd recommend you get a good lawyer. The police can help you if you need to find one.'

CHAPTER ELEVEN

<u>How to make glow-stick balloons</u>

What you'll need:

Glow-in-the-dark bracelets

White balloons

Push one or more bracelets into each balloon, inflate and tie as normal. They should glow for hours – shut the curtains, turn out the light and bat them to each other. This is especially good on gloomy, rainy days when cabin fever starts to take hold. Be prepared for your kids to send the balloons off to places from which they cannot easily be retrieved, but where they'll give off surprising amounts of light when you're trying to get the children to sleep. And however long it takes you to get them down, your mother will certainly think you should have started trying half an hour earlier.

I went home with one eye on my phone. All evening, I was on alert, waiting for it to ring and for someone to demand I appear in court. Throughout my career, I had sat on court media benches and rung police for early morning updates in a desperate search for news. But as the culprit, I had no idea how any of this would work. How long would it take for me to hear more from Macalister? I had handed him a conviction with my confession, hadn't I? He looked like the type of cop who could do with one.

Amy looked at me sideways as she got ready to leave the house for work. 'You okay? You seem shifty.'

I waved her question away. Thomas was running at full speed in circles around the living room, and it was only a matter of time before he landed on the coffee table. I'd get up the courage to tell someone what had happened another time.

She frowned. 'Well I know you won't want to admit it, but if you do decide you want to talk about whatever it is, I'll be home about midnight. Okay?'

I scooped Thomas up as he completed another circuit. 'Okay.'

My phone buzzed with a text half an hour later as I was overseeing Thomas's bath. My heart leapt with fear but it was Luke. 'Fancy a drink tonight?'

'You have to be joking,' I replied, one eye on the phone and one on Thomas, who was making a shampoo-mohawk with his hair. 'I can't even leave the house to go to the supermarket alone. More chance of finding a pet unicorn than going out for a drink.'

'I could come to you?'

I paused. I had not had a man over to my parents' house since I was nineteen, when Amy and I would attempt to bring boys home without waking anyone up. My parents had promised privacy when I moved in – but as yet that had only extended to talking to me through the curtain while I was having a shower, not actually opening it. And there was Thomas's bedtime to get through first, assuming Amelia stayed asleep.

'Great,' I replied before I could talk myself out of it. 'Just give me a couple of hours to get ready.'

Thomas had piled another mountain of bubbles on his head. 'I'm a fireman,' he informed me. 'A fireman chicken.'

'That sounds reasonable. Are you ready to get out, fireman chicken?'

A deflated balloon bobbed in the bath, left over from our failed attempt earlier in the week to make some glow in the dark. We'd sat in the wardrobe for a good half-hour but hadn't been able to get the glow sticks to stay put.

'Not yet.'

'What about if we fly you to your room?'

He looked thoughtful. 'Okay. I spread my wings.' He stretched out his arms. 'Fly.'

I stretched a towel out to collect him as he leapt at me, covering my shirt in a mess of bubbles. Holding him under my arm, I manoeuvred through the doorway, turning him on his side so his wings did not clip the doorframe.

We zoomed down the hallway to his bed. 'Is Amelia asleep?' he asked as we went past her room. 'We have to be quiet! Amelia's asleep! Fireman chicken is quiet!'

I tried not to laugh and threw him on to his bed. When I had wrestled him into his pyjamas and read *Where the Wild Things Are* twice, he nestled into the crook of my arm and closed his eyes.

'Time for sleep.'

We lay side by side in the dark. My parents were talking in the lounge, and I could tell Thomas was trying to listen. I could not get the image of Sergeant Macalister out of my head. The way he seemed to have a bit too much saliva building up when he talked. And how he had looked at me as I had described logging into Stephen's account and seeing the pictures. Like he thought that Stephen had made the right decision choosing her over me.

Had I ruined my chance at getting full custody of the kids? Would we have to go to court? How was I ever going to afford that?

Thomas's voice snapped me out of the cycle. 'Mummy,' he whispered. 'Can we go home?'

'What do you mean?' I pulled him close to me and leant my face against the side of his head.

'Can we go back to our house? With Daddy?'

My heart sank. 'Honey, it's a bit different now. Daddy is staying with Alexa. Remember? You went to the playground with them. You said she was nice.'

That had stung. But I had bitten my lip. Two and a half was a bit little to understand the words 'cynical ploy', especially in relation to his father.

'You be there too. We all be there together.'

'I'm sorry, sweetheart, it doesn't work like that.'

'I miss Daddy.'

I pulled him closer to me. 'I'm sorry, darling. I'm sure he misses you, too.'

If there was any justice in the world, he did. I hoped he felt a pang every time he walked past the doorway to Thomas's now-empty bedroom. 'You'll see him again soon, I'm sure. Maybe more fishing.'

'Mmmm.'

Thomas's breathing was becoming slower and deeper with each intake. I watched the profile of his face in the dark, his long eyelashes fluttering on his cheeks. The thought of not being there when his eyes closed at night, or imagining him sleeping in another bed in another room on the other side of town – even if it was the bedroom he had been in since he was born – ripped through me like a physical blow.

When I was sure he was asleep, I removed my arm slowly from around his waist and rolled back so that I could half-somersault off the bed. I crept backwards towards the door, and pulling it to, sidled out of the room.

I checked my watch. I had about half an hour to get ready. What state was the living room in? Had the dinner dishes been done? Did I have any snacks that were suitable to feed an adult? I did not know Luke well enough to know whether he would be pleased at the offer of a plate of Wotsits. I checked my reflection in the mirror. There was a smudge of something green along the side of my neck. A shower would have to be the priority.

*   *   *

Luke rang the doorbell right on 8.30 p.m. I had struggled with what time to agree to – too early, and I risked landing him in the middle of bedtime chaos. Too late and there was a real chance I would have fallen asleep before he even arrived.

I gave myself a final check over before I opened the door. As far as I could tell, there were no bodily fluids from children left anywhere on me, and I had managed to dry my hair properly this time. I had planned to quickly read as many news sites as possible before he arrived, to arm myself with adult conversation topics, but had run out of time.

He had two bottles of wine in his hands. 'I wasn't sure what you would feel like, so I brought both,' he said. He thrust a bunch of hot pink gerberas at me. 'And these. Hope you were telling the truth about liking them.'

My parents had tactfully disappeared to their bedroom, my mother a ball of excitement. I stepped aside so he could come in. 'You've missed the madness.'

We sat awkwardly on the sofa, side by side but trying to turn ourselves so that we half-faced each other. There was a rerun of an old episode of *QI* on the television. We watched in companionable silence for a few minutes while I got used to the smell of him and the feeling of his body taking up space next to mine on the sofa. Even the air felt different when we were sharing it alone.

I was suddenly self-conscious. Was it hot? Was I starting to sweat? Was my outfit acceptable? It had been hard to find something that I had felt would look okay but also not look overdressed for what was basically an evening in front of the TV at home.

'Would you like something to eat?' All I had been able to find in the fridge was an old pot of hummus, but I was sure there would be a pack of salt and vinegar crisps at the back of the larder somewhere if I looked hard enough. I'd stared to regret turning down my mother's offer to go to the supermarket for refreshments.

He gestured to his glass. 'I'm happy with my drink.'

I had to concede he had good taste in wine – each bottle was well out of my normal bottom-shelf-at-the-supermarket budget. We had made a good dent in the first one, and I was already trying to work out whether it would be inappropriate to suggest we opened the second.

When we had marvelled at the fact that one in six British mobile phones were contaminated with faecal matter – I had thought that number far too low, and Luke was disgusted that it was that high – and that Dolly Parton had once lost a Dolly Parton lookalike competition, I tried to strike up conversation.

'What are your plans for Christmas?'

He frowned. 'It's September.'

'Oh, you know, some people are super-organised . . .' My voice trailed off.

His smile was kind, and his eyes had a mesmerising way of flashing when he was making fun of me. 'I'm just kind of taking it as it comes at the moment. I don't even know where I'll be living. The "for sale" sign goes up tomorrow.'

'That soon? Where will you go?'

'Once it sells I'll probably move back to my apartment in town. It's a better fit considering it's just me. Limbo doesn't mind the inner-city life.'

He cracked open the second bottle and topped up my glass. 'I hope that won't mean we will see any less of each other, though.' He coughed. 'Sorry, I hope that doesn't sound pushy. I'm a little awkward with all this.'

He was giving me an intent look, which was increasingly hard to return. I played with the hem of my skirt.

'You don't seem awkward.' I cleared my throat. 'I'm sure we'll still be in to annoy you in your music class.'

His tone had become serious. 'I'd like to see you more often than that. I've really enjoyed the time we've spent together.' He caught my eye. 'Even with your parents.'

I ducked a glance at him. 'Really? And the kids?'

'The kids are wonderful. Truly. But maybe we could even go out alone, one night? If that works for you? From what I know about you, you don't get a lot of time to relax.'

'I'm sure there's a way to make that happen.' I wasn't sure but I resolved to find one.

He grinned at me again in that way that made my spine tingle. 'I'm just going to get a glass of water. Stay right there.'

I watched as he walked out of the room. Two hours had already slipped past. Usually, I twisted myself into knots wondering what to say and then beating myself up for getting it wrong. With Luke, his gentle way of listening made me feel like my observations of the world were witty and insightful – not the rantings of a sleep-deprived mother who hadn't spent enough time in the real world for months.

His phone jingled on the arm of the sofa. A text message. Why was it always so tempting to look at other people's phones? Surely I had learnt my lesson from what happened with Stephen. It trilled again. I leant over nonchalantly, trying to seem as if I was reaching for a magazine. The message was displayed on the screen: 'Any news on the hot girl?'

My heart sank. Hot girl? I should have known that someone like Luke couldn't have been totally single. I ducked back from the phone as he came into the room, a glass of water in each hand. 'Here you are.' He handed one to me. 'My speciality – lukewarm tap water.'

He reached for his phone and, seeing the message, rolled his eyes and shoved it in his pocket.

I decided to play dumb. 'Do you need to call someone back?'

'No, it's just my friend, Brett, being an idiot.'

I took a deep sip of water. Why did I invite him over? What did I expect? 'Nothing important?'

He looked at me out of the corner of his eye. 'Did you read it?'

'I got a glimpse. Something about a hot girl. Sounds exciting. You'd better spill.'

He raised his eyebrows. 'He's talking about you, you dork. I told him I couldn't go to his poker night because I was coming around here.'

'Oh . . . right.' I could come up with nothing more to say in reply. It had been a few years since anyone referred to me in those terms. What would his friend say if he realised the 'hot girl' was a mid-thirties gentle-parenting-failure mother-of-two with a tired collection of maternity bras? He leant over. I could smell the soap he'd used in the shower. 'Would it be okay if I kissed you? I've been trying to work up the nerve all night.'

I nodded mutely. I had thought about what kissing him might be like a few times over the past weeks and had not been able to imagine anyone else's lips other than Stephen's. He was not the first boy I had ever kissed but after so long I was not sure I would remember how to do it with anyone else.

Luckily, I didn't really have to. Luke leant forward and sort of melted into me, his hand behind my back pulling me in closer.

His face was completely smooth under my fingertips, still soft from the shaving cream he must have used before he came over. It was definitely different to kissing Stephen, who rarely remembered to shave more than once every three days.

This was more urgent and meaningful than I had experienced in a long time. I breathed in his woody scent.

I could feel his hand drifting across my back and around towards my bra. When would it be appropriate to tell him that region was firmly off limits? You only had to look at my breasts too long, and they would start leaking. I could already feel my nipples prickling – but not in a good way. Soon that telltale wet warmth would begin to spread across my chest, and a trickle would dribble out of my bra. I coughed and tried to move subtly, so his hand was on my side.

And what if he was expecting more than that? After Thomas, I had waited about six months before Stephen and I had tentatively attempted to have sex – I had not mentally prepared myself to give that area a workout again yet, post-stitches. He pulled back and looked at me intently again. I attempted a smile, my stomach bubbling.

We turned our heads to a noise in the doorway.

'Mummy?'

Thomas had appeared with his comforter blanket in hand. He shuffled across the room to me, dragging it over his shoulder. His eyes were sleepy and his hair was a mess from the pillow. He clambered up between us. 'I can't sleep,' he whispered and curled on to my lap, his arm around the back of my neck. His stripy pyjama top was riding up to expose the smooth skin of his back. I locked eyes with Luke over the top of his head. 'I'm so sorry,' I mouthed. Then, to Thomas: 'Do you want to sit with us for a while, honey?'

Luke reached out and ruffled his hair. 'It's frustrating when you can't sleep isn't it?'

Thomas buried his face in my chest.

Luke patted his arm. 'I'd better be going, buddy. I'll leave you to your mum.'

Disappointment washed over me. 'Are you sure? Thomas might only be up for a little while.'

'I think that's a boy who needs you more than I do. I'll see you tomorrow.'

I reached out for his hand as he stood, holding the tips of his fingers until he moved too far away for me to reach. 'I'm so sorry.'

'Don't be silly. He's got a lot going on. I'll see myself out.' He waved to Thomas, then me. 'I had a really nice night. Let's do it again very soon.'

As I shut the door behind him, I realised I had not thought about Sergeant Macalister or Alexa for at least two hours.

My mother rapped on the bedroom door at 7.30 the next morning. I had to check the clock twice – it was the latest we had slept in, in all of Amelia's short life. 'I forgot to tell you.' She stuck her head around the door. 'Helen Connolly from next door is coming over for morning tea.'

What? 'When?' I pulled a pillow over my face. I could feel the left side of my breastfeeding camisole was soaked.

'Not for a couple of hours but I thought you might like some time to get ready.'

Mum had made it clear many times that she thought our mornings could be a little more organised. My phone started buzzing. I checked the screen – a number I did not recognise. I pressed the button to answer it.

The woman's voice at the other end was high-pitched, and she was speaking fast. 'Rachel? I don't know if you remember me, but we once worked together. I'm Jessica, a reporter at the *Sun-Herald*.'

I tried to rustle up a mental image. She might have been the skinny blonde one who started just before I had Thomas and began working from home. Or maybe the smaller brunette who had been too nervous to interview politicians for a year. I'd found her practising her interview questions in the bathroom one morning.

'Hi, lovely to hear from you.' I sat up. Maybe someone had left in a hurry and they needed me to fill in for a day or two. 'How's everything going?'

'Sorry to bother you but we've had a call from Alexa McKenzie, who says you're responsible for a naked photo that's being spread online. She's starting a new blog, trying to use her profile to raise awareness about the issue of revenge porn and privacy more generally and I was just hoping to get your side of the story before I write about it.'

I coughed. 'What? I'm not going to comment on that.'

She persisted. 'I'd just like to be able to make sure we present all perspectives – give it a fair run.'

'Sorry, no. I'm not interested in talking to you. That's private business.'

'You know how these things go, you're a journo, yourself . . . I understand your relationship has broken down . . .' she tried again.

I pressed the button to end the call. A minute later she sent a text message: 'If you change your mind, please do call me. I just want to give you a chance to say your piece.'

My stomach was somersaulting. It was bad enough that the police were looking into it, but if Alexa had gone through with the threat of going to the media, there was no way I was going to be able to keep this quiet.

Right on schedule, I heard Mrs Connolly arrive and traipse through to the kitchen with my mother. Amy had headed out for a perfectly timed walk. No matter how old we were, my parents' neighbour made us feel like six-year-olds – I still could not bring myself to use her first name. I'd always felt as though she was comparing me to her own sporty, brainy daughters and I was coming up short. The only consolation was that Amy was usually worse.

As the kids and I sidled in, the jug was boiling and the oven humming. My mother never baked but I could smell something warming in there. The two women looked up as we entered the room, Thomas peering out from behind my leg. Mrs Connolly beamed. She still wore the same shade of purple lipstick I remembered from my childhood but her lip liner was now working overtime to keep it from fading into the lines around her lips.

'Rachel.' She put her hands on my shoulders. 'You look wonderful. And these are your gorgeous children.'

She stooped to pat Thomas on the head. I willed him not to shrink away. He did.

'He's a little shy.' I reached down to grab his hand as he tried to turn and run back to the lounge to practise his forward rolls over the arm of the couch.

Mrs Connolly was already inspecting Amelia. 'What a tiny little thing you are.' Amelia screwed up her face.

My mother brought a plate of cheese scones out of the kitchen. They would have passed for homemade if they had not been such uniform sizes. She ushered us to the table. I watched as she and Mrs Connolly lowered themselves into their seats. They both winced as they sat. Since when had my mother become such an elderly person? When I thought of her, I still pictured the forty-something part-time bank clerk who used to pick me up from school. Now she was very definitely a pensioner and not even always a sprightly one at that.

'Now, darling, Mrs Connolly has a suggestion for you. I hope you have a minute to hear her out?' My mother gave me a hard glare that made it clear that she expected me to listen, and closely. So there was an ulterior motive for this reunion. I folded my hands to wait.

Mrs Connolly, for her part, at least had the decency to look embarrassed. 'It's lovely to see you, dear,' she said. 'I don't want you to think I've only come over for this.'

I waved it away. 'It's fine.'

'Your mother only thought that you might need some work. And Veronica – my daughter, do you remember her? She needs some help with her business, and we thought you might be perfect for the job.'

Work? Wasn't managing two small children and an imploding life work enough? If I told them I might soon be dealing with police charges and my own fifteen minutes of infamy, that would shut them up. I kept quiet.

I vaguely remembered Veronica. She was about ten years older than me so had been impossibly grown-up when I was a child, and then she'd left home when I was old enough to start talking to her in any meaningful way. I doubted she would still be rocking the leopard print leggings and fluoro scrunchies I had found so impressive when I was nine.

My mother put her hand on mine. 'Veronica is trying to get some more customers for her yoga business. I know how much you like yoga, and she needs an administrative, marketing sort of person – I thought you would be a perfect fit. You know about all that social media sort of thing. You're good with words. You might get her going viral, or whatever you call it.'

My mother is an eternal optimist, especially when it comes to Amy and me. The idea that we might actually not be very good at something never seemed to cross her mind. We only needed to 'try harder', or 'be a little bit more organised', and we'd be fine.

'I don't really do a lot of yoga these days . . . What would I do with the children?'

Amelia jiggled on my knee and cooed with perfect timing.

'Oh, Veronica knows what it's like,' Mrs Connolly said. 'She won't mind at all if you have the little one with you. She's very keen on promoting work–life balance.'

'Maybe Amy could even pitch in a bit too, help you out if she leaves that job,' my mother offered.

I pushed back my chair. 'Can you help me with something in the kitchen, Mum?'

She followed me until we were out of Mrs Connolly's earshot. 'Are you worried about me paying board? I'm probably going to get a decent payout from the house at some stage, and I've still got some savings, so if that's the problem . . .'

She frowned. 'No, darling. Of course not.'

She pulled some glasses out of the cupboard and a pitcher of water from the fridge. 'I think you'd benefit from having something else to think about at the moment, so you're not just rattling around here all day with us.'

'But the kids. After everything that's happened, don't they deserve my full attention?'

She sighed. 'You deserve to be happy. You like working; you used to love yoga. Give it a go?'

I sniffed Amelia's hair. It still smelt like the baby cereal she had rubbed through it. I had almost discussed Thomas's latest gastro problems with Luke the previous evening but thankfully had thought better of it.

'Okay,' I managed to find the words at last. 'Talk to Mrs Connolly and let me know when Veronica would like to meet. I'm not promising anything, but I'll hear her out.'

I tried to smile as I scooped Amelia up to carry her out

of the room. 'If she doesn't mind a convicted felon,' I muttered under my breath as I closed the door behind us.

Amy was in the hallway, slowly closing the front door behind her so the click couldn't be heard. She looked up as I pushed the kitchen door to behind me. 'What is this all about?'

I rolled my eyes. 'Mum finding me something to do again. Apparently she and Mrs Connolly have been scheming.'

She gestured to the smock she was pulling out of a carrier bag. It was covered in splashes of paint that had probably been there since she last wore it to finish a painting while she was at university. 'It must be "sort out the daughters month". She's bribed me to get back to painting.'

'What are you working on?'

She shrugged and gestured to the garage. Through the open door, I could see a huge canvas leaning against the wall, still wrapped in protective plastic. Boxes of paints lay next to it.

'Remember Frank?'

'He of few showers.'

She waved a paintbrush at me. 'Apparently he's just sold a painting for like half a million pounds. Can you believe it?'

I couldn't. His paintings had always looked a bit like someone had thrown the liquid you find at the bottom of a compost bin against a canvas. Then he'd had the gall to tell Amy that her work was too simplistic.

'You'd better get a full million for yours, then.'

She grinned. 'I fully intend to.'

I kissed her cheek and whispered in her ear. 'Good luck, you know I secretly think you're great.'

She swatted me. 'Remember that time you told me you

thought my paintings looked like the work of a deranged chimpanzee.'

I winked at her. 'Just keeping you on your toes. What are big sisters for?'

CHAPTER TWELVE

How to make your own foaming snowman

What you'll need:

Baking soda

Salt

Washing-up liquid

Water

Vinegar

Some accessories to dress your snowman

Measure out two cups of baking soda and add two table-spoons of salt. Get your kids to mix them together. Add a teaspoon of washing-up liquid and make a dough. Add eight tablespoons of water and mix until the mixture forms a ball. You can then use it to build a snowman. When you're ready to start it foaming, pour over some vinegar. Depending .

on how much you use, you can almost make your man disappear. It's a pity this doesn't seem an effective solution for ex-husbands.

It had been a while since I had a job in an office but Veronica's workplace offered a work environment that was unique by anyone's standards.

She was exactly what I expected. There were no fluoro scrunchies to be seen, but she was tall, impossibly slim and seemed to have an unending supply of colourful second-skin leggings – all of which featured patterns that inevitably drew attention to her perfect bottom. She wore tightly fitted singlets that showed a sliver of flesh just above the waistband.

When Amelia and I arrived for our first day on the job, there were three elderly women in very tight pants trying to contort themselves into awkward positions in the hallway outside the main classroom. They watched me fumble for the set of keys that Mrs Connolly had left in the letterbox from Veronica, trying to unlock the office, and hissed – 'tree pose' or 'trying to perfect my warrior'.

Other people were reclining on the bolster seats outside the smaller treatment rooms. I soon realised they were awaiting various impending treatments. There was a Reiki practitioner once a week, and a Bowen Technique therapist who worked two half-days a week. I still wasn't exactly sure what either of those things were, but I'd find out soon enough. The waiting clients gave me a dirty look as I banged my laptop down a little too heavily on the overloaded desk. Amelia made a noise that sounded like an angry cat.

I got the feeling Veronica was determined to single-handedly help me find the mental fortitude to get through my separation and newly single motherhood. Whatever her mother had told her, she obviously thought much of the answer lay in motivational quotes and positive thinking. When I settled into my office chair for the first time, I noticed a little handwritten note propped on the corner of my desk, telling me: 'You can't control what they do. You can only control how you react.'

I manoeuvred Amelia through the gap between the desk and an enormous, overstocked bookcase and placed her travel cot on the room's only other chair. Every shelf was covered in boxes with stray bits of paper poking through the cracks. Some were scrawled with dates or what I assumed were tags meant to indicate certain types of yoga class. A laptop sat on the desk beside a dusty amethyst crystal. An oil diffuser was set up in the corner next to a small Buddha statue. A Himalayan salt lamp sat disused in the corner.

After her last session of the morning, Veronica arrived in my office, a cup of tea in each hand. Propping her feet on my desk, she gave me an unnervingly searing gaze.

'I can't believe you enjoy this stuff,' she said, as I showed her printouts of her bank statements for the past six months. It was one of the first things I needed to get sorted, but it was not pleasant reading. There were bill payments missed, teachers paid more than they should have been, rent not turning up on time, and students' payments going missing.

'It's just part of running a business, I guess. It's satisfying when you do get it into order. It just takes a while to get there, sometimes.'

I shuffled the pile. 'I thought I might make a list of the things we need to do to get some of this working as it should.'

I pulled my iPad out of my bag, ready to show her the spreadsheet I had drawn up. The potential for the business was amazing. Those five people leaving the classroom could be thirty-five. There could be hot yoga on offer, Pilates, a class for newbies who were worried about kicking someone when they tried to do a lunge or falling asleep in savasana. Maybe we could offer classes just for women . . . Why did she stick with the plain and boring?

She shrugged. 'I just can't get into it. I don't mind doing the classes and dealing with the people, but the whole admin and marketing side of it just leaves me cold. I'm happy for you to do what you think is best. I'll set you up, so you have all the access you need.'

'Maybe there's an essential oil for a dislike of admin.' I was joking, but she didn't seem to notice.

'You need some more for your diffuser.' She gestured at the machine lying empty in the corner. 'There are some great options for emotional balance. I'll pop some in to you tomorrow. You know, you're welcome to join in on any classes you like, any time. And I'll set you up with a session with Fern and Lorraine, too, so you get a sense of what it is they do.'

'Oh.' I stopped. 'Thanks, but . . .' I gestured at Amelia, who was sitting in a patch of sunshine, examining a cardboard box. 'She makes it a little tricky. Not very relaxing.'

Veronica seemed to notice my daughter for the first time. 'Of course, right. Well you know, just as you can. I'm happy to help if it's useful. How's it all going?'

'You mean single motherhood? It's a blast.' I regretted the

snarkiness in my voice immediately. 'He's off doing whatever he likes, and I just have to pick up and carry on.'

Veronica nodded. 'It can't be easy. I hope you'll find this is a really supportive environment.'

I quickly looked out the window, blinking back tears. She put her hand over mine. 'It's okay to be angry. Can you channel that into something helpful?'

'Maybe. I'd rather put my energy into making him suffer.' I caught her eye. 'Sorry. This is unprofessional.'

She laughed. Maybe she wasn't as scary as I'd thought. 'It's fine. But I would encourage you to try to shift that thinking . . . even a little bit. Maybe he's done you a favour. Given you the freedom to look for what might bring you joy?'

An image of Luke and Thomas eating ice cream together popped up in my mind. I waved it away. Meeting one good man did not let Stephen off the hook. 'I'm not at the acceptance stage yet. Come back to me in four years' time.'

She pushed one of the cups towards me. 'Ah well, it takes as long as it takes. Shout if you need anything – I'll be back for the 3 p.m. class.'

She gave me a wave, winked at Amelia and turned on her heel.

When she had left the room, I took a photo on my phone and sent it to Luke. You had to see the office to believe it.

A car I did not recognise was parked across the street when I arrived home. A tall, blonde woman loitered by my parents' letterbox. I realised too late who she was.

'Rachel!' She reached for me as I walked past. 'Can we please just have a word? The story is running in tomorrow's paper, and we'd really like to get your side of it. I'd hate to present it unfairly.'

212

I put up a hand to brush her away but a short middle-aged man – a photographer I recognised from the jobs we had worked on together – leapt in front of me, squatting between me and the house, blocking my path. His camera whirred as it rattled off shots. I put my hand over my face and pushed for the front door, leaning against it as it closed behind me.

Through the glass panel beside it, I could see Jessica ducking through the trees in the front garden, trying to get a glimpse into the house. I leant back against the cold wood, holding Amelia close to me. I knew how this would unfold. If it were me doing the story, I'd have one more go at knocking on the door, pop a note in the letterbox and follow up with a phone call. She rapped on the door behind me. 'I just want to make sure that I've given you every chance to respond to Miss McKenzie's accusations,' she shouted through the keyhole. 'Would you like me to tell you what they are?'

I pushed myself off the door and went into the bathroom, where the windows were frosted, and there was no opportunity for David to get another sneaky photo. I checked my watch: 4.30 p.m. Jessica would have to get back to the office soon if she was going to file the story today. Would they put it straight up online or hold off until printing tomorrow? My stomach somersaulted.

Amy was sitting at the breakfast bar when, convinced that Jessica and David had finally given up, I entered the kitchen. She gave me a half-wave. 'Who was that woman? I wasn't sure if you wanted me to tell her to sod off.'

I shook my head. 'Ignoring her was the right thing. She might have managed to get a quote out of you if you'd said anything.'

I propped Amelia on her play mat, where she batted at a

glittery toy. Amy had the remains of a glass of sparkling water in her hand, the liquid fizzing almost amber in the late afternoon sunlight. I pointed to it. 'Not like you to be drinking water.'

She glared. 'And what? I'm allowed to be good if I like.'

I knew better than to argue. 'I'll join you.' I watched her as I poured a glass. 'Can you keep a secret?'

'Probably.'

'Fine, well I guess it doesn't matter, anyway. Everyone's going to know soon enough. I've done something stupid. That was a journalist from the paper wanting to talk to me about it.'

Amy pretended to be astonished. 'You? The perfect daughter? What could you have possibly done?'

I scowled at her. 'I found some photos of Alexa. I guess you might call them private ones.'

'You mean . . .' Her voice trailed off as she realised what I was talking about, her eyes sparkling. 'That's fantastic.'

'Yes. You know what I mean. That kind of photo. So, when Laura was here the other night, we downloaded them, and they found their way on to Kyle's new website.'

'Found their way?' Amy raised an eyebrow.

'Well, she deserved some karma, didn't she? And we former journos have to stick together.'

Amy was watching me, wordlessly.

'So anyway, she's on some sort of crusade, "front-footing" it, and there's going to be a story in the paper.'

Amy snorted. 'That'll teach you.'

'What?'

'Isn't it kinda ironic that you're on the receiving end of a story for a change?'

I scowled at her.

'What's going to happen, anyway?'

214

'Dunno. It gets worse. The police have interviewed me.'

'They've what?' She sat up straighter.

'I haven't heard anything else yet.'

She guffawed so loudly that it startled Amelia, who wailed. 'Little Ms Perfect in trouble, who'd have thought it. Do Mum and Dad know?'

I recoiled. 'Don't tell them.'

We sat in silence for a minute. A pair of birds on the branch of a tree outside were involved in some sort of complicated dance that looked as though one was trying to push the other off. I gestured at them. 'Dad said that's something to do with mating. It almost looks easier than the human way, doesn't it?'

Amy snorted. 'You'd get pretty bored eating that seed stuff he throws out there for them. And I'm pretty sure she's not the same bird he was with yesterday.'

What did it say when you started to sympathise with a sparrow?

'It's okay, Rachel,' she ventured at last. 'It's hardly crime of the century stuff, is it? Though I guess it's a big deal for someone like you.'

I wasn't sure whether to be offended or not.

'You'll get through it. And I've got good news. If it makes you feel better. I've got a painting on display in an exhibition starting next weekend.'

'That's amazing, I'm so happy for you.' Her grin was infectious, and I realised I really was. 'The kids and I will have to check it out.'

She pursed her lips. 'Maybe don't come along to the opening night.'

Stephen might have spent the past ten years avoiding tax returns and refusing to learn how to configure an email account, but he was suddenly industrious when it came to the administration required to divorce me.

I was poring over Yoga Junction files at the dining table the next day, half-listening to the baby monitor and waiting for Amelia to wake from her afternoon nap, when my phone rang. It was my lawyer Louise Macintosh's office. Although calling her 'my' lawyer might be a bit of a stretch – we had not had any communication since I'd used her to help write my will after Thomas was born, and even that was all done via email and phone calls. But when Stephen demanded to know who his lawyer should be communicating with, hers was the only name I could remember.

'Rachel Murchison?' The woman at the other end sounded tentative. 'We seem to have some received some correspondence from you, but I've nothing about your case on file.'

I grimaced. 'Sorry. My husband – soon to be ex-husband – is suddenly a bit of an overachiever when it comes to getting things done.'

She made a noise that sounded a bit like a sigh. 'Right, so you'll be wanting to make an appointment to see Louise, then? How's Wednesday morning for you? Louise has some space about 10 a.m.'

'Sure.' I scrawled a note on the paper in front of me. 'That sounds fine.'

When I'd hung up the phone, I put my head down on the pile of notebooks. Someone once told me marriage was one of the hardest contracts to end. I didn't realise back then that I'd get a chance to test the theory out.

The sun was blazing as I pulled my car into a park behind the building where Louise's firm had its offices three days later. The spaces were, as usual, much too small for anyone driving anything larger than a Mini, and people on either side of the last empty one had interpreted the lines as more of a suggestion than a rule. But I was running late, so I did not have the luxury of driving around the block to look for a better option.

I checked my face in the mirror. I had deliberately not worn too much mascara, to avoid looking like a runaway racoon if talking about the demise of my marriage set off the tears again.

The dashboard alarm was still blinking where the weight of my bag had fooled it into thinking I was carrying a passenger who had refused to put on a seatbelt.

The bag was full to overflowing with wipes, nappies, the remains of a lunch I had packed Thomas for a trip to the aquarium, mail from last week and – I hoped – a notepad to try to keep track of what Louise was going to tell me. What sort of things did a divorce lawyer even say? Would she want bank statements? Childcare plans? Bills? I once watched a film where they had to get physical evidence of the man having had an affair before the woman was granted a settlement. I assumed things had moved on since that, although it would seem I had that comprehensively covered, too.

I had heard Louise was the best at this sort of thing, and not just because she was the daughter of one of my mother's friends, Marianne. The will had been done as a favour – she made most of her living helping women avoid getting screwed over when they got out of doomed marriages. Could she help me escape being sued by Alexa, too?

I slithered out of the car, pulled my sunglasses down over my eyes like armour, and hoisted my bag on to my shoulder. How could you live a life where each workday meant a succession of miserable women traipsing through the door, trying to salvage something from the wreckage of what must at one point have seemed like happiness? She must be single.

Outside the door, I took a deep breath, pushing the air out through my teeth. I hiked my shoulders back and my chin up, as I remembered a fierce schoolteacher instructing us to do. Whatever I felt, I might as well look confident. I was hit with a wall of air-conditioned cold air when I pushed the heavy door open. The woman behind the reception desk looked up and smiled. 'How can I help?'

I stalled. 'I'm here to see Louise.'

She nodded. Was that a pitying smile? 'Just take a seat, she will be with you in a minute.'

I tried to look nonchalant as I scanned the room. Did Alexa have an interior design scheme on her poorly written website called 'reception neutral'? The room was set up in much the same fashion as every professional services office I had ever been in. There was oddly patterned but inoffensive light grey carpet, dark blue couches, a bin with magazines only slightly newer than those at a dental surgery and a brightly lit tank with a bored-looking fish, swimming in slow circuits.

I watched the receptionist as she typed furiously on her clattering keyboard, avoiding my eyes. I checked my phone again – still no messages but it could not hurt to give the impression that one might arrive at any minute. I picked at the edge of a chip in my weeks-old nail polish.

'Rachel?' An impossibly tall and scarily slim woman strode into the room. She extended a perfectly manicured hand to me, her thin gold bangle sliding down her wrist. 'It's nice to meet you in person at last. I'm Louise, please come on through.'

Her office was similar to the waiting room. I was pleased to see there was nothing overly chic about it, despite its inhabitant.

I conducted a surreptitious scan for personal photos on the desk but there was nothing obvious. A family photo would have been too jarring, I supposed. But a photo of a girly weekend away somewhere exotic might have given me hope that there was fun in my single future. Or might I one day be able to go away somewhere with Luke? It seemed cheeky to even consider the possibility.

'Please, tell me how I can help,' she said.

I hesitated. How was I to know? That's what I was there to find out.

'Um, well,' I stuttered. 'My husband and I have separated – he left me. It's become pretty nasty.'

There was silence. She was waiting for the punch line.

'I'm sorry to hear that,' she mustered at last, when it was clear to both of us that that was the best I could come up with. It was not obvious whether she really was.

'Yeah, so I don't know.' I cringed. I sounded like a teenager. 'I want to make sure I can hold on to the children, and I need some advice on what to do with the house. He's also got a business. I helped him set that up – I guess that's relevant.'

She was busy taking notes. 'Yes, very.'

She sat back and looked me up and down. I folded my arms across my chest. I noticed that one of her eyes was slightly smaller than the other, which made me feel a bit better, although her hair was impossibly perfectly high-lighted with an array of different shades of blonde, from platinum to a sort of deep ash. It was mesmerising. It fluttered as she tilted her head, scribbling on her pristine white notepad. I was suddenly ashamed of my handbag-battered spiral-bound A5.

'I think he'd like to buy me out of the house. Immediately. And preferably never have to speak to me again.' I laughed in what I hoped was an ironic way, but she did not smile. 'His girlfriend is pretty focused on him moving on.'

She regarded her notes before pushing back her chair again. 'That's not easy to do with kids in the picture. Is that what you want?'

I shrugged. 'I don't want it to be easy for him.'

Louise turned her pen over in her hands. 'I like to come to agreements without a major fight. No one wins if we go to court for a long battle. It just gets really expensive. There are a few ways we could do it. You and he could have a conversation and determine what you think is fair, then come back to me . . .'

I must have pulled a face because she stopped. The idea of sharing the same air as him still made my stomach churn. The only thing I wanted to be doing if we were in a room together was throwing sharp objects at his head. Since my latest act of revenge, it was likely he'd be chucking them back, too. There was no way I would be able to calmly make my case.

'Okay, or not. We could also opt for mediation, or what I call collaborative law. We can sit down and hash it out with him and his lawyer . . .'

That was not much better. He would just get an extra line of defence. 'Things have really deteriorated between us,' I offered up weakly.

'I've had some communication from his lawyer already, actually, wanting to make an offer. If you'd prefer, he can do that, and we can counter-offer. That option can get quite expensive, with all the legal time involved, if an agreement is not reached quickly. And you want to make sure you protect as much of what you have as you can, if you know what I mean. You've got the kids to think about preserving your assets for.'

I ducked my head, a warm wave of shame creeping up my neck. Why wasn't I putting the kids first?

'But, just quickly, you should know the business is very likely relationship property, and you are entitled to a share of that, particularly if you helped him to get it off the ground. You've sacrificed your own career and earning opportunities for your children. The settlement will need to compensate you for that.'

I raised my eyebrows. 'Even if I'm still working, too?'

She drummed her perfectly painted nude nails on the desk. 'Have you given up evening work since Thomas came along? Do you think you missed out on promotions because of your need to be available to look after him?'

I snorted. 'Well. Yes. I've had to move into admin, actually, because I couldn't go into the newsroom and leave the kids behind.'

'And has he?'

I said nothing.

'Buying you out of the house is fine – if that is something you like the idea of – but that can't be the extent of the settlement.'

She was stern as she rattled it off but I was impressed. It was the first time anyone had acknowledged that there had been a sacrifice in the years Stephen and I had been together.

When Stephen started earning more, he'd made subtle jokes about supporting me and my so-called 'lifestyle' when I finished a little early to pick Thomas up, or juggled work and a playdate. There was never any mention of the time I'd spent writing extra freelance articles late into the evening to bring in cash when his workload was too light – or even acknowledgement that my slightly less intense work schedule was only driven by the need to have someone at home, keeping Thomas alive, and it clearly wasn't going to be him.

But if Louise could see I'd given something up, maybe Stephen did owe me something, after all.

She was still making notes quickly, and talking, almost to herself. She stopped. 'Have you thought about what custody arrangement you'd like?'

I stared at her. The ideal situation would be that none of this had happened. Or that Stephen and Alexa were struck down by some newly discovered rare illness that made them smell like old milk.

'I don't want the kids away from me.'

'I understand from his lawyer that he's pushing for 50/50 care.'

I ducked my head. 'I'm sure it's just to reduce the amount he'll have to pay me. Especially because I'm earning a lot less than him at the moment.'

She crossed her legs. There was a small hole in the knee of one of her stockings. 'If he owns his own business, I'm not sure how practical that much custody would be for him, anyway. Do you think he would be able to look after the kids on his own, half the time?'

Thomas's first intelligible word had been 'Dad' and he turned to his father whenever I denied him a sweet treat after dinner or when I told him I would not allow him to add to his collection of weird hatching dinosaur eggs when we were shopping. Stephen would often take him to the playground after nursery – but it was always described in terms of 'giving me a break' (to get some chores done) or 'giving me space' (to work when a deadline was near). He always grumbled when I booked in a hair appointment on a Saturday afternoon or if I talked about trying to get out for dinner with a girlfriend. It had only actually happened once.

He was genuinely mystified when I asked him to phone

the doctor to make an appointment for Thomas. 'How do I know which doctor he sees?' Having to get home in time to cook dinner for a small person each night would not be a welcome addition to his schedule. I couldn't see Alexa wanting to take over either, not that I wanted her to.

'When we were still on speaking terms, before his girl-friend got involved . . . he said one day a weekend was what he wanted,' I said, offering the only information I had. 'That seems more feasible, to me.'

Her face was inscrutable. 'Your children are very little. I think it's important that whatever we do, we try to make it as easy on them as we can. Usually that means a stable home environment, ideally with Mum.'

I took a deep breath. 'I have to tell you something else. The police have called me in . . .'

Her eyes widened. I imagined she didn't go home with lots of great stories from work – perhaps this was shaping up to be a highlight in a day of divorce settlements.

'I did something dumb. Sent a nude photo of his new girlfriend, she's Alexa McKenzie, you know, that designer . . .'

'From TV?'

I scowled. 'Yes, her. I posted it online and they went to the police.'

'That wasn't very smart.'

I rolled my eyes. 'Maybe. Ditching your pregnant wife isn't very smart, either.'

'No charges yet?'

I shook my head.

'Okay. I have someone in my team who can advise us if it does progress to that stage.'

Her face softened and she patted my hand. 'It might not come to anything. Why don't we do this . . . I'll draft up a letter telling his lawyer we are happy for him to buy you out of the house, at a price determined by an independent valuation. In return for getting that sorted quickly, I will try to dictate the terms of your custody arrangements and we'll come up with a child support agreement, between us. You deserve some help, no matter what you're being told.

'I think you need to focus on what's most important to you.' Louise's voice was gentler. 'And I don't think it's really the house or even getting your own back on them. Let's try to get as much as we can out of this for you and the children. You should end up with a tidy nest egg there – prices have gone up quite a lot since you moved in. Take some time to decide what you want to do with it.'

She stood up, ready to guide me to the door. 'Do you want to try to make a claim for some of his business? It's my job to tell you that you should probably fight for a share of it.'

My shoulders sagged. 'I'm not sure I've got the energy.'

CHAPTER THIRTEEN

<u>How to make elephant toothpaste</u>

What you'll need:

Dry active yeast

Hot water

Bottle

Hydrogen peroxide

Food colouring

Dishwashing liquid

Funnel

Mix one teaspoon of yeast into two tablespoons of hot water. In your bottle, mix half a cup of hydrogen peroxide and your choice of food colouring with a few squirts of dishwashing liquid. Using a funnel, pour your yeasty mixture into the bottle. Whip away the funnel and watch your elephant toothpaste take off. This is most fun when you can watch it twisting and turning in the sunshine. Your kids may never be satisfied with their own toothpaste, ever again. Never mind, though, you've got lots of time in the evenings to fight about these things now you're solo-parenting.

It was a text from Laura that woke me. The room was dark and Amelia was snuffling in her sleep on one side of me, Thomas jammed in against us on the other. I reached for my phone. The message was just three words: 'It's not bad.'

I pulled up the news site I was still mostly used to scanning for stories carrying my own byline. The story wasn't the lead – a possibility I had conjured up only in my most fevered fits of midnight panic. I scrolled down the page. There she was: 'Designer fights online abuse'. Alexa had posed prettily in a well-lit photo. She always seemed to take photos from the right side. Did she have some sort of complex about the left? I clicked on the story. It was short.

Alexa explained how she had been the target of 'vicious online bullying', her privacy had been assaulted and she had been too embarrassed to leave the house for days after her boyfriend's ex stalked her online with some sort of vicious, irrational vendetta. It made the acts of a few minutes sound like something I'd been working on for months.

The story went on to detail her new blog, a Facebook group she had set up for people who had suffered online invasions of privacy and acts of revenge porn to share their stories, and included a couple more photos of Alexa staring forlornly – but beautifully – out of a window.

I sat up. Was that it? I was in the clear? I replied to Laura: 'She hasn't named me.'

The response was almost immediate. 'I know. Relief!'

I was sitting in my office, Amelia perched on my lap, with the door propped open as the last class of the morning streamed out of the yoga studio. I let my eyes glaze over as I thought about how I could find a better way to get a handle on Veronica's relentless and seemingly futile expenses.

She had tried some Facebook ads that seemed only to get the attention of men in Eastern Europe who messaged her to tell her she was pretty. I wanted her to put some of her classes on to YouTube but I might as well have suggested she set up a class on a traffic island. 'There is no way you're getting me in front of a camera.' She was too awkward around children to attempt a kids' yoga class and she thought maternity yoga was boring. 'It's all little lunges and tree poses.'

After my failed attempt at the session with Lani while I was pregnant, I had to agree with her that it was best avoided.

I lifted my hand in response as a figure walking past my door waved. A few of the regulars had become used to me sitting, surrounded by piles of paperwork in my office, and came in to exclaim over Amelia. This time, the person stopped in the doorway. I sat back and squinted against the glare of sunlight. It was Luke.

'What are you doing here?'

He looked sheepish. 'I came to do a class.'

That was a surprise. 'How did it go? I didn't know you were into yoga.'

'Awful. I'm not. Can I come in?'

'Of course.' I watched as he slouched, leaning on an over-worked filing cabinet in front of me. It was not the posture of a regular yogi. 'What possessed you?'

He blushed and put his face in his hands. 'I thought, now you work here, yoga might be one of the things that I need to get my head around. Well, if you are going to want to spend time with me. I'm afraid I've been a bit of a failure on that count, though.'

I felt my own flush spread over my face. Had he really spent his morning with the ladies of the 11 a.m. class for me? I couldn't remember the last time Stephen had done anything to try to impress me. 'Hardly! I wouldn't know my swan pose from my cat these days.'

This was an exaggeration. I hadn't managed many sessions since we moved in with Mum and Dad but I still used the cat and cow sequence to stretch out my back when it locked up after too many hours squished up with Amelia in bed. But the attempt to reassure him seemed to work.

He had beads of sweat on his forehead, although the class he had finished was one that was meant to be about relax-ation rather than exertion.

'You have no idea how much of a relief that is. I was sure Veronica was going to tell you how terrible I was, and you'd not want anything more to do with me.'

A shimmery twinkle of happiness zipped through me. He had come in to impress me. It was almost as if he didn't realise he could have made my day just by ringing to ask me over for a bowl of cereal. 'Don't be ridiculous. I'm amazed that you'd do that for me.'

We looked at each other. 'Are you going back to work now?'

He reached in his bag. 'Actually, I picked up some sushi from that place you like on the way in. I was hoping you might have time to sit in the park for a bit before I head back.' He regarded it warily. 'It's been in my bag for the past hour but it should be okay.'

I watched him as he walked ahead of me out of the office. He might have felt like a yoga failure but his broad shoulders and defined calves looked pretty good in his gym gear.

We settled under a big tree away from the 'terrible two' of the park, as Luke called them – the playground and the public toilets. Children were liable to come hurtling off the slide at full speed into your lunch if you sat too close to the playground and the public toilets had a distinctive smell, even though they were some of the cleaner ones I had discovered as part of our toilet training escapades.

We sat, our backs against a broad tree trunk. I stretched out a blanket on the grass for Amelia, who kicked her legs in the warm air. The sunlight flickered across Luke's face.

'This is lovely.' I turned to watch him eat.

'Yeah it's good sushi,' he said, handing me another piece.

He was staring up at the clouds, which were zipping across the sky propelled by the autumn breeze. I pushed aside the twinge of awkwardness that still niggled every time I realised it was not Stephen occupying the man-shaped space beside me.

'I mean it's nice to sit in the park with you.'

He blushed. 'Ah right. You must need to get away from all that peace and relaxation every so often, try to keep your stress levels up.'

He reached for Amelia's foot and tickled it.

'You're good with her.'

He winked at her. 'She's pretty easy to be good with.' He paused. 'But I'm not very good at all this, though, sorry.'

'How do you mean?'

230

'I mean, spending time with you. Not that you're hard to spend time with, it's just . . .' He shifted awkwardly. 'This isn't coming out how I was expecting.'

I laughed. 'I know what you mean. This is all a bit unusual. I bet the last time you had sushi in the park with a woman, she didn't have a small human attached.'

He lay back on the grass. 'No, it's more that I was with Angela for so long . . . My brother tried to get me on to Tinder a year or so ago and I just couldn't face it. It takes a peculiar kind of bravery, putting yourself out there.' He coughed. 'So just bear with me.'

I touched his hand. 'You're doing just fine. Tell me about your family – is it just you and your brother?'

He reached for his phone, flicking up a photo. 'I have a sister, too. She's in London. Working in advertising. My brother, Simon, he's a lawyer. I'm the drop-out of the family. The opposite of you.'

'Hardly!'

He stroked my hair. 'Well, you're the one holding it together for everyone there; on my side – since Ange – I've been the one who's being held.'

I frowned. Was that really what it looked like from the outside? Some days it barely felt as though I was managing myself. If I was expected to be the guiding light for the rest of my family, they could end up very lost.

He quickly changed the subject. 'How's it all going, living with your parents and all that?'

'It's not as bad as I thought it would be. I've discovered a new appreciation for daytime television, I now know my hydrangeas from my agapanthus and my laundry is being done for me on a regular basis.'

'Sounds like amazing service. Do you think you'll move out, or are you getting too comfortable?'

'Nowhere near comfortable! I am looking – I've got one to check out this afternoon, in fact.'

'If I'd met you earlier maybe it would have been a good idea to rent my place to you,' he said, looking at me sideways. 'It seems a shame that I'm trying to sell a rental property just as you are trying to find one.'

I was not sure what to say. Living next to my parents would be useful but maybe not ideal in the long term, and did I really want to be Luke's tenant?

He seemed to read my mind. 'It might be a bit weird living in a house that's owned by me. I might come around and get stuck checking you've mowed the lawns properly or something.'

I pretended to be affronted. 'Hey, who says I would invite you around?'

Amelia had fallen asleep on Luke by the time we returned to the studio after lunch. When she slept, her little bottom lip jutted out, as if she were slightly unimpressed at whatever she was dreaming. One tiny fist clutched the front of his shirt. He looked at me. 'What do I do now?'

I stroked her cheek. 'I think you have to wait until she wakes up.'

He looked stricken. 'I'd love to but work . . .'

I laughed. 'I'm only winding you up. Here.' I gently dislodged her fingers and hooked my hands under her armpits. She sighed heavily as I nestled her against my front. 'It's perfect timing. I want her to sleep. I've got a Reiki session with Fern.'

He raised an eyebrow. 'Enjoy that.'

I reached over to kiss his cheek but he turned his face so that our lips connected. He smelt expensive and soapy. I pulled back as a woman opened the door behind us and squeezed past, down the front steps. 'See you soon?'

He waved to Amelia, walking backwards, so as not to

break eye contact with us until he was almost at the street. 'I'll call you later on.'

I settled on to the table in Fern's room, listening to Amelia snore in the Moses basket I'd placed in the corner. Fern smiled at her. 'She's looking very peaceful.' Fern was about my age, tall and gangly. Her dark brown hair was cut in a pixie style that made her neck look even longer than it really was. She was wearing big peacock feather earrings that moved when she talked.

I caught her eye. 'Let's hope it lasts.'

She positioned herself behind me and placed her slim, cool hands on either side of my head. 'Have you ever had a Reiki session before?'

I subtly shook my head. 'Never. But I'm working here now so I thought I should get to know the whole business. You seem to have some loyal fans.'

'Would you like a light touch or no touch?'

I paused. 'Um, I guess light?'

Was no touch a thing? How would it even work? Fern pressed a button on her oil diffuser and a waft of vetiver and lavender swept over me. 'Try to relax. I get the sense you're not particularly used to seeking treatment for yourself – is that right?'

The room was starting to feel uncomfortably warm. 'I guess you could say that. But I don't think I'm avoiding it – just relatively healthy and injury-free, touch wood.'

She moved her hands down my body and pressed them gently on my face. 'It doesn't have to be a physical ailment. Sometimes it's helpful to take a more holistic view of wellness, just take a moment to ask for help, to nurture yourself.'

'Maybe I'll find it easier to find time for that when the kids are a bit older.'

She moved her hands on to my shoulders. 'It takes practice.'

I was sure my mother was trying to sabotage my attempts to find a place for us to live. First, she deleted all the real estate listings I had saved on my laptop, while she was using it under the pretence of printing a recipe. Then, when Thomas told her that he liked staying with her, she told him he was welcome to stay 'forever and ever' and she never wanted him to leave. When I had told her that morning, as I was leaving for work, that I would look at a house on my way home, her face fell.

'What's wrong?' I looked over my shoulder as I clipped Amelia into her car seat.

She was determinedly looking away from me. 'Nothing. I just didn't realise you'd be moving so soon. It's a lot of change for the children to cope with.'

I stood up. 'Soon? We've been here for five months. Surely you're getting sick of us.'

She gasped. 'I would never! We love having you here.'

'You're totally overrun. You've more *Paw Patrol* books in your living room than anything else and I'm sure Dad is sick of getting woken early every morning when Thomas clumps down the stairs.'

Mum threw up her hands. 'No! It's lovely. This house is best when it's full of children. And you're such a good influence on Amy. Do you know, she told me she's looking for a job that will give her more time for her mad painting.'

'Mum! I thought you loved her painting.'

She made a dismissive gesture. 'Oh, you know, it's wonderful. It's just a bit . . . modern.'

I had to swallow a giggle. The orange and green piece on the centre of my parents' beige living room wall was about as restrained as they got.

Mum's face was alight. She reached around to stroke Amelia's cheek. 'She'd never have done it without you around setting such a good example, reminding her what she used to love to do.'

I snorted. 'She'll be fine.'

She looked away. 'Sorry, darling. You do what's right for you. I'm sure the place will be lovely.'

In the rear-view mirror, I watched her walk back into the house as I drove down the driveway. She looked small and slightly hunched. There was a flicker of a feeling that was almost maternal in my chest. Then I remembered something Stephen had said one Christmas: 'When you're with your family, it's like you're the mother.'

I'd thrown a tea towel at him, thinking he was making fun of me for fussing over the place settings for dinner. Now I could see there might have been more to it. I put my foot on the accelerator. If Amy could get out of the rut she had been in for years, I could get out of mine.

As we approached the open viewing later that evening, I started to allow in a niggle of hope that Mum might have been right about the house. After lunch with Luke and the mystifying Reiki session – which Amelia had entirely slept through – I'd started to feel that it was possible not every ball would always fall into the worst-case scenario gutter.

The neighbours seemed reasonable – gardens were a little overgrown but there were no rusted heaps of cars on the front lawn or menacing dogs ready to jump the fence. I spotted a couple of trampolines and swing sets, so it was possible that we might be able to have a playdate with the neighbours. A woman walking her dog waved to the children as we passed.

But as we got nearer, I saw the crowd. There were at least

235

ten couples in the front garden of the house. Most of the men were dressed in suits and all the women were in high heels. There was not a child among them. I looked down at my skinny jeans and sneakers. I had thought this was an acceptable house-hunting outfit. Perhaps I was wrong.

'Please sign the register,' the property manager trilled as we wandered through the front door. The paint was peeling around the doorframe, revealing a coat of dark green beneath the white. She was looking over my head, towards a couple in the living room.

'You'll notice the original fireplace is still intact,' she shouted. 'This house has retained many of its character features.'

People were crammed into the narrow hallway. Someone seemed to be inspecting the gas heater fixed to the wall. I stuck my head into one of the bedrooms. The single bed stretched from one side of the room almost to the other. There was a flimsy IKEA-style pop-up wardrobe in one corner. On the other side of the hallway the second bedroom was a little larger but there was still no evidence of a wardrobe or storage cupboard anywhere. I could only imagine stacking Thomas's boxes of toy trains up in the lounge.

'Mummy, I need to go to the toilet.' He was looking up at me, pleadingly.

'Really? Right now?'

'Yes.'

I had been so looking forward to getting him out of nappies but the reality of a mostly toilet-trained small person was somewhat different to what I had imagined. We were constantly dropping everything for a dash to the bathroom or trying to cajole our way into the toilets at restaurants or shops.

Here, the bathroom was not just occupied, it was

crammed with at least two couples nodding approvingly and admiring the artful floral decoration atop the cistern. The room was quite big compared to the bedrooms and had a big claw-foot bath on one wall. I could imagine trying to vacuum under it.

'We'll have to go outside,' I hissed at Thomas. 'Hold on.'

I picked him up and 'excuse me-ed' my way back to the front door. We ducked along the path and a couple of houses down the road.

'Okay you'll have to do it here on the hedge.'

'What?' Thomas giggled. He was mid-stream when I heard footsteps behind us. I looked up. It was the property manager.

'You left so quickly, I just wanted to see if you had any interest in the property.' Her lip had curled with distaste. 'But I see you are busy.'

I wiped my hands on my jeans and stood up. 'Oh . . . yes. We are interested.'

Thomas had turned around and was facing her, his pants and underwear around his ankles.

'I'll give you a form to fill in.' She determinedly held my gaze, as Thomas wrestled with his clothes. I bent to help him. 'We will pass our recommendations to the landlord this evening.'

That night, when I finally crawled into bed, it was only to stare at the patterns on the light fittings. I had given Veronica a deadline of the morning to sign an agreement to have a massage therapist move into the Yoga Junction rooms as well, but she had left it on my desk. Could I forge her signature? Would Amelia ever be able to fall asleep without someone lying in bed with her? I pictured us at fifteen and fifty, still twisting around each other to get her to nod off.

It still perplexed me that it was possible to be so bone-tired that I daydreamed about sleep – but then I could not get any rest when I finally got the chance. I forced myself to shut my eyes and remembered my mother's advice dished out when I was a sleepless child – to picture myself somewhere wonderful. Where was wonderful now?

Wonderful seemed to be an image of Luke that flashed up in front of me. His smiling eyes and the way he smelt as he sat on the grass next to me. The way he would massage the bridge of his nose under his glasses when he was thinking about something vexing, and the way his muscles moved across the bones in his forearms, under the rolled-up sleeves of his business shirts. When our limbs accidentally brushed, my skin would zing. I was constantly trying to engineer ways to do it again.

It was like he flicked a pressure-off switch that I had never known how to find.

With him, I did not have to pretend to be a fabulously organised mother whose children were perfectly nurtured and intellectually stimulated. I did not need to stress about my career going down the toilet. There was none of the defensiveness of my marriage to Stephen – I'd pretended for ten years that I could drive a manual car because he'd told me early on it was the only 'real' way to drive. Then he'd bought one. But I admitted to Luke within the first ten minutes that I still sometimes had to check my hands to remember which way was left.

What would it be like to share this bed with someone else, after so long with Stephen? When we had kissed, I had been startled by how familiar was that warm syrupy feeling in the base of my stomach. I imagined his hands tracing my sides and drawing me to him, what it might be like to lie here and look up at him hovering above me. He was so gentle and thoughtful – would he be the type to want to hand me full control? Or might I see another, more forceful side of him? After years of knowing exactly which paint-by-numbers move Stephen would deploy, I was suddenly desperate to find out.

CHAPTER FOURTEEN

<u>Art with medical supplies</u>

What you'll need:

Big piece of paper

Pen or marker

Cotton balls

Cotton buds

Paint

Have the kids lie on the paper and trace around their bodies. Use the cotton balls, cotton buds and paint to colour in their body shape. If you're feeling creative, you can make a mosaic out of your first-aid kit, glueing the supplies to your outline. You may be surprised at the gruesome injuries your kids try to inflict on 'themselves' when it comes time to decorate. Take turns treating each other's injuries. This could be good practice for the kids if their parents aren't great at accepting help.

There was a café around the corner from my parents' house that offered that elusive combination of good coffee and a decent play area for the kids. Usually you had to choose between a fast food franchise with weeks-old instant coffee perennially reheated but a full play area to keep the kids entertained for hours, or a good coffee and half a puzzle stashed on a bookshelf somewhere. Salt was renowned in parents' groups within a twenty-mile radius and Laura and I had started to make Saturday brunch with the children a regular spot in our diaries.

I arrived just after 8 a.m., pushing Amelia in her stroller, Thomas on my hip. His bike was carefully balanced on the handle above Amelia's head. Laura was already sitting in our usual spot by the playground. She raised her hand in a half-wave. Thomas spotted Lila climbing a rope ladder and squirmed so that I would put him down. He sprinted towards her.

'Sorry we're late.' I dangled a small packet of sugar in front of Amelia as an improvised rattle. 'I tried to go for a run this morning. Taking Veronica's advice to channel my negative thoughts into something positive.'

'No good?'

'Thomas decided he wasn't up to pedalling about halfway, so it's been a little challenging. Still, better than our attempt to do a living room yoga session yesterday.'

The waitress appeared beside me, my latte in her hand. She placed it on the table in front of me. I grinned at her. 'Am I that predictable?'

She didn't smile.

I waited until she was back at the coffee machine. 'What's up with her?'

Laura shrugged. 'Dunno. Bad morning, I guess. How's the new job?'

'Actually, surprisingly pretty good. It's just admin and basic marketing stuff but it's nice to have a change. It could be a good little business and you know yoga is a bit of a guilty pleasure when I can find the time. Pay is rubbish though.'

Laura reached across to pass a sliver of brownie to Lila, who had appeared at the playground fence. 'How's Amy?'

'Well! Apparently she's had a bit of a life change. Focusing on her art again and being all smiley. Barely snarky at all. Who knows how long it will last but it's actually quite nice.'

Laura raised her eyebrows as she took a deep sip of her green tea. It smelt like grass clippings. A copy of the morning's paper sat next to us on the table. 'Do you miss it?' Laura gestured at it.

I leant back in my chair. 'Yes. A lot.'

I leafed through the newspaper's front section. There were a number of new bylines I didn't recognise. Getting rid of my work-from-home senior salary must have freed up space in the budget to hire a few more juniors. Laura reached for the glossy magazine that sat in the middle of the Saturday paper. As she pulled it from the pages, we gasped in unison. She dropped it on the table as if it had burnt her fingers. On the front cover, doe-eyed and forlorn, posed on a stool in an empty studio, was Alexa. 'Online attacks', said the headline, in what looked like 3000-point font.

Laura flipped through the pages of the magazine until she found the story. It was a four-page spread, in which Alexa talked again about how she had been the target of a vicious attack, which she had worried would ruin her career and reputation. How she could never imagine how someone could be so bitter and twisted that they would take advantage of something that was meant to be private. The way she described her relationship with Stephen made them sound like a determined Romeo and Juliet, fighting to be together with the world against them.

'Half of that couple was your husband just a few months ago,' Laura wailed.

'I've started up a website to raise awareness about how big a problem this really is,' Alexa had told the journalist. 'I'm hoping to campaign for stricter laws – at the moment you really only usually get a fine and I just don't think that's enough. I'm asking people to share their stories of how they've been hurt. We're building up a wonderful online community. What seemed like the most awful thing has really had a silver lining.'

Then further down the page, I saw it. 'McKenzie says the attack was instigated by her husband's ex-wife, Rachel Murchison, who hacked into his Facebook account to spread the images. Murchison, a former journalist, refused to comment. A source said she was now unemployed and living with her parents.'

Inset into the text was the photo of me arriving home from work. It had been cropped so you could not see Amelia in my arms. I just looked as though I was huddling defensively, scowling at the photographer. My hair had been caught by the wind and was jutting out perpendicular to my head. I had huge bags under my eyes and there was a stripe of something white on the shoulder of my black blouse. If they had scoured the archives for a stock photo of a deranged woman who was the complete opposite of well-coiffed, elegant Alexa, they could not have found a better one than me.

I put my head in my hands.

'Look.' Laura's eyes were wide. 'It says at the bottom she's going to be in a TV item tonight.'

I moaned. 'This is so much worse. I thought we were off the hook but she's really milking it.'

Laura put her hand over mine. 'I'm so sorry,' she whispered.

I shook her off. 'I've got to get home.'

My mother was on the phone when I arrived back at the house. 'Oh no.' She had one hand on her cheek. 'I don't think it was like that.' She paused to listen to a reply. 'No, she's not a vindictive girl, you know. I don't know how this has got so out of hand.'

She looked up as I sank on to the couch. 'Okay, I've got to go.'

I tried to arrange my face into a smile. 'Sorry, Mum.'

She scurried over and, sitting beside me, pulled me to her. 'That was Margot, you know, Fred's wife. She saw the article and just wanted to make sure you are okay.'

'Wanted the dirty details more like.' I let my weight rest against her. 'I'm sorry I didn't tell you.'

She murmured something I couldn't make out. It sounded reassuring.

'I didn't want to disappoint you. It was a stupid thing to do. But it wasn't like Alexa says. I just needed to do something . . .'

She rested her head against mine. 'I know. How that woman can say you've hurt her is unbelievable.'

'I guess Stephen's the one I should have been focused on.'

'What does she expect?' My mother's tone was clipped as she cut me off. 'Sending photos around. I can't imagine you ever being silly enough to do anything like that.'

'Maybe that's been my problem all along.'

Thomas had found his favourite rubber Tyrannosaurus rex and was trying to scare his sister.

Mum pushed a piece of hair back off my face. 'You always say yourself that today's news is just tomorrow's fish and chip wrapping, darling. This will all blow over. Just focus on the children.'

I rested my head in her lap, the kids staring at us from the floor in front of me. She started to stroke my hair. I closed my eyes. 'I might be in trouble with the police, too.'

She was quiet for a minute. 'It'll be all right.'

I let her play with the length of my hair in the same way she had when I was a grumpy eight-year-old. Thomas reached over and patted my leg.

'Can you believe she's actually got Stephen on her blog? Big photo and everything?' Amy walked in, looking at her phone. 'She's so posey.'

My mother must have waved to her to be quiet because she stopped. 'Oh, sorry, Rachel. But he'd hate that, wouldn't he? He wouldn't even let me take photos of him with the kids at Christmas.'

I pulled out my phone. 'I wouldn't think he'd be too pleased.'

Messages had been pinging on my social media accounts for the past two hours. Some suggested what a sad head case I was for picking on a woman as wonderful as Alexa. I deleted some of the newer ones. 'Probably just jealous because you're fat,' wrote one paunchy middle-aged man. 'It's so sad when women suffering a mid-life crisis bully those who are fortunate enough to be in a better position,' one concern-troll offered up. It was not the first time I had been on the receiving end of online vitriol – just a few months before a story I had written about a scam had meant my inboxes filled up with angry messages from people who had been taken in but not yet realised it. But this time the attacks cut deeper. Who was Sandra from Highbury to tell me that I was a terrible mother? Or Denise from Winchester to suggest I deserved a cheating husband?

'I guess you don't want to watch the programme,' my mother ventured as we cleared the table after dinner. Amelia was still in her high chair, throwing her food on the floor.

'I think that's literally the last thing I want to do.' I scooped Thomas up and carried him to the sink, where I tried to wipe his face. He wiggled away.

'Can't catch me!' He ran for the spare room.

'Shall we watch a silly film instead? I could find *Love Actually* for you, I know that always cheers you up.' My mother tried to catch my eye as we loaded wine glasses into the dishwasher. I'd always had a soft spot for Colin Firth.

My father groaned. 'Not that again. I thought we only had to sit through that when your sister was around.'

I put my hands on his shoulders. 'Don't worry, Dad. I don't know if I can stand watching another cheating husband,

248

anyway. I'll probably just give these kids a bath and have an early night myself. I've got to go into the studio tomorrow morning.'

He was still cradling his drink and looked up at me. 'How are you enjoying that?'

I stretched over to wipe Amelia's face. She grabbed the cloth in her fist and shoved it in her mouth.

'It's different. Not what I expected I'd be doing. But it could work out.'

'She's got a good location there – lots of traffic.'

My dad had been a town planner before he retired. He probably already knew exactly how many people drove past the studio on any particular morning. 'She could do better with it.' I sat beside him, pulling faces at Amelia. 'Even little things – she needs a decent sign so people even know she's there and what she does. Half the people sitting in their cars right outside probably don't even know what's inside.'

He patted my hand. 'She's lucky to have a girl like you to help her. You'll get it all sorted.'

'Thanks, Dad.'

My mother was watching as I collected the children's belongings for their bath. 'Can I help you? I can put them in the bath for a bit. You go and have a break.'

I brushed past her. 'Honestly, I'm fine.'

She put her hand on my arm. 'You don't have to do it all, you know.' She pointed at Thomas. 'Look, he's ready to go. I'll bring him in for a kiss before bed.'

I nodded. The idea of skipping the shampoo fight and the post-bath sprint around the house trying to dry him was tempting. As I climbed the stairs to my bedroom, ready to pull my duvet over my head and hide from the world, my phone bleeped. It was Luke. 'Are you free for a coffee in the morning?'

'Of course.' I'd been wondering about inviting him round for dinner with my parents – it was monthly roast beef night and he'd mentioned a craving for Yorkshire pudding. 'See you at the library café before work?'

'Bring Thomas and we'll see what he can do with maple syrup this time.'

Luke had snaffled a table in the corner and was staring at his phone intently when I arrived. The library café is a strange beast. It is always packed with people who might have splashed out on a cup of tea (half-price between 7 a.m. and 9.30) first thing but then spend the rest of the morning using the desks and the free Wi-Fi to get their assignments written or their sales pitches finished. I had a strong suspicion that a number of businesses in town were saving on their rent costs by encouraging their staff to get all their paperwork done under the assumption they were having a coffee at the library.

I found out after Luke and I had had a couple of quick coffee dates to escape the studio – there was only so much of the positive affirmation, deep breathing and living in the moment that I could handle in one day as my world melted down around me – that he and the woman who ran the café had briefly almost dated. He seemed to think it had all ended amicably before anything had the chance to happen but I could sometimes feel her dark eyes, behind her statement-framed glasses, staring at the back of my neck.

He looked up as I settled into the seat opposite him, Amelia tucked awkwardly into my elbow. Thomas had stopped at the cabinet and had his nose pressed against the glass, eyeing up a slice of brownie. Amelia gave Luke a big, gummy grin.

'That's the most pleased to see me anyone has been all week.'

I kissed the top of her head. 'She's got good taste.'

'I ordered a coffee because I felt like I was going to die.' He ran his fingers through his hair. 'But just chuck what you want on my tab.'

I paused. 'Is everything okay?' He wasn't meeting my eyes and seemed to be swallowing frequently. 'I guess you saw Alexa got a bit of attention yesterday. Bet she's loving it.'

The force of his sigh made his shoulders wobble. 'That's what I wanted to talk to you about.'

I pulled Amelia to me, as if it were she who needed protecting from whatever was coming.

'I only know about it because my in-laws, sorry my former in-laws, I guess, Angela's parents, were watching the TV last night. They saw the photo of us.'

I raised an eyebrow. 'What?'

'Apparently when they mentioned you in the item, they flashed up a photo of us that you put on Facebook, one we took at the beach with the kids.'

He paused, folding a paper napkin back and forth in his hands. 'It was a bit of a surprise to everyone.'

'Oh.' I felt as though someone had punched me in the stomach. 'I'm so sorry.'

'They were pretty upset. They didn't know I'd started seeing anyone – though of course, it's not anything to do with them really. And now they think I'm all caught up in this online madness.'

He looked at me at last. 'It's coming up to the anniversary of Angela's death and it's so hard for them. It's just all made me realise that maybe the time isn't right, you know? Maybe I was wrong about being ready.'

I swallowed hard. 'I'm . . .'

He waved my impending apology away. 'I know. Alexa's been awful. I know you're angry. But maybe it's best for you, too, if we just scale things back for a bit? Just friends.'

'No . . .' I started to protest and reach for his hand across the table – but what would I say? It was mad. Why would anyone want to be involved with this if they didn't have to? 'Alexa, she's doing well out of all this . . .'

His voice was soft. 'Maybe. But, Rach, I was pretty surprised that you'd do something like that. It's . . . well. I didn't expect it.'

I put my head in my hands. The silence seemed to hum between us.

'I just didn't want them to think they could get away with it,' I spluttered at last. 'Trying to take my kids. Leaning on me while he built up the business then just walking away.'

'But revenge like that? Isn't that a bit high school?' I couldn't read his expression as he watched me struggle for a reply. 'I'd better get to work.' He gathered up his notebook, newspaper, phone and wallet and tucked them under his shoulder. With a half-smile at Amelia and Thomas, he ducked his head to bid goodbye to me, looking back just once over his shoulder as he shut the door to the staff room behind him.

'Where's Luke gone?' Thomas looked after him. 'Can I have a brownie?'

I could feel a tear leaking out from the corner of my eye. I willed myself not to cry, especially in front of the café woman with the severe haircut. I grabbed a serviette and dabbed haphazardly at my face, trying to organise our things into my bag.

Thomas started to clamber on to my lap. I moved Amelia to make space for him. He put his arms around my neck. 'What's wrong, Mummy?'

I kissed the top of his head. 'Nothing, sweetheart. Just a bit sore in my chest.'

He eyed me. 'Breathe.'

It was what I told him to do when he was in the middle of a tantrum. Obediently, I inhaled deeply. It didn't help.

The studio was bustling when Amelia and I arrived at work. Something about the sun coming out seemed to motivate people to get moving, even if it was to a yoga class rather than a circuit workout.

I forced a smile at a couple of the regulars and pushed the door open to my closet-cum-office. The pile of papers on my desk was still stacked to an almost-toppling height. Amelia had fallen asleep so I tucked her in her basket, before steeling myself to tackle my admin mountain. I'd thought getting the paperwork sorted for Stephen's business was exasperating at times but this was another level entirely. It was made worse by the fact Veronica seemed to think that being carefree about the running of her business indicated she was not shallow enough to care about something as tawdry as money.

All the time, I was going over the disastrous meeting with Luke in my mind. His face as he looked back at me. The way he'd said 'just friends'. Should I have tried harder to argue? The idea that he had decided I was not as good a person as he'd thought I was, that I was some sort of high school mean girl, was tough to digest.

I was running through the log of clients' bookings and casual class numbers when Veronica wandered in with a folder. I raised an eyebrow. 'I hope that's not what it looks like.'

'Receipts.' She cringed as she handed the plastic folder over and faded bits of paper fluttered out of the side on to the floor. 'I think you need it for that tax date that's coming up . . .'

I dropped the folder on to my desk. 'Yep. Why aren't you taking that class?'

'I'm giving a new teacher a go. See if she might be able to give me a day off from time to time if she's any good. Shall we grab Mary and Elise afterwards and get them to rate her out of ten?'

I avoided her eye. We had agreed that we would start on the marketing plan and some social media strategies once I had got her tax in order – but it seemed that the stuff that I had actually been hired to do, the stuff I might be slightly good at, was still out of my reach. Instead, I was swimming against a paper avalanche of receipts and attempting to appraise a teacher of a class I had never even done, all while biting my tongue to stop my tears. I was not in the mood for her flightiness.

'I'm not being paid enough to do this,' I muttered into my second coffee of the morning.

Veronica stared at me. 'Is everything okay?'

What could I say? I had rejections for houses coming in faster than I could apply for any more, my estranged husband was swanning around with someone who looked like she had stepped out of the pages of a glossy magazine, the world thought I was a crazy stalker. Even my no-hoper sister who was usually guaranteed to make me feel better by comparison had paintings on display in an exhibition. And I might have a court date looming. I would like to hear her try to 'everything happens for a reason' it out of this one.

'Just having some tough times at the moment.'

Her face was kind. 'Still angry?'

I stared at my computer screen. 'Maybe just sad now.'

Veronica nodded. 'That's normal. He was a big part of your life, your husband. Everything's different.'

'It's not just that. I've done some stupid stuff.' Now I sounded like a teenager, too.

'Yeah I know. It's okay. There's no guidebook to get through these situations. Have you spent some time setting your intentions lately? Focusing on some smaller goals?'

I rested my chin on my hands. 'Thanks but I'll be okay. I'm booked in with Lorraine. Maybe Bowen Technique is the answer.'

I was joking but she just smiled. 'You never know, right? I'll watch Amelia for you.' She pulled the door to behind her.

Amelia stirred. I gritted my teeth. While Thomas had been known to sleep for at least a few hours when he was her age, I was lucky if Amelia settled for more than thirty minutes. It was usually just long enough for me to start getting focused on something.

I lifted her up and placed her on my knee. She broke into another wide grin. I kissed the top of her head, where a crust of cradle cap was sticking determinedly, despite my best efforts to dislodge it. 'Gently massage,' the websites said. I worried that if I was only gently massaging she would go to school with a fine layer of orange showing through her hair. I picked at an edge with my fingernail.

'I'd better get everything sorted for you, hadn't I?' I asked her as Veronica left.

She gurgled and stuck her thumb in her mouth.

'You didn't sign up for a mother who's a total train wreck.'

I picked up the pile of client files and a printout of Veronica's bank statements. 'Let's lie on the floor and sort this out.'

I placed Amelia in a patch of dappled sunlight. She screwed up her face. 'Just give it a minute, it's actually quite nice.'

I felt weird talking to a baby at first. When Thomas was first born, I would look around self-consciously before I whispered 'this is a banana' to him as we wandered through the supermarket. Over the months I got better at prattling away. By the time he was able to form some of his own words in response, I was so used to keeping up the stream of chatter that it was almost a nuisance to have to wait for his replies.

Veronica had written some notes about each of her clients, which I guess were meant to help her remember their names. 'See-through tights' was one – on a woman who had signed up for a twelve-month membership and seemingly stopped her payments for it three months in. 'Chase this – is she paying?' I scrawled on the sheet of paper.

'Very intense. Possible lecher,' she had written on another – a man who had done two classes and then disappeared. He did seem to have paid for both of them.

Veronica appeared not to have made any effort to chase any of her clients for a payment – ever. Sometimes she did not even turn up to her classes on time and I had to assure the people waiting outside that there would be someone there to help them learn to let go of their stresses – and that they were not doing themselves any favours getting het up about it. I made uneven piles of things to attend to in order of importance, all the while making faces at Amelia.

I had made a rule with myself – when I had spent more than half an hour jiggling and singing rather than getting any actual work done, I would go home. Some days this happened before lunchtime and I had to pile everything into my battered nappy bag and cart my files and laptop back in the car with me to work once the kids were in bed. Other times I managed to make it to the middle of the afternoon before I started dropping balls in my desperate juggle.

I counted the minutes, singing the *Fireman Sam* theme song, trying not to let any thoughts of Luke enter my head. Amelia was lying on top of me when my phone rang. It was my mother. She was breathing as though she had run to the phone. 'There's been an accident. Amy's hurt.'

CHAPTER FIFTEEN

<u>How to make your own mini-microscope</u>

(a plaster-friendly activity)

What you'll need:

Scissors

A plastic cup

Cling film

Rubber band

Water

Something to examine

Quick reflexes to grab the cup when your child tries to pour the water on the floor

Cut a hole in the bottom of the cup. Cover it with cling film wrap and secure it with your rubber band. Put your interesting thing in the cut-out hole in the bottom of the cup. Pour some water on top of the cling film. Your water should magnify your specimen. Be prepared to spend much of the next few weeks studying the ground as you walk, desperately trying to find little microscope-friendly items, and whipping small bits of rubbish away from mystified friends. Make the most of having small things to worry about when the bigger ones seem too much to deal with.

'What's happened?' I pulled myself to my feet, clutching Amelia to my chest.

'She crashed her car leaving work. Her boss called me – they've taken her to the hospital.'

I looked down at Amelia. 'I'll be there as soon as I can.'

When it was Thomas being sent to the doctor after his fall, anxiety had propelled me there on autopilot. This time, anger drummed in my head every inch of the way to the hospital. What was it about my sister that compelled her to self-destruct every time things started to go right for her? My memories of my teenage years were a procession of my parents' worried faces – when she dropped out of school just before final exams. When she disappeared for a week to stay with a friend rather than submit her portfolio for an art scholarship. The time she faked glandular fever to stay behind while we went on a family holiday.

My parents were sitting on hard plastic chairs in an empty emergency ward cubicle when I arrived. 'She's having an X-ray.'

My father stood as Amelia and I tore through the curtains that separated the cubicle from the rest of the teeming department. A doctor was shouting instructions at an elderly patient in the next bed and I could hear a couple having an argument across the other side of the room.

'How did it happen?'

Dad started pacing the three steps from one end of the cubicle to the other. 'It seems that her car was the only one involved. Although maybe something caused her to swerve off the road – we don't know. No one seems to have seen it happen – the woman who called the ambulance just heard the smash and came out of her house.'

'Whose car was she driving?'

'Your mother's. Insurance will cover it.'

He put his hand on my mother's back and started to knead the muscles in her shoulder.

'Where was she going?'

'Home, I guess. She didn't make it very far.'

A growing feeling of unease spread across my chest. 'Had she been drinking?'

My mother put her head in her arms.

'We don't know but it does look a bit like it, doesn't it? They have a few drinks after they finish a shift most nights. They've run some blood tests so we'll know soon.'

'Stupid.' I positioned Amelia's legs around my waist and balanced her on my hip. 'Serves her right.' A surge of anger fired through me.

'Rachel . . .' My dad gestured towards my mother, whose face was grey. 'We just want to make sure she's okay. We'll deal with the rest of it after that.'

'Sure,' I snapped. I pointed to the posters on the wall, trying to get Amelia's attention. It took all of three minutes to work from the healthy eating one that wanted me to give her more vegetables to the poster that told doctors how to rate a coma.

I settled into the seat that my father had vacated and bounced Amelia on my knee. She reached for a shelf of plastic-wrapped syringes above my head, and I ducked down so she couldn't grab them. A nurse appeared around the edge of the cubicle curtain, looked at us for a couple of seconds, made a note on a pad in her hand and disappeared again.

Another twenty minutes later, there was a clatter outside the cubicle and a pair of orderlies pushed their way in, dragging a bed behind them. Amy lay on top of it, her arms lifeless at her sides. Her hair had been swept back from her face and a gash on her temple throbbed amid the pallor of her face. The orderlies moved her bed against the wall, gave us an awkward nod and backed away. My mother reached for Amy's hand and rubbed it between hers. She was murmuring something under her breath.

A doctor wrenched back the curtain. 'The X-ray shows we're dealing with a bad break in Amy's left femur – we'll need to operate on that today,' he told my parents. 'She's also badly sprained her left shoulder. We've given her some pain relief to keep her as comfortable as possible in the meantime. I'll ask someone to show you up to the surgical ward as soon as we can.'

She seemed to only notice me as she was turning to leave. 'We only allow a maximum of two visitors in the emergency department, and they should be next of kin.' She raised an eyebrow and waited.

I shrugged. 'Okay, we'll get out of here. I need to get Thomas anyway.'

I turned to look at Amy, who had still not moved. Her breathing was shallow but the monitor that clung to her beeped reassuringly. I leant in to make a show of kissing her cheek, her breath sour in the menthol-scented air.

'What a stupid move,' I whispered in her ear. 'I guess you are the messy one after all.'

As we made our way out to the front entrance of the hospital, an elderly woman was approaching in the opposite direction. Her upright posture and brisk gait were familiar. Mrs Connolly. A memory jangled in my mind – something my mother had said about her having a niece in hospital.

She shot us a bright smile as we locked eyes. 'Hello, dear.'

I groaned inwardly. I would not have ventured out in public in my current state, were it not for Amy's situation. I was not prepared to talk to anyone, least of all a woman who always made me run a mental catalogue of my inferiority to her stylish, sophisticated daughters. My heart started to beat quickly. She would have seen the media coverage; it seemed that everyone in the city had. She must regret having convinced Veronica to hire me. Or perhaps she just pitied me as the kind of woman who could not keep her husband around when she needed him.

One of the online commenters had suggested that if I'd 'just been willing to have sex a bit more often, he probably wouldn't have left'. Another said it was because I had 'dared to have my own career' and 'hadn't spent enough time focusing on his'. When had I started to ignore my own advice never to read the comments? Probably about the same time Luke had looked at me with his almost-pitying eyes.

'Hi.' I half-waved.

She stopped. 'How are you?' She fixed me with a piercing look that indicated I was not going to get away with a platitude. I reluctantly stopped walking.

'I'm really enjoying working with Veronica,' I spluttered

at last. I looked at the window, avoiding her eyes. 'It's good, with everything going on . . .'

She put her hand on my arm to cut me off. 'I saw the television piece. Are you holding up okay?'

I made a weak gesture towards Amelia. 'Kids have a knack of making our failings seem a hundred times worse, don't they? But they also mean I have to carry on regardless.'

She nodded. 'Try not to let it get to you, dear. Everyone does silly things sometimes.'

'Me more than most, it turns out.'

At home, Thomas worked his way through hundreds of sheets of paper as he produced 'artwork' after 'artwork' for his poor bedridden Auntie Army.

Poor Saskia hadn't known what she was in for, inquiring about whether anything was going on at home. As I collected his things, I'd told her to take her pick: new baby, father leaving, moving house, now aunt in a car accident. We'd agreed that if the worst the teachers were dealing with was the occasional bout of rebellious nakedness from Thomas, they were probably getting off lightly.

As Thomas drew, Amelia kept trying to wrench his pens from his fists. I sat between them, attempting to pull together a couple of sentences for Veronica's new website. Somehow, I needed to entice a new breed of clientele in – there were still too many over-seventies – without creating an environment that might put off the dedicated regulars. I looked down at Amelia, who wiggled her way over so she was propped against my chest and started chewing my nipple absent-mindedly. 'I wonder if we should consider including naked yoga? Apparently that's a thing now.'

My phone buzzed. The caller ID showed it was my mother. I pondered ignoring it. There was only so much 'poor Amy' I could indulge in before I snapped and shouted at someone.

'Hi, Mum.'

'Rachel, darling.' I could tell from the echo that she was standing in the hospital hallway. 'Do you plan to come to visit your sister this evening? Your father and I were thinking about ducking home for a bit and I don't like the idea of leaving her on her own. Visiting hours are until 8 p.m.'

I gritted my teeth. 'She's a thirty-year-old woman, she'll be fine on her own.' I pushed my keyboard away. 'She got herself into that mess.'

My mother sighed in the way I remembered from when she'd mediated our fights when we were warring teenagers. 'Well actually, the test results have come back clear. She hadn't been drinking.'

I sat back. 'Really?'

I could hear my mother smiling. 'Yep, it looks as though our concerns were unfounded on that front.'

'Don't hang up, Mum.' Guilt twisted my stomach. 'I'll head across in about half an hour. Do you want anything?'

Amy was awake and poking at her iPad when we reached her room. She only looked up when Thomas tried to climb up the side of her bed. 'Careful.' She reached out to keep him at a distance. 'There's all sorts of wires and bits here.'

I arranged Amelia on my lap and sat in the only chair. Thomas dived under the bed to examine the mechanics that allowed it to move. 'How are you feeling?'

She shrugged. 'They're giving me good drugs. Mum and Dad won't stop hovering.'

'You gave them a fright. When are you going to be allowed home?'

She scowled. 'Who knows? No one tells me anything.

266

Food is crap. And she . . .' she gestured at an elderly woman in the bed across the room '. . . snores. A lot. How anyone is meant to get better in a place like this is beyond me. Missing my exhibition opening night, too.'

She winced as she moved her arm, bashed the call button and shouted: 'I need some more painkillers.'

I piled a stack of magazines on the bed. 'I thought you must have been drunk. I was ready to come in here and shout at you.'

She grinned at me. 'Nope, just a really bad driver. They reckon a tyre blew out or something. Save your shouting for someone else.'

She lay back on the bed. I flicked through one of the magazines, showing Amelia pictures of deserted beaches in a travel article. Amy coughed. 'It's time for us to accept the new normal. Me sane, you nuts.'

I sighed. 'Can we not?'

'Sorry, it's just taking some getting used to.'

The room smelt of antiseptic and some sort of air freshener scent that was probably meant to resemble freshly cut flowers. I squeezed her hand. 'Sorry for giving you a hard time. It's just with all this Alexa business . . .'

She didn't even bother to pretend to listen to me. 'I bet you haven't even seen her Instagram account.'

She was holding out her iPad, with the app open. It was covered in photos of Alexa's face, Alexa's body – in a bikini – or Alexa working out, without a drop of sweat in sight. The only photos that weren't just of Alexa were her and Stephen. In one, he had his hand on her breast. In another, she was licking his ear. She had more than 200,000 followers, posting comments. I grabbed the tablet from Amy. 'What is this? What's going on?'

I could tell Amy was enjoying it. 'Turns out our girl is

pretty good at cashing in. She does a live video chat every night where she reads out all the emails she's had from her fans. She's getting marriage proposals. Someone suggested she run for president.'

'This is crazy.' I scrolled through the page. At the bottom, a familiar grin stopped me. There was a photo of Thomas on his dad's shoulders, Alexa posing prettily beside them. It was captioned 'our family xx'. 'What is she thinking?' I threw the iPad at Amy. 'Thomas isn't her family.'

Amy smirked. 'Stephen will be loathing it, I told you.'

'He'd better bloody be,' I muttered through gritted teeth.

Veronica was waiting for me on the front step when I arrived at the studio, with both children in tow, the next day. She had a KeepCup in one hand and an enormous bag slung over the other shoulder. I wasn't sure if it was the intended effect, but it made her look minuscule in comparison, in her skin-tight shiny bright blue leggings and singlet top.

'Morning.' I tried to sound breezy as I hauled Amelia out of the car and placed her on the grass next to the pavement so I could lift Thomas out of his seat.

Veronica gave me a half-hearted wave. 'Can you let me in? I've done something with my keys.'

Thomas ran ahead of me and tried to open the door. 'It's locked,' he informed her.

She looked over his head to me for help.

I tossed my keys over the stroller. 'My sister's still in hospital but I'm booked in with Lorraine so I thought I'd better come in.'

Veronica paused, the key in the lock. 'I'm sorry to hear that. Nothing serious?'

'She'll live. I might just need a bit of a hand juggling stuff for the next few days.'

When we finally got into the foyer, Veronica sighed point-edly. I ignored her while I tried to work out what I needed to collect from my office. She tried again. 'I need to tell you something.' She dropped her bag on to the floor. Something rolled out and under the door to my office.

Exasperated, I gestured for her to go ahead. I directed Thomas to a space next to my desk and placed Amelia on her blanket on the floor. He was already fidgeting and shifting in his seat. I nudged my iPad over to him and opened his favourite game. 'Pop some bubbles for a bit, okay, honey? I just need to talk to Veronica.'

He began swiping and tapping furiously. Veronica watched him, open-mouthed, for half a minute. I waved away the question. 'It's fine. The evils of screen time are totally overrated.'

Composing herself, she turned to me.

'I've decided I don't want to do this anymore.' Veronica was still on her feet but had started to collapse against the wall. 'I'm not cut out for running a business. I watch what you do with it and you're so good, but I just can't bring myself to care.'

I snorted. 'I kind of got that impression. It's okay though, we've been getting there.'

Why was she bringing this to me now? I owed her for giving me a shot with the job but while my position description covered a lot of things, business coaching was not one of them. 'What are you going to do, close up?'

She shrugged. 'I talked to my accountant. He has been telling me to do something about it for a long time – ever since I started losing money. It's not a fixed-term lease and there's hardly any gear or staff so there aren't any ongoing things to worry about. I could just walk away.'

I pulled my notebook out of my bag, as if I planned to

269

take notes, to buy me a minute of time. I had suspected she was losing money but I figured, were quitting an option, she would already have done it. I felt a little sorry for her as I watched her sag against the faded beige of her surroundings. She must be in her early forties, although she did not look it. The idea of starting again in the middle of your working life was daunting.

'What were you hoping for when you started it?' I found I was genuinely curious.

She frowned, then offered me a conspiratorial smile. 'I kind of did it as a bit of revenge of my own, I guess.'

I had been prepared for an accidental entrepreneur story, but a spiteful one? I waited for her to continue.

'My sister and I inherited a bit of money from our aunt a few years back. But I didn't realise at the time that my partner could take half of it if we split. I knew it was looking likely so I decided to buy this place. I didn't think he'd be motivated enough to fight for half a business. Turned out, I was right . . . That's not very zen, is it?'

I was impressed by the dedication. And really, when it came to revenge, who was I to judge? 'I get it. Is it all gone? The money?'

'Pretty much. I feel pretty stupid.'

I shrugged. 'You can't change it. What will you do? If you don't have this place?'

'I would love to go back and study. I've always wanted to be a social worker.'

I looked at my fingernails. You would think, this being the second time I'd lost work within a couple of months, I'd know the protocol. I had been wondering how I would manage to muddle through with Thomas starting to struggle and a full workload, but now the studio was slipping out of my grasp, I felt my instinct was to try to hold on to it.

'There's nothing I can do to change your mind? I'm sure I can help . . .'

She shook her head. 'You're sweet but no. I've been thinking about this for months.'

I exhaled. 'I guess I might as well take these two and clear out after my appointment, then. Not much point getting it sorted if you're going to close it up. Your accountant can do all the tidying up.'

She pulled a file out of her bag and thrust the battered collection of paper at me. 'Actually, I wondered if you wanted it.'

She waved it when I did not immediately take it from her. 'The business. These are the annual financial reports from the last couple of years – you've pretty much seen it all already, of course. It's not worth much but I'd sell it to you for the cost of the gear if you want? And I'll come back and teach classes while I'm studying. You don't have to pay me if you can't afford to. You'll be amazing.'

It took me a second to realise what she had suggested. Would there even be space in my brain for this place? But I had a list of ideas for the business stuck in the front of my binder and jotted all over the notes in my iPad. The idea of throwing them away made me almost teary. And there should be money coming from Stephen for the house eventually that would more than cover the amount Yoga Junction could be worth. With Amy injured she might have more time to be favourite aunt to the kids.

I knew how to run a business, although helping Stephen through those early years had been thankless. I'd stayed up until midnight some nights trying to bash things into shape for him and he had only rolled his eyes at the extra workload when I asked him to start invoicing properly. I had felt a flicker of schadenfreude when Laura told me he'd missed out on a contract in recent weeks because he'd forgotten to submit his tender on time.

'Can I think about it?'

She grinned. 'Of course. I can't think of anyone who would do a better job of it. Now, you've got your session with Lorraine. You'd better go. The kids can hang out with me.'

I looked to Thomas for approval but he was still immersed in his tablet. 'You're sure? I can ask her to keep it quick.'

She pushed me out the door. 'Go. Thomas seems perfectly happy and I'll walk around the building with Amelia if need be. If she can't see it's me, I'm sure she'll be fine.'

Lorraine had set her room up in much the same way as Fern. A single massage table sat in the middle, a heavy net curtain hung over the window and there was a strong woody scent in the air. The central heating was working overtime to keep the room at a tropical temperature.

Lorraine was in her mid-fifties, short and round, wearing a bright floral dress. She beamed at me as I shut the door behind me. 'It's wonderful to get a chance to meet you properly.'

She rubbed her hands together. 'Do you know anything about Bowen Technique?'

I spread my hands. 'This is all new.'

'Take a seat. It's a hands-on type thing, but it's not intense at all. I'll just gently manipulate your muscles and joints to send your body some messages to help it heal itself. Are you suffering any injuries or illnesses at present?'

I focused on her notepad. 'Nothing physical.'

She nodded. 'You don't have to tell me any more than you want to, but this can be a good treatment to help you relax and generally feel better in yourself. That can only be a good thing, right?'

When I was on the bed, she started to gently walk her hands up my back. 'You're carrying a lot of tension.'

I buried my face in the rose-scented sheet. 'I'm having a bit of a rough time at the moment. My marriage ended recently.'

She made a soothing noise. 'I'm sorry to hear that.'

She moved her touch out to my shoulders, a gentle rolling motion that seemed to glide across my skin. I relaxed the muscles in my arms to allow her to move them. 'Then a man I thought I was falling in love with ended our relationship.'

She kept up her steady movements. 'That's terrible.'

Then she paused. 'We just need to leave some space for the treatment to work.'

Soon, the rolling began again. I listened for noises outside the room. Amelia was babbling in response to something Thomas was saying. He chortled.

'And I had to move in with my parents and my sister and my kids,' I muttered into the sheet.

She shifted her touch to my neck. 'Be kind to yourself, won't you? You deserve happiness.'

I let her move my head. 'I am trying. It's harder than you'd think.'

I was not sure whether Amy had actually healed enough to go home or whether the nurses just got too sick of her to keep her around, but she was out of the hospital within a week.

She set up a TV in the corner of her bedroom, an array of chargers in the multiplug in the wall so she would never have to be without her phone or tablet, and even had a bell on her nightstand so she could call for help if she needed one of us. After a couple of hours, I was already dreaming up ways to throw the bell out the window.

'Are you going to come out and eat dinner with us?' I

had to shout from the kitchen to be heard over the sound of her TV.

'Can't move,' she hollered in reply.

'Starving to death, then,' I muttered into the steam of the boiling potatoes.

'I'll bring you something in a minute.' My mother came to her aid. 'A plate of something nice.'

The bell jangled again. 'What do you need now?'

Amy's reply was muffled. Her bell jangled again.

'For goodness' sake.' I wiped my hands on a tea towel and strode across the room.

'There's someone at the door,' Amy shouted as I got nearer. I turned. I could make out an outline of a man through the frosted glass of the front door.

He was turning to leave as I opened the door. 'Stephen?'

'Ah.' He wiped his hands on his jeans. 'Hi, Rachel. Have you got a minute? Sounds a bit busy in there.'

I stepped outside, shutting the door behind me. Could Amy see us through her window? I wasn't sure.

'Sorry not to have rung. I was on my way past and I thought I'd call in.' He was moving his weight from one foot to the other. Why was he suddenly speaking to me like a normal person again?

I waited. There was no way he was just driving past. He must have thought I would ignore his call. What was it now? A new website picking up the photo? A new documentary on poor Alexa and her ordeal? Surely whatever it was, it could be left to the lawyers.

He spoke at last. 'I was hoping I could restart my days with Thomas – I know we haven't got anything formal in place yet but . . . would that be okay with you?'

'Oh!' I had to fight the urge to laugh with relief. 'Yes, he'd love that.'

Stephen ducked his head. He looked as if he might be going to cry. 'I miss my little guy.'

I bit my lip. 'He misses you, too. Do you want to see him now? Amelia's asleep or I would bring her out, as well.'

Stephen beamed. 'Can I?'

'Wait there.'

I leant into the house and gestured to Thomas, who was still playing with his Transformers on the living room floor. He frowned and crawled over to me. As I pulled him through the doorway, his face transformed. 'Daddy!'

Stephen picked him up and swung him over his head. 'Hey, buddy, how's it going?'

Thomas buried his face in his shoulder. 'Good.'

'I can't stay for long, but I just came over to see if it was okay with Mummy if you came over to hang out with me this weekend. Would you like that?'

Thomas nodded, his face still in Stephen's shirt.

'Okay we'll think of something fun to do. Just us.'

I couldn't help myself. 'No Alexa?'

He looked away. 'No.' Patting Thomas on the back again, he half-waved to me. 'I'd better be off. Thanks, Rachel. See you soon, T.'

As soon as I shut the door behind us again, Amy's bell was ringing. 'What is it now?' I leant around the door to look into her room.

'Who was that?' she demanded.

'None of your business.'

She pouted. 'I'm the invalid. You're meant to keep me entertained.'

I pulled the door shut. 'Let's hope for all our sakes I get the house I'm going to look at tomorrow.'

'I heard that,' she shouted from her bed. 'There'd better be room for me. Hey come here!'

I stuck my head around the doorway. 'What's up?'

She grinned. 'Guess what?'

'What? I'm busy.'

'I sold a painting.' Her eyes lit up as she shuffled around, trying to sit up on the bed. 'That big pink one that Mum was trying not to roll her eyes about. Michelle just rang to let me know.'

I reached across to give her a gentle high five. 'That's awesome. Well done.'

'And the best bit is they paid asking price for it. Can you believe it? When Michelle put it on there I thought she was dreaming.'

I kissed her cheek. 'Fantastic, you and your mad paintings deserve it.'

'What about you?'

I waited. What about me?

'You really need to do something brilliant and amazing, too. Show Stephen what he's missing out on. I bet he's missing you already.'

I pulled my foot up into tree pose. 'Actually there might be something surprising on the horizon. Give me a few days to work it out.'

Thomas shrieked in the kitchen. 'But first I'd better go and sort that out.'

'You can't leave me hanging,' she protested.

As I walked away she shouted after me: 'Has he broken up with her? I bet he has, hasn't he? Does he want you back? What are you planning?'

CHAPTER SIXTEEN

How to make a time capsule

What you'll need:

Pens or pencils

Some paper

Photos

A jar

Somewhere to store it

Have your children draw (or write, if they can) on scraps of paper. Make notes of their favourite things – films, activities, friends. Note how tall they are and what they're wearing. Print out some recent photos. Label the jar with the year and seal everything within it. In ten years' time you can look back and wonder at how crazy your life was then and hopefully how much has changed since. Just make sure your kids don't add any food when you're not looking – a decade might not be kind to a cupcake.

I arrived at my accountant's office early the next morning. My hands were shaking as I pulled my handbag over my shoulder and fixed my hair in the reflection of the window. I still could not quite believe I was taking Veronica's mad proposal seriously. I was a journalist not a yoga teacher. Wasn't I?

But I had left my kids with my parents and jotted out a brief business plan on my iPad. The excitement was creeping in. Ten years earlier, I'd wanted to start up my own studio, with glamorous weekend retreats for people with time and money to spend on yoga at the beach. Now I was planning to take over a struggling suburban studio catering for the middle-aged of the neighbourhood. And I still wasn't getting a full night's sleep. But if Amy could sell a painting after fifteen years of trying, surely I could do this, too.

The receptionist gestured for me to come in as I fought through the heavy door that always seemed to push when you wanted to pull, and vice versa. She was mid-fifties with bright dyed red hair and seemed to have a collection of voluminous kaftans on rotation in her wardrobe, no matter what the weather. She had watched Stephen's business grow from the first time we walked into this waiting room, wondering if it were even possible to set up a new building company. I half expected her to ask where he was but she just smiled. 'He's ready for you, go on through.'

I knocked tentatively on the open door of my accountant Jason's office, down a long hallway with what looked to be a staff kitchen at the end of it. He was sitting at his meeting table, a stack of folders on either side of an A4 notepad he was scribbling on. He looked up and grinned. 'Rachel, hi, come in.'

He gestured for me to sit opposite him. 'I've had a look at what you've sent me.'

I laughed nervously. 'You probably think it's mad.'

He made a dismissive gesture, searching for the sheets of paper in the stack. 'It's not the maddest thing I've heard this week. But there are a few things to consider. Hey, first I wanted to say how sorry I was to hear that you and Stephen had separated. I've always enjoyed dealing with you both.'

I squirmed. 'Thanks.'

He gave me a conspiratorial grin. 'You were always the better businessperson of the two, though, I must say. Not nearly as painful as most of my building clients.'

He spread the pieces of paper out in front of him. 'Okay. As I'm sure you're aware, this yoga business is not making a lot of money at the moment. It looks like she didn't actually make any profit in the last financial year and very little the year before. There's no guarantee you're going to make enough money from this to pay yourself anything.'

'Mm.' What could I say?

'But there's not a lot of overheads. The rent is low. It looks like there's a fairly solid client base there. You have good experience in communications and running a business. You

280

might be able to turn the place around in a way that she hasn't been able to, if the business side of things is not really her forte.'

'I hope so.'

'Her accountant says she wants £20,000 for it.' He tapped his pen on the table.

'Yes, that's right. She just wants to cover the equipment, really.'

'I'll put it bluntly, I don't think it's worth that. I've done a few calculations and I think the most she could justify asking is about £5000.'

My heart headed for my shoes. 'There's no way she'd accept that. She wants to get out but I don't think she's that desperate.'

'No, you're probably right.'

He leant back in his chair and looked at me. 'You seem disheartened. Do you really want to do this?'

I really did. 'It's not just the business. It's become a fresh start in my mind. Doing something that's just for me, not for Stephen or the kids or my parents, or anyone. Just something that's me in my new life. Before I started working with Veronica, I spent more time talking to Peppa Pig than I did conversing with real adults. I don't want to go back to that.'

He put his hands behind his head. 'All in all, it's only the price of a car, right? The worst that happens is the business doesn't work out and you lose that money. If you can afford it, and you've indicated that you can, based on the house payout coming through before too long, then don't let me stop you. The emotional stuff matters, too. Your happiness is worth something.'

I watched as he placed his pen on the notepad. 'I never thought I'd hear you say that.'

'I know. Don't tell anyone. But, you know, you've been through a lot. You deserve to have something that's just for you, if that's really what you want. Some people go on an expensive holiday when they've been through a divorce. This isn't necessarily a total waste of money.'

I bit the rough edge of my thumbnail. 'How about we offer £15,000 and see what she says?'

For all his dream-killer reputation, Jason had kind eyes. 'If that's what you'd like to do, I'll support you in that. Would you like me to make the offer in writing now, for you?'

Back in the car, my hands were shaking. I pulled out my phone before I realised I wasn't sure who to call. I settled on Laura. 'You'll never guess what I've just done,' I told her as she answered.

After she'd hung up I stared at the phone. I was desperate for a reason to talk to Luke. If I sent a message he might not reply or – worse – he might reply with that pleasantly absent-minded tone he used when library mothers told him stories he didn't believe. But it was a big deal and he had been to the studio. Surely he'd want to know.

I opened a new email message. 'I might trade journalism for a new career as a yoga magnate . . . I'm negotiating to buy Yoga Junction. Hope you're well.' Should I sign it off with a kiss? That seemed a bit desperate. I sent the message before I could talk myself out of it.

I sat in the car, refreshing my inbox. There was no immediate reply. I checked the time – Amelia would need a feed so I couldn't drag it out any longer. At a red light, I refreshed again. There it was – a message from Luke. 'Sounds exciting. Hope it comes off.'

Was that it? No questions? Nothing to reply to. A horn behind me beeped. The light had gone green.

Each year, my son's nursery holds a games morning. It's as mad as it sounds – a melee of two- to four-year-olds working their way around a stadium full of sports equipment that is always just a little too big for them.

In a fit of enthusiasm, I had volunteered to be parent help for the next day's event. We pulled up outside the gym in the morning with a couple of minutes to spare. Bundling Amelia into the carrier, I helped Thomas out of his seat. He protested as I passed him his shoes.

'Honey, I can't carry you. We're late.' Other mothers looked at me sympathetically as I trotted across the car park, falling through the doors of the stadium just as the centre's head teacher was stepping up to the microphone. She shot me a grin. 'Welcome, everyone.'

The idea was that they would move around the room in groups. The first activity was a basic folk-dancing type exercise. Thomas was handed a drum to keep time. I tried to make eye contact with a teacher – this could be a terrible idea, like one of those Greek numbers where it keeps getting faster and faster until all your drunk relatives fall over. He soon started drumming as fast as he could, chortling as his classmates tried to keep up. I sat on my hands to stop myself reaching out to slow him to a more appropriate rhythm.

The next one was a sort of football training exercise, where the kids took turns running and jumping to crash into some pads. Thomas took the opportunity to have me run up and down the course as fast as I could with him, shouting: 'Faster, Mum, faster!'

As I navigated my way along, weaving in and out of other running children, for the third time, my phone beeped. I pulled Thomas over to the side to check it. 'Mum!' he protested loudly. 'Keep going! Stop working!'

It was at the bottom of my bag. I fished around under a packet of old wipes, a few nappies and a muesli bar to find it. There was a text from Veronica. 'Congratulations!'

I regarded it for a minute. Did this mean what I thought it did?

Another followed: 'I've just told my accountant to say yes to your offer. Welcome to Yoga Junction.'

How do you reply to that? 'Thanks,' I tapped back. 'I'm really excited.'

She sent me a smiley face.

I put my phone back in my pocket. I would see her when I went into the studio later in the afternoon. She was down to take the 4 p.m. class.

Thomas shrieked. 'My arm-bow!'

He was holding his elbow, which another child had knocked, running full-speed past us back to where they were all returning to sit, cross-legged in front of a teacher.

'Are you okay?' I dropped to my knees, trying to hold Amelia upright in the carrier, and landed a kiss on the wounded joint.

'Kisses don't fix.' He scowled.

A few hours later, Thomas back with my parents, I sat in my car outside the yoga studio, watching a group of women advancing up the path to the front door. There was a faint rumble of pride in the base of my stomach, although a jangle of nerves quickly followed. This was my business. Those were my clients.

I pulled Amelia out and wandered up and into my office. I caught the eye of Diane, a regular who was taking her shoes off and placing them by the wall. It looked like a display at the world's strangest shoe shop – old sandals, battered sports shoes and a couple of pairs of corporate heels that belonged to those who had come straight from work.

'You look well.'

I blushed. 'Thanks. Makes a change from tired, I guess.'

I settled behind my desk, Amelia with her toys at my feet. When Thomas was a baby, I had been cornered by a woman at playgroup who had lectured me at length about the benefits of heuristic play – how it was better for kids to play with pegs and kitchen utensils than it was to load them up with plastic toys. Something must have stuck because Amelia now had her own Yoga Junction box of goodies that I had found lying around. She was delighting in rubbing a spatula on her face.

I pulled up my master plan for the studio. I could finally start putting some of this into action. Before long I was interrupted by a cough in the doorway. I looked up. It was Diane.

'Sorry to bother you . . .'

'It's fine, what's up?'

'I think Veronica is meant to be taking our class? She hasn't turned up.'

I looked at the clock. It had just ticked past 4 p.m. 'Give her a minute. She's not always the most punctual. I'll try to get her on the phone.'

Veronica's phone went straight to voicemail.

The clock flicked over another couple of minutes. I retrieved the phone numbers for the relief teachers she had trialled from the pad left on my desk. Hannah answered on the first ring.

She sounded stricken when I explained. 'I'm sorry, I'm away on a course.'

I bit my lip. 'Do you know anyone else who might be able to help me out?'

'No,' she said slowly. 'But you know, maybe you could handle it? I'm pretty sure all Veronica does is follow yoga routines from her magic folder. You know what you're doing.'

I laughed. 'Thanks but I don't think I'd be very convincing.'

'Okay. Well. Good luck?'

I stared at the phone after she hung up. Even with Amelia beside me, there was no way I was going to turn away thirty paying clients as my first act as owner of Yoga Junction. I switched my screen to Google and tapped: 'Hour-long yoga routine.'

Five minutes later, with notes scribbled in shorthand on a scrap of paper I hoped no one could see, I was in front of the class. They all gazed at me attentively, awaiting my first instruction.

'Let's start with a few deep breaths,' I commanded them. You couldn't go wrong with breathing, surely. Amelia took in a deep breath of her own but Diane lifted her from her spot in the corner before she could wail. 'Think about your Sankalpa – a few words to focus on through our practice today.'

Usually mine was 'I am getting back at Stephen' or 'I am making him pay', or – when I was in a better mood – 'I am surviving'.

'Today I'm going with: "I am strong",' I told them.

The rest of the group lifted their arms above their heads and raised their faces to the roof. After years of having every command I uttered ignored by Thomas, it was amazing to have a crowd hang on my every word. I realised too late I'd forgotten to shave under my arms. I pushed the thought away.

'Now forward-fold,' I instructed smoothly, leaning forward so that my palms brushed the floor. I wasn't able to get my forearms to the ground as Veronica might, but it was a pretty decent pose, nonetheless. 'Take this moment to centre your emotions,' I suggested. 'Get in touch with your intention.'

I guided them almost seamlessly through another twenty minutes. But by the time I'd made it to the bottom of my paper, I froze. I had been writing quickly, and with a gloopy gel pen. I could not make out the words. My atmospheric music was still twinkling from my phone.

'Deep breath,' I commanded the class as I racked my brain. 'See if you can extend your arms a little more. Be strong, be calm. Remember, the only thing you can control in the world is yourself.'

Sword pose? Sworn pose? Whatever it was, if I could not read it, there was no way I could remember how to do it. A swan pose was about the closest I was going to get. I sank to the ground, the class following me. 'Now tuck your front leg around . . .' I wiggled '. . . and kick up your back leg. See if you can rest your head on your back foot.'

That was a joke but most of them seemed to miss it.

'Does it matter if my knee isn't flat on the floor?' one of the women in the front row asked.

'Oh. Um.' I stalled. 'Take a deep breath in. If you feel resistance, see if you can relax a little until the muscle accepts the pose. Just go with your own flow. The last time I got into this pose, I had to be helped out of it.'

They thought I was joking. What would Veronica say next? 'The most important thing is that it works for your body. Work with what feels good for you today. Don't compare yourself to your neighbours, focus on your own flow. Now another deep breath, everyone. And relax . . .'

I sat on my mat after the class and watched the group file out of the room. Last to leave was Diane, still carrying Amelia. 'Not too bad.' She smiled.

'I'd better come up with a better babysitting plan.' I cringed. 'Unless you'd like to join the staff.'

She kissed Amelia on the cheek and handed her to me. 'She's no trouble at all.'

I lay back on my mat, Amelia astride my chest. She leant forward, dropping a long strand of saliva on to my face, then giggled. I blew a raspberry on her arm. 'You think you're so funny.'

The old building that housed Yoga Junction was quiet. I could hear the wind buffeting the wooden frames of the sash windows. Somewhere, the roof creaked. It could all do with a fresh coat of paint, although I gave Veronica points for the big, sparkly chandelier in the middle of the room. The way the sun sparkled through it was captivating even on a late autumn afternoon.

Amelia cooed at me, trying to stick her fingers up my nose. 'You did well, little one.' I traced the curve of her round cheek with my finger.

My back clicked as I strained to sit up, Amelia's weight pressing against my chest. I was still waiting for my core strength to return post-pregnancy. Grimacing, I fished around in my bag for my mobile. There were three missed calls from my lawyer, Louise.

I am sure some people spend all day ducking their phone calls. I had been trying to pin down a builder to get a quote to make a new sign for the front of the centre with no success. It took me a whole morning to get a computer tech to answer the phone when my laptop had been felled by a virus.

But that was nothing on my attempts to return Louise's calls. It was like she had tried fervently to ring me for about half an hour, then decided she never wanted to hear from me again. I called her as we left the studio. In the car at the red lights. Every time, she was out of the office or on a call.

When I arrived home, my parents were standing in the middle of the living room. My father looked up and grimaced as I walked into the room.

'Now, don't worry, darling.' My mother took my hand.

'We've misplaced your son,' my father finished for her.

I put my bag down. 'You've what?'

She swallowed hard. 'He was performing a bit. Having a bit of a tough time. Maybe overtired from his exertions.'

Maybe stressed out because his whole world has changed, I added silently.

'Anyway, he told me he was running away. I ignored it because I thought he'd just need a bit of time to calm down. But now we can't find him.'

She was rubbing her hands together. 'He must be around here somewhere.'

My heart started to beat faster. 'Did he leave the house?' I thrust Amelia into my mother's arms and ran back to the front door. Leaning out to the street, I looked each way. There was no sign of him on the pavement. 'I'm going to go and look around the back.'

I could hear my father wandering around inside, opening cupboards and doors, shouting Thomas's name as I scoured around the garden. I started to call for him, checking under the deck, in the garage, behind the spiky Phoenix palm Dad had been promising to pull out for months. I looked over the fence to Luke's house. There was no way that Thomas could have squeezed in there.

'He's not even three yet. He can't run far,' I repeated the mantra under my breath. 'Where would I go if I was an angry little boy?'

I was walking in circles, retracing my steps. Each time I rounded a corner and didn't find him, my heart rate seemed to increase a notch.

After ten minutes lurched interminably by, my mother appeared in the garden waving frantically. She was holding Amelia, who happily patted a rattle. 'We've found him.'

My hand instinctively went to my chest. 'Where is he?'

'He's in the cupboard under the stairs. Absolutely refusing to move.'

I should have known. It had been a favourite hiding place for Amy and me, when we were little. The gap created by the staircase was hot and stuffy and smelt like old woollen blankets but it was the perfect size for a hiding place. I followed her back into the house. My dad was on his knees, imploring Thomas to come out. Thomas resolutely kept his back to him. 'Here's Mummy,' my dad said, reaching out for me. 'Come out and see her?'

Thomas shook his head.

'Darling, is everything okay?' I tried. He did not turn around. 'What can I do?'

'Not coming,' he shouted and scurried further away into the corner of the cupboard. Even if I hunched down on to my hands and knees and squeezed through, I was not convinced I would be able to manoeuvre him out if he was unwilling.

My parents and I sat, looking at each other awkwardly. If he had been a teenager sulking I'd have had no problem leaving him there all evening. But an almost three-year-old? It was five minutes before I tried again. I peered around the corner. 'Do you want Daddy?'

'No!'

Amelia stretched away from me and let out a bellow. I bounced her on my hip, jiggling in the way that sometimes placated her. She shrieked louder.

'Please come out, darling. Amelia would like to see you.'

There was no reply. Amelia was rooting about on my shoulder, looking for my breast. 'Honey, I'm going to need to get your sister to bed. Are you going to come out?'

He crossed his arms and glared up through his eyebrows.

I looked around, searching for something to entice him. 'What about a treat?'

'No!'

There was a crash from Amy's room. She emerged, leaning heavily on one of her crutches. Grimacing, she limped across to the opening to the cupboard. 'Hey, favourite nephew . . .' she called. 'Come hang out with your Auntie Army.'

She lowered herself on to the floor. My mum put a hand on her shoulder. 'Don't hurt yourself.'

She pushed her away and started slithering back into the cupboard, wincing as her injured leg brushed against the edge of a rolled-up carpet stored in the corner. Soon she was lying, her head next to Thomas. She started whispering to him.

'What's she saying?' My dad craned to hear.

'I don't know.' I paced the floor with Amelia.

At last, I heard Thomas giggle. 'Okay.' There was scrabbling as he turned around and crawled back to the opening of the cupboard.

'Meet you in my room in five minutes,' Amy called after him. Then more uncertainly: 'I just have to work out how to get out of here.'

I watched her as she edged her way out.

'That was amazing.' I allowed myself a pang of jealousy. 'What did you tell him?'

She grinned. 'Oh just that we'd hatch a plan to play a prank on you.'

I laughed. I hoped she was joking. 'Whatever works, I guess.'

'Yep, I'm not such a dead loss aunt, after all.' She smelt sweet, a new frangipani-ish perfume. She must have ditched the pop star one she had been wearing for the past decade.

'No you're not.'

CHAPTER SEVENTEEN

<u>How to make rainbow roses</u>

What you'll need:

Glass jars

Water

Food colouring

White roses

Fill each jar with a mix of water and food colouring. Pop your roses in and watch as each picks up the colour of the water. This is a great opportunity to talk about absorption and get your kids to discuss what colour they think each rose might end up. Bonus points if the coloured water doesn't end up all over the carpet. Arrange your roses in a jar in the middle of your dining table. You'll realise that, while everything changes when you put it into a new environment, some of those changes can be for the better.

By half-past four, Louise's assistant was not even bothering to hide her exasperation with me as I tried to get her on the phone. 'I've passed on your message,' she told me firmly. 'I'm sure she'll call you when she gets back into the office.'

'It's just, I'm worried, you know . . .'

She cut me off. 'I understand. But Louise has a packed schedule today. She'll phone you when she can.'

Everywhere I went, my phone came too. I checked for messages as I changed Amelia's nappy, as I sang silly songs. I made up excuses to call Laura twice to check that the network was still functioning.

Finally, my phone buzzed as I tried to slide some limp chicken nuggets on to Thomas's plate for dinner. He watched me reproachfully, half-leaning on the table, one hand on Amy, who had limped over to sit with him. He was exhausted but fighting hard to convince me otherwise. 'Careful,' he said. 'Don't burn your fingers.'

'I'll try not to, honey.'

With one hand, I shuffled Thomas's dinner towards him

and frantically tried to swipe across my phone to answer the call.

It was Louise. 'Sorry I've been out of range.'

I grimaced. There must have been fifteen missed calls from me on her mobile. 'Sorry for hounding you. I was just a bit concerned . . .'

'Don't be, I've got good news,' she cut me off. 'My colleague did a bit of investigation. The police have decided not to continue with the case against you.'

The ground seemed to wobble under my feet and I sank back against the kitchen bench. 'Are you serious?'

'I just got off the phone with them. I think it was looking to be more trouble than it was worth. The guy who seemed to want to make a bit of an example of you has moved off the case. I reiterated how remorseful you are and that there is no chance of any of this sort of trouble in future.'

'No, of course . . .' My mouth had gone dry. 'That's fantastic. Thank you.'

'Don't thank me. I wondered whether Ms McKenzie or your husband might have said something to them, do you know?'

The memory of Stephen's face when he came over to see Thomas danced in front of my eyes. He had been a lot less angry. 'I'm not sure. But thank you for ringing. It means so much – it's such a relief.'

'No problem at all. We've still to sort the last details of your settlement with Stephen but you can expect that within the week. Then you can really get on with things.'

My heart was beating so hard I could hear it and feel it in my temples. I shook my arms. I had not realised how much I had been holding tension in my shoulders.

It was not until my parents pushed open the door that I discovered I had tears rolling down my face.

'Is everything okay?' My mother pulled out a chair next to Thomas, who was driving his fire engine back and forth across the tablecloth.

I was choking on tears that were becoming heavy sobs.

'Yes.' I managed to squeak it out before putting my head down on my arms on the bench top.

My dad patted my back awkwardly.

I straightened up and rested my head against his shoulder. 'The police are not going to pursue my case.'

My mother leapt up and ran to me, throwing her arms around my neck. 'That's brilliant news. I am so pleased for you. What a relief.'

She rocked me back and forth in her arms, in a motion similar to the one I used to get Amelia to sleep. The tears were still flowing. I tried to catch Thomas's eye to send him a reassuring smile.

'Don't worry, darling.'

He shrugged and returned to his plate of food. 'Silly Mummy.'

'Yes, very silly Mummy. I'll try not to be so silly again.'

Both the kids were in bed when Laura knocked on the door later that evening, a bottle of champagne under her arm. I laughed when I spotted it. 'We aren't making that mistake again.'

She giggled. 'Definitely not, but we have to celebrate our good fortune.'

She pushed past me into the house. 'I'll get us some glasses.'

Our eyes met as we clinked them. I could hear the bubbles popping in the wine.

'I'm so sorry.' Laura grasped my hand. 'I should never have put you in that position, especially with everything else you're going through.' She looked desolate.

'I'm an adult. You didn't make me do it. I'm just so incredibly relieved it's all over.'

We each lay back on the couch cushions, our eyes on our wine glasses.

'If it makes you feel any better . . .' she dipped a chip into the bowl of dip I had found in the back of the fridge '. . . I ran into Luke at the library.'

How was that going to make me feel any better? I tried to keep my voice neutral. 'How is he?'

She gave a dismissive wave of a hand. 'Fine, I guess. I didn't really ask. He asked how you were.'

A little shock of electricity zapped me. 'What did you say?'

'I told him you and Stephen are probably getting back together.'

'We are not!'

'I'm joking. Just wanted to see what you'd say.'

My stomach heaved. I missed everything about him: the way he made Thomas smile, the emails he sent me every time a child did something awful in one of his classes. It had cheered me up enormously one day when he told me a toddler had vomited behind the books. That would have been bad enough but no one found it until the next day.

'What did he say?'

'Nothing really.' She regarded me for a minute. 'You're still quite keen on him, aren't you?'

I gulped my wine. 'Maybe. Yes. Definitely.'

'Now it's all over with Alexa, maybe you could try again,' Laura said. 'He was a total fool to bail on you but maybe he's realised.'

There was a scrabble and a thump from my sister's room. She pushed the door open and, leaning heavily on her crutches, hobbled over towards us. She feigned surprise to see Laura on the sofa with me. 'Planning your next attack?'

Laura took a deep breath, as if she planned to unleash a tirade. I put a hand on her arm to stop her. 'I'm reformed, Amy. Would you like to join us for a drink?'

'I'm giving it a rest for a bit. Might have some good info for you though.' Her eyes twinkled.

'Go on then?' Laura was sat back against the couch, watching her.

'Well.' Amy gestured to Laura's phone. 'Pull up old sparkle-pants's Instagram account.'

'Alexa,' I told Laura. 'Amy doesn't approve of her wardrobe.'

Laura tapped on her screen. 'Okay. Got it.'

'Now, scroll down. What do you see?'

Laura exhaled heavily. 'No . . .'

'What?' I grabbed the phone from her hand. 'What is it?'

'Alexa looks like she's grabbed herself a new fancy man,' Amy crowed.

There were four new photos posted. In each one, Alexa was cheek-to-cheek or lip-to-lip with a man who looked like an extra from a Beyoncé music video. He was tanned, chiselled and much, much younger than Stephen. 'Wow.'

'He didn't say anything, I guess?'

I was suddenly burning with anger. 'So, it's over, then.'

Amy stumbled back on her crutches. 'I thought you'd be happy.'

'Why?' I swallowed my champagne in one long gulp. 'He tore apart our family for what – six months of good sex? Fifteen minutes of social media fame?'

I closed my eyes. My poor kids.

Laura watched me as she topped up my drink. 'Do you think he did you a favour, though, really?'

My mind skipped back to Luke. I took a deep breath and a more moderate sip. 'Maybe. It's just a pity there was so much fall-out in the process.'

Laura nodded. 'I do feel a bit sorry for her . . .'

Amy cocked her head. 'What? For Alexa? Why?'

'She didn't deserve it,' I ventured.

Amy gave a dismissive wave of her hand. 'Whatever. It's probably the best thing to have happened to her career in years. She's admitted as much herself, virtually.'

I was up early the next morning. Everything seemed a little brighter now that the threat of court action wasn't hanging over my head. My father was at the kitchen table, drinking a coffee, when Amelia and I arrived downstairs.

He looked up as we entered the kitchen. 'Good morning.'

'Yes, I think it is.' I twirled Amelia around the room.

He smiled, watching us. 'I'm glad things are coming right for you.'

I fished out a bag of baby cereal from the larder. It was almost time to move her on to breakfasting on something that was more like real food and less like the kind of thing you'd use to hang wallpaper.

'We were going to go and look at another house today,' I ventured, before he could return to his newspaper. 'But Mum seemed a bit distressed at the idea of us moving out. Maybe we should wait.'

He folded the paper and put his glasses on top of it. Leaning back in his seat, he frowned at me. 'Don't worry about your mother, I'll deal with her. You need to be happy, Rachel. You can't stick around here for the rest of your life worrying about what Mum thinks of what you're feeding your children.'

'Dad!'

He shrugged. 'I've noticed. She finds it hard to let you be the mother. Of course you're welcome here but if you think it's time to move on, we'll support you in that. Both of us. Maybe you could take Amy with you.'

I opened my mouth to reply but he laughed and returned to his paper. 'I was kidding. She's moving out herself once she's back on her feet, apparently.'

From the outside, it looked much like the other houses in the street. Smallish, brick, with a scrap of grass out the front. The letting agent was advancing down the front path as I pulled my car into the driveway. Weeds were sprouting between the paving stones.

She smiled as she saw Amelia. 'How sweet, how old is she?'

'Only five months.' I caressed her cheek. She really was sweet when she was asleep.

'You're brave, moving with such a small child.' She had already turned and was striding ahead of us up to the glass-panelled front door, jiggling a ring of keys in her hand. She had what looked to be a grown-out perm and a grey parting in her auburn hair.

'Not much choice.'

She did not answer but swung the front door open for us. 'Please have a look around. I'll just be out here if you have any questions.'

She immediately buried her face in her phone, tapping furiously.

I adjusted Amelia in the carrier on my front. Thomas and I took a tentative step towards the house. The front door opened straight into the living room, where there was a white shag pile carpet underfoot that had seen better days. In the corner of the room there was a small, faded green kitchen.

A hallway led to another wing of the house, where the dark wooden doors gave the whole place a vague school camp feel. There were three bedrooms, with small wardrobes and a bathroom with a shower over the bathtub. It was adorned with a plastic shower curtain covered with pictures of dolphins.

One of the bedrooms had a stain on the floor in the shape of North America, possibly from red wine. I figured it was probably where a bed would go.

But the sun was streaming in, the garden was a reasonable size and there was a deck out the back where I could imagine myself sitting with a coffee on a sunny summer evening, if I ever got to the point where I could reliably get the children to sleep before me. Maybe I could even have friends around after a day at the yoga studio.

It would suit us perfectly, at least until I worked out how I could ever afford to buy a place of my own again.

We traipsed back to the front door. 'I'd like to put in an application,' I told the agent.

She barely looked up from her email. 'Don't worry, I've got your details on file from the other houses you've looked at.'

There had been several. At one, competing tenants had bid the rent out of my price range as I stood behind them and watched.

She dropped her phone into her bag and stood up. 'I'll run it past the landlord this afternoon and let you know. You can do a bond, letting fee and two weeks' rent in advance?'

It was about all I had in my main bank account but there was enough – just.

I had Stephen on my mind as I got ready for work the next morning. With Alexa gone, would he expect me to try to patch up our marriage? I knew Thomas had written a letter to Santa, already, asking for his dad back for Christmas. But I couldn't do it. He wasn't the guy I'd married. This new Stephen might turn out to be an okay father for the kids but he wasn't someone I'd be able to share my life with. I'd always wonder when he was going to ditch me again.

The house was quiet. Thomas had already gone out with my parents and Amelia was surprisingly relaxed, chewing the corner of a board book. She was leaning back against the pillows on my bed, after a restless night as her first teeth tried to poke through her gums.

I pulled out my phone to send Stephen a message but dropped it back in my handbag when I realised I had no idea what I wanted to say. I had a lot less desire now to fire abuse at him but I was not sure I was ready to invite him round for a conciliatory cup of tea, either.

I regarded myself in the mirror. Would he even like the new me? I felt like a different person to the one he had left half a year earlier. Even at the most superficial level, my perception of what was acceptable work attire had changed since I had become surrounded by a sea of Lycra. It just felt weird to wear what I previously would have considered workwear – a nice tube skirt and a blazer maybe, or a pair of pants and a blouse – when everyone else was firmly in activewear.

My maternity leggings would not cut it, so I had started up a subscription for leggings from an online outfit that sent a pair a month for £10. I would then put on a huge, bum-covering sweatshirt when I had to leave the confines of the studio and venture out into a world where I suddenly felt very underdressed and much like a too-tightly packed sausage.

I was trying out my latest pair, a white get-up with a huge lotus flower across the thighs, for a yoga class with Hannah. Since my panicked phone call, Hannah had been very attentive. I wasn't sure if she had had feedback from the students, but she seemed keen to make sure that I did not end up having to cover any more classes. Veronica still had not returned, although someone had deduced from her Facebook account that she was having a mini-break on an island somewhere. Laura and Lila had volunteered to spend the hour with Amelia.

I settled into a spot at the back. It was against the unofficial rules of the centre, but I had my phone with me. Laura was eminently capable but my nerves were hard to shake. Hannah called the class to attention with a peal of a bell.

'Good morning,' she said, in her heavy German accent. The room seemed to be captivated.

She guided us through a gentle warm-up. To my surprise, I found I was fairly confident as long as I was taking the class and not leading it. I knew what all of the poses were before she demonstrated them and I did not wobble as she directed us on to one leg. I even managed to focus on my breathing for a full ten seconds. Was a Sankalpa of 'I am happy' too much to wish for?

As she encouraged us down into a deep swan dive, I took the opportunity to discreetly check my phone.

There was a message from Laura. 'Meet you at the library. Babies' music class after yoga. Perfect for Amelia – crucial development.'

I groaned, loudly enough for the woman standing next to me to turn to stare at me. Laura was nothing if not determined.

'Breathe deeply and let all your stress go,' Hannah commanded. 'Sink into warrior two and look ahead to the fantastic future that you will manifest.'

I gazed down my fingertips. I had already decided that my baseline for success in this new life would be the kids' contentment. If I could get them through with a decent house to live in, time to spend together and plentiful cuddles to snuggle into whenever they needed them, that would be enough. I hadn't allowed myself to hope for more – but the prospect of seeing Luke again sent a ripple of butterflies through me.

I gratefully descended back into a downward dog as Hannah commanded, sneaking a chance to look at the message from Laura again. If I was going to go, I had less than forty minutes to get ready.

As Hannah set up the room for savasana I took my opportunity to leave. 'Sorry, excuse me,' I muttered as I navigated past the feet of people who were trying to enter a deeper state of relaxation. I gave Hannah a shame-faced wave as I backed out of the room.

I arrived at the library just as the class was starting. Laura and Lila were pacing the concrete outside, showing Amelia a bee buzzing between flowers on a hibiscus. 'Here's your mummy.' She thrust her at me.

'How's she been?'

'She's missed you but she's been great. We've had a lovely time. How was the class with the skinny hippy?'

Laura had not been impressed with the social media exploits of the new addition to the team. Hannah had an Instagram account full of photos of her perfecting poses in front of sunsets in tropical locations. The thigh gap was probably the final nail in the coffin of her potential approval. 'It was okay. The regulars seemed to be into it, which is the main thing. This request made it decidedly less relaxing.'

Laura was unapologetic. 'It had to be done. You'd never have turned up here under your own steam.'

'You're probably right. Amelia's first music class without Thomas. Wonder how believable this is.'

We found a seat at the back, Amelia trying to breastfeed through my shirt. I had just let her latch on when Luke appeared. I felt sick. He looked exactly as I remembered him, down to the wry smile he offered the crowd as he settled in front with his guitar.

'Now, the babies won't be able to join in a lot,' he told us. 'So, I'll need you parents to help them.'

'This is so good for their little brains,' I heard a woman sitting in front of us say earnestly. She positioned her baby, sucking on a rusk in a way that brought to mind expensive Cuban cigars, so that he was facing Luke. He duly started to bawl.

By the end of the class, Amelia was asleep.

'This is too awkward,' I hissed at Laura, who was still avidly tapping her foot to the beat of Luke's now-finished last song. 'We have to go.'

She shook her head and gestured to Amelia, fast asleep in my arms, a trail of dribble dropping from the corner of her mouth on to the front of her floral onesie. 'Amelia's clearly enjoying this. Don't deprive her of such an important sensory experience. Anyway, I promised Luke you'd be here till the end.'

'What?' On cue, Amelia let out a sleepy snort.

As the parents in the class, who were obviously regulars, started to pack up, Luke held up his hand. 'I'm going to do one more special song today.'

He looked down at his ukulele as he picked out the opening chord. 'It's called "Sorry". Maybe the babies want to apologise for keeping you all up all night?'

There were a few obliging giggles.

'But there's someone here to whom I owe an apology.' He locked eyes with me across the other parents' heads.

The song was horrendous. 'Sometimes we do silly things/ Sometimes we make mistakes/But if we can apologise/it can all turn out really great . . .'

He should never deviate from the kids' nursery rhymes

that require three chords and half an octave. But I could not break eye contact with him as he warbled. It felt as though every one of the parents in the crowd was looking at me, fixed smiles on their faces. I allowed myself to grin and stood up so I could get a better view of him.

When he had finished, the crowd parted for him to make his way over to us.

'Rachel. I'm so happy to see you here.' He was so close I could feel his breath on my cheek as he looked down at Amelia's sleeping face. 'She's grown.' He looked at me.

'That's what babies do, I guess.' I wondered as soon as the words were out of my mouth whether they sounded ruder than I had meant them to.

'I'm sorry that I missed it.' He traced the lines of her hand with his finger. 'I want to say I'm sorry for the way I treated you.' He reached for my hand, too. 'You didn't deserve to have me disappear like that. I freaked out – I was only just getting used to the idea of meeting someone new and then it all got a bit messy . . .'

He gestured at the room.

'I'm sorry if that was a bit much. I've been trying to think of a way to apologise to you. Laura and I thought that was a good idea at the time, but now I'm not so sure.'

I shot her a look. This was all her idea? 'It was very sweet, thank you. I think you might have surprised a few of your fans, though.'

He grinned ruefully. 'I'm trying to give up this class. It's such a tough ask, trying to get babies to sing.'

'I think you do very well.'

We regarded each other, shifting our weight from one foot to the other. Laura had slunk out of sight.

'I'm sorry, too,' I managed at last.

'You were dealing with a lot.'

'No – you were right. It was immature. I promise if anyone ever cheats on me again I'll deal with it in the normal way. I'll just key his car.'

He looked up quickly.

'I'm joking!'

He grinned. 'I can't imagine anyone else being stupid enough to cheat on you, anyway.'

I blushed. Amelia was stirring. 'I had better go; my mum is dropping Thomas off at the studio.'

He kissed my cheek as I turned away, landing his lips on my ear. 'It's been so good to see you. Can I call you?'

I nodded. I felt a little light-headed and giddy. The room swam in front of me as I turned to try to find Laura. She reappeared from behind a stack of books as Luke edged his way around a group of children lying on the floor, back towards his office.

'So?' She looked at me expectantly.

'So what?'

'Is it all back on again?'

I shrugged. 'No! I don't know.'

She grinned. 'I think you like him,' she said, putting on a silly sing-song voice. 'I think he likes you.'

I hit her with a book. 'You're so ridiculous.'

The second morning yoga class had already finished when we made it back to work. I positioned Thomas in front of my desk with a notepad and dug a couple of coloured pencils out of my drawer. 'Can you do a picture for me?'

He started to concoct a pattern of lines crisscrossing the page. 'I'll write my name.'

I lowered Amelia into her cot, holding my breath as she turned her head to the side, as if searching for a breast again, before she settled off to sleep.

'Mummy,' Thomas said as I opened my invoicing program. 'Can you lay an egg?'

'What? No.'

'Please?'

One of his rubber high-bounce balls was lying on the floor. I quickly tucked it into my shirt, stood up and let it fall out. I did my best impression of a chicken squawk.

He guffawed.

'I'm drawing Amelia,' he told me earnestly, introducing a hash of black lines into the blue.

'That's great, darling.'

I turned my attention back to my screen. I had intended to organise a business networking event at the studio to start building its profile – I was going to try to have a sort of stretchy tea party for the local mums with a guest speaker to talk about the benefits of yoga. But every time I started a new sentence my mind would wander back to Luke and his song. When would he call? Would it seem desperate if I got in touch first? What would I say?

'Mummy?' Thomas chirped again.

'Yes, darling.' I was using my not-really-listening voice.

'My stomach hurts. Inside. I think there's a baby coming.'

I had to stifle a giggle. 'I think you're safe there, sweetheart. Do you need to use the toilet?'

'No.'

'Okay.'

'Yes.'

'Okay hold on a minute.'

I gave up any attempt at work just as the first afternoon class was settling down for meditation. Try keeping a small boy quiet through that. I resolved to get a quote for sound-proofing insulation in the walls.

* * *

I was clipping Amelia into her car seat when I became aware of a vehicle pulling up across the street. A familiar shape was getting out, making his way towards us. But no one should be coming in to the studio – unless Fern had scheduled a one-off. As the man came nearer, I saw it was Luke. He waved, a bunch of bright pink gerberas in one hand. Under the other arm was my sister's big pink painting.

As he got nearer, he held the canvas out to me, buffeting in the wind. 'I thought this might look good on your wall. Sorry it's taken me a while to get round here to give it to you.'

I took it from him. 'You're Amy's secret buyer?'

He looked embarrassed. 'I realised I'd made a mistake as soon as I went home from work that day. I thought buying the painting would help make it up to you. But then I saw Amy in the street and she was so excited about a stranger loving her work . . . so I just kept quiet.'

I smiled. 'You're so awkward.'

He pushed a strand of my hair off my face. 'You know me so well.'

As I reached up to peck him on the cheek, he pulled me in for a kiss that sent a warm rush up my spine. 'I think you were absolutely right to buy it,' I murmured as I leant my head against him. 'It's totally perfect.'

He inhaled deeply. 'A bit like you.'

THE END

Acknowledgements

My mum, for reading every draft and always saying nice things; the NZ Society of Authors, for accepting me into their CompleteMS programme; Diana Menefy, Steph Matuku and Mary Novak, for helping me get my ideas in order; the Brilliant + Amazing + Mothers + Writers, for their support; Victoria Oundjian and Rachel Faulkner-Willcocks, for taking a chance on me, and Sabah Khan, for her work to promote the book; and my kids, for sometimes going to bed on time so I could write.

Read on for an exclusive extract from
Susan Edmunds' next book . . .

Mummy Needs A Lie Down

Spring 2020

CHAPTER ONE

So, ladies: what should I pack in my hospital bag? This is my eighth baby, but I can't remember what I did for any of the others. Do they provide nappies these days?

Renee

Age: One day

It was a hospital midwife with stains under her cuticles who handed me my baby, freshly expelled from the warm, wet indoor spa pool of my uterus into the overly air-conditioned delivery suite. You'd think you wouldn't notice those details, but after 36 weeks of waiting, I'd developed some high expect-ations of what that particular moment should be like.

The baby's face was puffy and pink, like an aged woman with a sinus-twisting case of hayfever. Her fingers were weirdly out-of-proportion long and completely white. They looked like the hands of a waxwork witch who had terrified me at an amusement park when I was a child. All those years ago, they had been curled around a purple crystal ball. This time they were forming angry fists as if the child – my child, I pulled myself up, *my child* – had realised a bit too late that this was not where she had meant to end up, and was trying to protest her way back to safety.

The soft bone of her skull had been pulled up at the back by the ventouse machine that sucked her into the world. Another woman in light blue scrubs reached over and slid a hospital-issue woollen beanie over it to cover the peak. Should I tell her the point was actually vaguely appealing? Like I'd delivered a child who was extra streamlined, designed for speed. I pressed my lips shut. That could be the last of the gas talking.

I leant back on the narrow hospital bed. It had been cranked into a seated position some time between when I summoned the energy to fire one last desperate push through my pelvis as the obstetrician pulled with her appliance stuck into my nether regions, and when I'd been handed the little bundle of anger.

I could relate to my daughter's outrage. If I'd been picking a place to come into the world, it wouldn't have been this corner nook of a public hospital – sorry, world-class delivery suite – where the lights above looked like the engines of an alien spacecraft and everything smelt of cheap disinfectant. How well did they clean the floor in this place?

'Mum'll know she's got this one around.' The midwife winked at me as the sound of my baby's cry cut through the air. I'd known there was a noise happening, and I knew she was distressed, but it had taken me a minute to realise that it was my daughter producing the wail. I forced a smile, but I seemed to be moving a beat behind the real world. It was like I was swimming in a fish tank while everyone else wandered around on dry land, peering in on me.

'I'm cold.' I looked for my partner, Nick, who was two steps away from the bed, his gaze locked on our baby in my arms. Was he trying to avoid looking at some other part of me? I was aware of a distant tugging as the obstetrician finished her perineal embroidery. Odd that she'd bothered to put a local anaesthetic on for that when everyone had been so keen to coach me, drug-free, through the ventouse and baby's head creating the rip in the first place.

Nick pointed at me, looking at one of the women for help.

'It's not cold, Renee.' She was brisk, whipping a blood-and-something-else-soaked sheet out from under me and replacing it with a crunchy plastic pad. 'Your body's in shock. It won't last.'

Too right, I was in shock. Where I'd been used to a bump taking over my midsection, there was now a wobbly pouch of skin, being pulled down by gravity like a collapsing tent. It was shaking like a plate of jelly as my body trembled. The child I'd grown used to as a foot poking into my ribs or a head doing lazy somersaults in my uterus was gone. I missed her even as she snuffled around at my chest.

The hospital midwife took hold of my left breast and angled it at my daughter's face. 'Let her have a go at latching. Does she have a name?'

I avoided Nick's eyes. We'd still been debating in the car on the way to the hospital, although his arguments grew less strident as my contractions became more severe.

'Holly,' I said, settling on the most decisive tone I could muster. They didn't need to know he'd told me it sounded like something you'd name a dog.

Contractions had started to niggle at me at 6pm the previous evening, while Nick and I were having dinner. We had been on the type of schedule that fits the parents of toddlers since we'd moved in together three years earlier, because he decided, mid-life, to ditch his day job to retrain and run a gym with his mate, Sam. While, before we met, I had grown used to a habit of working until late and then sleeping until just before I was due at work in the morning, his alarm clock would bleep at 4.30am most days to prepare for his first client sessions at 5. It was a time I considered to be firmly the middle of the night. I was just relieved that he'd stopped his habit of setting the alarm for 4am and then snoozing it every ten minutes until half past.

By 8pm, I was no longer able to convince myself that the muscle convulsions were practice Braxton Hicks, or just the complaints of worn-out ligaments.

My midwife, whom I'd been seeing since I emerged bewildered from my first-ever-in-my-life positive pregnancy test, had counselled me the deliveries of first babies were unlikely to be quick procedures.

'You can expect eight hours of active labour,' she'd said as our consultations switched from fortnightly to weekly. Her offices were around the corner from the offices of the events management firm I worked at and I dutifully trotted there on my lunch breaks. 'You'll need to rest at the start to ration your energy.'

Nick called her as I clambered into the bath an hour later. I could hear muttering and his footsteps pacing the length of our poky two-bedroom flat. Then he put his head around the door. 'She's gone away for the weekend.'

I struggled to sit up, bracing myself against the slippery plastic of the bath. 'What?'

'Something urgent. Apparently, the hospital have systems in place – we'll just head in there and there will be a duty midwife who will take care of us.' He was clearly parroting the lines she had given him. 'But she reckons we should try to get some sleep first.'

I slithered down further into the water. We'd discussed

this as a possibility, but I had filed it away in the same best-not-thought-about category as the possibility of induction if I was still pregnant at 41 weeks. 'Can I talk to her?'

He shook his head. 'She's just got on a plane. She'll call you when she gets to the other end.'

Another contraction sucked at my cervix, sending a wave of heat up my body. I cringed. The steam from the bath was making me nauseous. 'Can you help me out?'

We hobbled to the bedroom, his arm supporting me under my shoulders, a towel draped inadequately around me. I'd felt big before but now it was as if I needed my own moon. The distance between my hips seemed to have doubled in a matter of hours. I flopped into our bed, drawing my knees up to my chest. Nick crawled in beside me, tracing the bumps of my spine with his fingers. The movements became slower and less regular until they stopped entirely after about 90 seconds and his breathing deepened. I turned over. He'd fallen asleep. How perfectly on-brand. Another contraction socked me in the stomach. There was no way I could stay in bed.

Nick appeared from the bedroom, wiping his eyes with the back of his hands at 1am, as I was curled in a ball on the sofa, moaning into my hands. 'Should I be timing them or something?' He screwed up his face in the light of the living room.

'Could have started doing that five hours ago.' I looked up at him through my fingers. 'Half an hour more, then we'll go.'

The hospital was less than ten minutes' drive from our home, but you could have told me, as I curled up in the passenger seat, that we were driving the length of the country and I would have believed it. We stopped at every red light and with every contraction I pulled myself up on the door handle, trying to scramble away from the pain. Nick had started to count down the time between them – one of the few practical domestic uses of his personal training skills I'd ever seen. I pushed out of my mind the thought that he could have the chance to use his first-aid certificate for a roadside delivery.

'Another one in 20 seconds,' he intoned as we pulled into the hospital carpark.

'No, no, no . . .' He hoisted me out of the car, and we stumbled through the doors of the maternity ward. The midwife on duty was sceptical and took her time pulling on the blue latex glove she would use to examine me in the same manner that you might remove the giblets from a frozen chicken. Her blue-gloved hand buried to the wrist, she nodded – almost impressed. 'Advanced labour,' she hissed at the nurse who was to join us in the suite.

Half an hour later, the magic 10cm of dilation had been reached. The midwife whipped away the gas machine I'd been sucking desperately every minute. 'Now, you need to push. Like you're on the toilet,' she said, her voice firm. 'It sometimes takes a few goes to get the pushing right. Next contraction, go for it.'

Nick was still counting the seconds. 'Get ready.' He squeezed my hand as it hit. I pushed as if I wanted to shove my intestines out through my urethra on to the bed. But at the end, the midwife was still looking at me. 'Try again next one.'

Nick patted my shoulder. Was this what he did to his clients? 'See if you can sort of push down more in the middle of your body?' He pointed to something he'd found on his phone. 'I see here it says . . .'

The trainee caught his eye and he stopped. The world

wobbled. 'She's doing great, isn't she? Maybe you could rub her back?' she said.

I seemed to be stuck in an unending loop. Contraction. Try to push. Everyone watching. Everyone sighing. A monitor strapped to my stomach beeping. I'd lost track of time, either through pain or too much nitrous oxide. I became aware of the first midwife staring at me more intently. I was fighting to keep my eyes open between each contraction. 'I think we should get an obstetrician in here, see if we can get you a bit of help getting this baby out, okay?'

An intervention. My antenatal class had spent an hour on the various methods that could be used to 'help' deliver a baby: forceps that looked like giant salad tongs and might cause irreparable damage to you or your baby; a ventouse that looked a bit like an electronic toilet plunger . . . and might cause irreparable damage to you or your baby. I'd written a birth plan making clear exactly how much I wanted to avoid an intervention, but I couldn't summon the energy to care. I just wanted it to be over. To go back home to my own bed and sleep.

I would later see 'poor maternal effort' scrawled on my maternity notes. As if it were a lack of trying on my part that stopped a 3.5kg baby from gliding through my size eight pelvis.

After all that, I knew that Nick wouldn't put up too much of a fight over our baby's name.

I watched Holly snort and snuffle, trying to find her spot on my breast. Finally, her little mouth, which looked like one I'd seen on a kitten when I was a child, connected with the tender, newly brown skin of my nipple. The suction was firm.

'She's not on right.' The midwife who'd manhandled my

breast into position leant over, sliding the tip of her little finger into the edge of Holly's mouth, breaking the seal. When was the last time she washed that hand? The latch had looked fine to me.

She smelt like the perfume my high school maths teacher had put on after each lunch break to mask the smell of cigarette smoke. She gestured for me to try again. There had been a handout at the midwife's rooms with a photo of a small baby suckling at a voluminous, veiny breast. They'd said something about lining up the baby's nose to nipple. I waggled my breast at Holly who opened her mouth. The midwife watched, scribbling in my maternity notes book. 'That looks better, well done. Does it feel okay?'

I could see Holly's jaw moving as her eyelids fluttered shut. I reached out for Nick who was hovering at the side of the bed. 'Do you want to hold her once she's finished?'

He nodded. The clock ticking on the wall tapped out the seconds in the silence. Someone had scrawled across its face that it was hospital property, as if you might try to sneak off home with it like some sort of low-rent souvenir. Clearly many of the people giving birth on this ward were not getting high-calibre baby gifts. Holly's sucking slowed into a butterfly tickle. I wiggled, trying to dislodge her. When she slipped off, asleep, I tucked a hospital issue blanket around her and passed her to her father, a bit like the Christmas ham my grandmother used to wrap in a trusty blue-and-white tea towel.

Nick grasped her in the crook of his arm, making her seem even tinier against his gym-honed bicep muscles and veiny forearms. He looked worried she would slip from his grasp. With a twitch of his body he turned her so she was stretched out on his forearms, her head in his hands. Her nose wiggled as if she were smelling something unpleasant.

322

I shifted my weight on to my left thigh and inched off the bed, finally swinging my legs around so the soles of my feet connected with the cold lino of the floor. 'I'm going to go and find a shower. I need a wash.'

Nick gestured to the gym bag he had thrown over his shoulder as we'd run for the door. It was overflowing, one zip only half-closed, a nightie making a bid for freedom. Somewhere in there, there was an old smartphone loaded with rainforest sounds and soothing beauty spa melodies. There might even have been a rollerball full of essential oil that my mother sent after she missed my baby shower. I extracted the nightie, slid my feet into a pair of worn-in slippers and placed one tentative step in front of the other out the door into the deserted hallway. In one of the rooms across the corridor, a woman was shrieking. Had I made that much noise? I felt like a lolloping hippopotamus, my midsection moving pendulously with each tentative step. The obstetrician had been down below for a long time with her big needle and black thread. Walking should hurt more than it did – the local anaesthetic must still be doing its job.

The communal bathroom was at the end of the corridor. I pushed open the heavy door and sidled in, still moving as if I was carrying a baby bump in front of me. The stalls were all empty.

Before I fell pregnant, I used to joke I could never have a baby because I couldn't manage nine months without a glass of wine and plate of stinky cheese in the evenings.

It turned out that I had swapped one habit for another – social media had become my pregnancy vice.

One online mothers' group in particular had become the safe place I would delve into in the evenings, discussing everything from the merits of various car seats to the intricacies of trying to conceive a second child while your first is still sharing your bed most nights.

The women in the group had warned me to be well prepared for my first attempt to urinate after birth – one even told me it was worse than the actual labour itself. I'd been told to do it in the shower to wash away the sting. Little had they known I'd have anaesthetic coming to the rescue. The shower cubicle was at the far end of the room, a sectioned-off space with a swinging half-door to shield it from the rest of the room, as if, having been laid out on the bed like a roast chicken mere minutes earlier, you'd be willing to give up most privacy from then on once the baby had been evacuated.

I stripped off my hospital gown and threw it in the metal-topped laundry bag in the corner, hanging my nightie on the hook on the back of the door. There were no mirrors in the room, which was probably fortunate judging by what I could see of the tracks of dried blood smeared across my thighs. I coaxed the tap on and slid under the lukewarm jet of water. The trickle running down the drain turned pink with blood and a clump of something that looked like burgundy compost. I let the water run over my face. The rhythm of the shower pressure melded with the pulse in the hospital air-conditioning into a sort of hypnotic thump-thump. I crossed my arms in front of my chest. My fingertips were still buzzing with the flood of adrenaline that had delivered Holly into the world.

I poked at my stomach. I didn't know what I expected, but it wasn't this. It looked as if I'd eaten a big dinner every day for the last six months. Where had my taut basketball of baby gone? Maybe I'd thought the bump would slowly descend until my body was ready to suck it all back in again. By the end of my nine months of pregnancy, I couldn't lie on my stomach, walk up steps or fit in the car. But now I kind of missed that bump.

I turned the water off when the door to the bathroom opened and someone else traipsed into the room.

Pulling my nightie down over my hips – had I really thought I'd be straight back into a size small? – I shuffled out of the shower cubicle. The newcomer was brushing her hair, a toothbrush jammed between her teeth. She turned and grinned at me. 'Sorry, I didn't mean to disturb you.'

I waved it away. 'You didn't. I should be getting back to the baby, anyway.'

The other woman smiled. She was a few years older than me, but not many, perhaps in her late 30s, with a sensible bob haircut and kind eyes. 'How's baby doing?'

I opened my mouth and shut it again. Was leaving her behind the wrong thing to do? Maybe every other mother in here was refusing to give their baby up to even go to the toilet in the first few hours and there I was, wandering away and hiding under the shower jet.

I gestured vaguely to the other end of the hospital. 'Good, I think. She's with her dad.'

The woman caught my eye in the mirror as she spread toothpaste on her brush. 'Mine too. Gotta take a break while you can. Who knows when there'll be another?' She smiled, brush in her mouth. 'You okay? First time?'

I nodded. I hadn't announced my pregnancy until 14 weeks, reluctant to believe the midwife's assurances that the baby was pretty likely to stick it out. Even though I was only 30 I had always suspected it might never happen for me. Who makes it that far in life without any sort of pregnancy scare? But there it was. Nick had almost fallen over when I had showed him the stick with its two lines.

Since then, there had been a relentless parade of people

wanting to tell me how hard motherhood would be. A workmate, part-way through helping me prepare a client presentation, had told me not to stress about being busy because soon I would not be able to breathe at home without inhaling a piece of dirty baby laundry desperate for a wash. When I complained about a niggly ankle, a woman in the supermarket had told me not to complain about the pain because I'd soon have to go through the torments of hell in childbirth.

I realised the woman with the bob was still waiting for a response. 'Yes, first baby.' I forced a laugh. 'Don't know what I'm in for, right?'

She shrugged. 'I'm sure you'll be great. They just need someone to love them, don't they? All the rest is just a bonus.'

She swished the water around in the sink, clearing out the smears of toothpaste, then retrieved a lip gloss tube from her pocket. 'Is your man any good?'

I raised an eyebrow. 'At what?'

'Does he help out around the house and stuff?'

Neither of us was up to much when it came to housework. Laundry piles tended to become a colour feature on our beige sofa. The kitchen bench was a dumping ground for things we couldn't find a home for and as long as it was in piles and not spilling out over the entire surface, I'd count it as clean.

'We're pretty even, I guess.'

She moved to hold the door open so we could both leave the room. A trolley rattled down the hallway somewhere in the distance.

She patted me on the shoulder as we prepared to set off in opposite directions across the ward. 'Hope it lasts. Whatever you do, don't break up in the first year. You're both basically officially crazy for the first 12 months.'

Waving back over her shoulder, she laughed. 'You think I'm being melodramatic, but you wait. You'll want to wring his neck in a month. But then somehow in a year's time it'll all be sort of okay again.'

I watched her wander off down the hallway, limping slightly. It had better not take a year to get back to 'sort of okay'.